DETROIT PUBLIC LIBRARY

3 5674 05783517 6

W9-BUH-005

Insurrections

WILDER BRANCH LIBRARY
7140 E. SEVEN MILE RD.
DETROIT, MI 48234

OCT   2017

INSURRECTIONS

Stories

RION AMILCAR SCOTT

UNIVERSITY PRESS OF KENTUCKY

The following stories were originally published in slightly different form: "Good Times" appeared in *Joyland* as "The Party." "202 Checkmates" appeared in *Fiction International*. "The Legend of Ezekiel Marcus" appeared in *Crab Orchard Review*. "A Friendly Game" appeared in *Specter Literary Magazine* and also in *Literary Orphans*. "Party Animal: The Strange and Savage Case of a Once Erudite and Eloquent Young Man" appeared in *Confrontation*. "The Slapsmith" appeared in *Stymie Magazine*. "Everyone Lives in a Flood Zone" appeared in *Bluestem Magazine* as "The Flooding." "Juba" appeared in *New Madrid*. "Boxing Day" appeared in *Catapult*. "Klan" appeared in *The Teacher's Voice*. "Three Insurrections" appeared in the *Kenyon Review*.

Copyright © 2016 by The University Press of Kentucky
Paperback edition 2017

Scholarly publisher for the Commonwealth,
serving Bellarmine University, Berea College, Centre College of Kentucky, Eastern Kentucky University, The Filson Historical Society, Georgetown College, Kentucky Historical Society, Kentucky State University, Morehead State University, Murray State University, Northern Kentucky University, Transylvania University, University of Kentucky, University of Louisville, and Western Kentucky University.
All rights reserved.

Editorial and Sales Offices: The University Press of Kentucky
663 South Limestone Street, Lexington, Kentucky 40508-4008
www.kentuckypress.com

Library of Congress Cataloging-in-Publication Data

Names: Scott, Rion Amilcar, author.
Title: Insurrections : stories / Rion Amilcar Scott.
Description: Lexington, Kentucky : University Press of Kentucky, 2016.
Identifiers: LCCN 2016024715| ISBN 9780813168180 (hardcover : alk. paper) | ISBN 9780813168203 (pdf) | ISBN 9780813168197 (epub)
Subjects: | GSAFD: Short stories.
Classification: LCC PS3619.C6833 A6 2016 | DDC 813/.6—dc23
LC record available at https://lccn.loc.gov/2016024715

ISBN 978-0-8131-7440-2 (pbk. : alk. paper)

This book is printed on acid-free paper meeting the requirements of the American National Standard for Permanence in Paper for Printed Library Materials.

Manufactured in the United States of America.

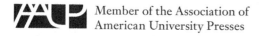 Member of the Association of American University Presses

To Pop

Contents

Good Times

I

Walter caught the sight out the corner of his eye one hot July day, and for so long afterward he asked himself what if he had never seen those dangling legs from the balcony above, kicking, kicking, kicking against the open air.

He watched them first with confusion—what an incongruous vision, a man's legs in baggy black jeans flailing against the open blue of the sky. He next watched with interest, and then with terror when he heard the gagging and hacking. A man hanging. A man dying.

Laura! Laura! Walter called. Laura, come! Laura come now! Laura come!

She didn't answer right away. He wondered whether maybe she hadn't forgiven him their last argument the hour before. He couldn't recall why he had shouted and dismissively waved his hands at her. When she didn't respond, Walter figured his voice was making her nerves twitch, and she was turning up the television and ignoring him as she did when the neighbors' baby wailed from above.

Those legs. Those kicking legs. When Laura came out onto the balcony, Walter was already climbing a stepladder, the biggest, sharpest kitchen knife in hand.

Laura, he called. Come and help me!

What do you want me to do?

Don't just stand there! Grab his legs. Grab his legs.

Laura gathered the man's legs in her arms and dragged his body over the railing. He pulled and jerked her from one side and then the other.

1

Hold still, she said. Stop kicking. It's going to be all right, she said, though it was obvious that things wouldn't be right anytime soon.

There, there, Walter said, projecting a sense of calm for the first time. There, there, buddy. Try to hold still. He sawed frantically at the rope. The man's neck had turned a bruised purple.

When the rope snapped, the man's body dropped, heavy and lifeless. Walter and his stepladder tipped over onto the concrete of the balcony floor. The man's ribs banged against the railing before he landed atop Laura's small frame. There was a moment while the hanging man dropped when it seemed they'd all go falling over the side into oblivion. Laura pulled from beneath the motionless stranger to lean into a corner.

Oh God, she said. Oh God. Oh God.

Walter reached to touch him, this man who lay all bunched like a pile of dirty laundry. As Walter's hand hovered over his shoulder, the man let out a cough, the first in a series of them. One dry and the rest phlegm-filled. They rattled in his throat, in his chest and his gut. The man rolled side to side, clutching his stomach and then his ribs.

He sat up and placed his head against the metal bars of the railing. Laura brought him a glass of water and a wet rag to wipe the spittle and phlegm from his face.

Say, what the hell was that all about? Walter said. You scared my lady nearly to death. We could have all tumbled over the side—you know that, right?

The man hid his face behind the rag, coughing softly and then loudly.

What's your name? Walter asked.

Rashid, he replied in a strained wheeze, lowering the rag. Walter noticed the man's yellow-red eyes. They nearly glowed against the night-dark of his skin.

My name's Walter, and this is my wife, Laura.

Thank you, Walter, I got tangled in the rope. I thought that was it—

You got tangled? You telling me you weren't trying to hang yourself?

Hang myself? Commit suicide? Naw. Naw. Hell no. I got tangled in the rope trying to fix the wood up there. Ricca been on me about fixing that wood. You seen my little boy running around. Rashid coughed softly. He be giving me hell. I know you seen him. Growing so fast, probably looks different every time you see him probably. That's all I was thinking about when I was hanging there.

Rashid, you must take me for—

Before Walter could finish, Laura cut in, her voice as smooth and as sweet as velvet cake. Now, Rashid, you need to take care of yourself. All these dangers out here, you almost left your—what's his name, your little boy?

Luce, name's Luce. He'll be three in September.

You almost left Luce fatherless, baby.

Rashid nodded and took a sip of water, his hand trembling. Walter thought of the things he wanted to say, but he let them rest on his tongue. Sometimes Laura's wisdom was infinite, he thought, that's why he had stayed with her for all those years upon years.

Rashid shook Walter's hand and hugged Laura. He hugged her long and tightly, as if she were a great-aunt he loved and would likely never see again. Then he walked out the door and Laura and Walter could hear his feet tap up the hallway stairs and they listened for his door to open and slam. Finally they heard the thumps of his feet on the ceiling above. They listened to the music of Rashid's steps until his wife and son came home. And Rashid's taps blended into Ricca's, and even the awkward footfalls of Luce and his frequent screams weren't an annoyance this night.

All week they waited for a sound, a gunshot and the thump of a falling body perhaps, or a sight: those legs dangling again from the balcony above. There were only the screams of a child, which now sounded like music. Screams and nothing else. They heard nothing, saw nothing, and that nothing was perhaps the most unsettling thing of all.

II

A week passed and then another week and yet a third without some dramatic incident, so Laura and Walter stopped listening for the end of Rashid's life. A few times Walter mentioned Rashid and the strange afternoon. Why would that young boy with a pretty wife and baby want to do something like that? he'd say, and Laura would shake her head and reply, Not our business. Twice Walter left the house and saw Ricca struggling with Luce. The first time, the toddler rushed from her as soon as she set him down on the sidewalk. She screamed his name while tussling with full grocery bags. Walter wanted to grab the boy or ask to carry her bags. Anything to lighten the load. Then he'd ask about Rashid. But all that was so forward; not his style with strangers. The other time, she carried Luce in her arms as he slept on her shoulder. Except for that puffy, smooth face, he looked like an armful of crumpled shirts. That time Walter opened the door for her. Howdy, he said, and she smiled, but he couldn't bring himself to say more. What was there to be said, anyway? Say, Ricca, your husband dead? He off himself yet? Not yet, huh? You know it's gonna happen, right? Right? How you plan to get on as a single mother once your husband's dead, huh?

No, he let her trek up the stairs unmolested by inane questioning. Life is for the living, he told himself, and if Rashid didn't want to live, to hell with him. Maybe he'd say that to her the next time he saw her. Just that first part, *life is for the living*. He'd smile as he said it, maybe gesture toward Luce if he was there. When Walter opened the door for her, he noticed that Ricca's smile sat on her face like a kitten on a windowsill. Then she disappeared and her smile was all that was left, like the Cheshire Cat. Something about Ricca and her grace was so feline. Why would Rashid want to take himself away from that? Life is for the living, he thought again one afternoon sitting on the couch daydreaming about opening the door for Ricca and about Rashid's dangling legs and probably a hundred other things. Then he turned on an old episode of *Good Times* and fell asleep laughing.

Walter awoke later that afternoon to a pounding at his door. He jumped and looked toward his balcony, thinking that again he'd see dangling legs kicking through the air. Then a second set of banging. Walter stared at the door for a moment. Yeah, who is it? he called. Then he peered through the peephole. There stood Rashid. Walter opened the door and Rashid strode in with his shoulders thrown back and a smile that showed all his teeth.

Walter. Walter, Walter, did I wake you? he asked as he peeled a can of beer from a six-pack and pressed it into Walter's hand. We need some light in here.

Rashid flicked a switch, and bright white jabbed Walter's eyes.

Come on, have a drink, Walter, it'll help bring you back into the land of the living.

Rashid, right?

You know my name, man.

What is this all about, Rashid? Walter looked at his beer and then shrugged and cracked it open and took a sip.

Man, I never thanked you for saving my life. I mean, I said thank you, but let's face it, if not for you I'd be dead. Saying the words *thank you* is not enough in the face of that.

So you bring me a beer?

I brought a whole pack.

That's funny, Walter said before taking a second sip. Really funny.

But you didn't laugh, Walter.

I'm laughing in my head, believe me.

Rashid laughed so loud that he closed his eyes and his torso shook and he began to cough. It reminded Walter of the deathly cough Rashid released after being cut down, too close to dead, nearly spent.

What I like about you, Walter, is how deadpan you are. Funny as shit, man.

We've barely said two words to each other, Rashid. It's too early to tell what you like about me. Besides, there's nothing funny about me. You should meet my daughter. She's the funny one.

Yeah, but I can tell what kind of dude you are. Maybe I felt your soul when you saved me.

Come, Rashid, have a seat. I want to talk to you. Me and Laura have been really worried.

Worried?

Look, Rashid, Laura tells me all the time not to say anything. She's all concerned with your dignity, but I'm concerned with your life. You all right?

Walter watched to see if even a tiny piece of recognition had seeped through. Rashid's face was a blank hillside freshly covered with sod.

For Christ's sake, Walter said. When I met you, you were hanging by your goddamn neck from a balcony.

That beer is having some effect on you, Walt. You turned from friendly to all volatile and shit in a sip or two. I never seen that.

And I never seen a man hanging from a balcony by accident.

You seen one hanging on purpose?

Goddammit, Rashid, don't play with me. On your baby boy's life, I saw you hanging and it wasn't no goddamn accident, you were trying to kill yourself. I'm not a fool, don't try to make me out to be one. You come in here with beer and a smile, but if you can't admit that to yourself and to me, it'll come back to haunt you. You'll be up there again and I tell you what . . .

Walter trailed off as he stared at Rashid raising the can of beer to his lips. Rashid looked to the floor as he slurped slowly. Walter stood.

I don't know if you have admitted it to yourself. Or if you've admitted it to your wife. You can just . . . Rashid, I don't know you, not really, but I . . . Look, man, just admit it to me. Here. Now. Tell me the truth. First step you have to take.

Rashid sat back, folding into the couch, the blankness returning to his face, flatness overtaking his eyes. He said nothing. He sipped. He kept saying nothing.

Good goddammit, get out of my house, Walter said. I don't need this. I tell you what, don't be hanging from my balcony when you do this again. I don't appreciate that, and I won't come to save you, I'll let you swing. I didn't ask for this and I didn't need to watch a suicide attem—

Suicide, Rashid said. Man, look Walter. I'm sor— Shit, I was about to bullshit you again. I was— You think it's just easy to say it like that? Suicide. That shit can just roll off your tongue because— You ever try to take— Man, this is just like the first time Ricca told me she loved me. It flapped off her tongue like she was saying hello. We was some kids. Babies. We still some kids to you, probably. She laid up right there in my arms. The thing about her is that she fits well. No other woman had fit in my arms that well. Can you imagine basing the rest of your life on something stupid like that?

Walter shrugged. Love is like that, he said, when it's new and you're young. Same thing almost with Laura. We been around forty-some years.

Yeah, but I just couldn't say it. I babbled about something for a while and she was patient. Said I didn't have to reciprocate. She loved me whether I loved her or not. When she went off to school that day I actually practiced. Practiced saying *I love you*. All this morning I was practicing what I was gonna say to you just like how I practiced back then.

You gonna tell me you love me?

Funny, Walter.

Wrong time, I know. Laura's always warning me about that.

Naw, levity's good. But I was practicing how I was going to tell you I was trying to suicide myself. Yeah, man. I was trying to kill myself that day. Something told me it was time to control my destiny, beat the Reaper to it, no reason to see this life thing through. I tried to kill myself, and the moment I went through with it I knew I had made a fucking fatal error. And yeah, I do love you, Walter. Weird thing to say to a stranger, but I do because you saved me and you saved Luce and you saved Ricca.

When he spoke of his family, his voice became high-pitched and the cracking cut sharp at Walter's ears and tears shot down Rashid's face. Rashid covered his eyes and cheeks with his hand. He became stuck between sobs like a disc caught on a scratch. Walter pulled a rag from his pocket and hovered over Rashid.

This the first time you tried taking your own life? Walter asked.

Yes. Rashid nodded through sobs. Yes. I've thought about it off and on for twenty years, but—Luce and Ricca. Damn, the same things that make you want to kill yourself also save your life. I swear all I was thinking about when I was hanging was that boy and that woman.

Walter watched Rashid, stone-faced. Rashid's words seemed to him a comforting lie. He didn't attempt to take his own life because of Luce or Ricca. Such a selfish thought, such a heavy thing to rest upon their backs. And it was Walter and Laura who had cut Rashid from the end of a rope, not a toddler or a woman who was elsewhere at the time. Rashid suddenly struck him as ungrateful and self-pitying. Walter put the rag back into his pocket.

It's like, I been preparing Luce to live without his daddy, Rashid said. Now, isn't that sick? I went out and got a DVD of this old episode of *Sesame Street* where Mr. Hooper—you know, the guy who runs the store— yeah, on that episode he passes away just like the actor who played him, and I showed it to Luce over and over. He be reciting lines from that episode around the house just out the blue, but that first time he was mesmerized. Big Bird's all distraught and the humans are trying to explain why he's never going to see Mr. Hooper again. I thought the shit might be too heavy for Luce, but then I remembered why we was watching. I said, Son, you understand what's happening? He nodded and ain't take his eyes off the TV and he said, Yeah, Mr. Hooper went to the store. He gets quiet, just staring at the screen and I ask him again. He says, Big Bird is sad because Mr. Hooper is lost. I'm like, Do you think he's coming back? Luce is like, No. He's lost. He's not coming back. I kept thinking of Luce walking around the house saying, Daddy's lost. He's not coming back.

They both finished their cans of beer at the same time. Walter peeled another off the rings and handed it to Rashid. Then he peeled one for himself, cracked it open, and began to drink.

Rashid, he said. All that crying got to cease. I'm not going to say that men don't cry. I cried like a baby over every damn little thing in the first couple years of my daughter's life. Children do that to you. Make you weak and strong at the same time, but yeah . . . man up. Look, tell me something. You a Riverbaby?

Riverbaby?

Guess not. Were you born here? You from Cross River?

Oh, yeah, Riverbaby. Naw, but at Freedman's University they say I'm an expert in Cross River history. Yeah, I come from D.C. Ricca's from up north. New York. But she moved to Maryland—not Maryland like Cross River, Maryland, but Maryland like right-outside-of-D.C.-Maryland—when she was in high school. We met when I was in college in D.C. She was an undergraduate, I was in grad school. Well, she dropped out and I told her to go back and she did. We moved out here because I got a job teaching at the college. But look, Walter, shit's one of those compromises where everyone loses. She wanted to move back to New York to be with her mother, I wanted to stay in D.C., so we moved to a neutral spot.

Marriage is compromise.

Compromising yourself. All your principles. Everything. Nobody wins.

Luce wins.

I guess Luce wins. He doesn't even realize some kind of cold war is going on all around him. Man, I'm talking all this shit—

I get a feeling you never said it to anyone before.

Rashid became quiet. Took a long sip from his can.

Hey Walter, let me tell you about this party, one we had back when we was living in D.C. It was a surprise. I didn't know. Ricca didn't know. Man, no one knew. Sometimes I think the people who surprised me didn't even know. Shit just happened. Like magic.

Walter settled into the couch and opened another beer, but he didn't drink. He was feeling lightheaded already, and it had been years since he'd been drunk. Many more since he'd been regularly drunk, weekly and before that daily. He imagined that Rashid, with his light frame and weak spirit, was far more gone than he. Who knew how many beers he had self-medicated with before ginning up the spirit to come downstairs.

It was the day after my graduation, Rashid said. Now I'm a historian with a Ph.D and shit. Dr. Rashid, Ricca keeps calling me. She graduated the semester before. And we're having a lazy Sunday, right? Just thinking about the future. Half happy I was done. Half anxious about getting a job and getting the fuck on with my life. Ricca's father was in the hospital. Last time, but we ain't know that. We had been talking about going to see him, but no firm plans. She says we did, but really we had no firm plans for nothing. I'm half sleep and Ricca is doing something, I don't remember what. I hear the doorbell ringing and then some pounding at the door and then the door ringing again and I'm all like, what-the-fuck.

I lived in this neighborhood in the northwest part of town off this street called Georgia Avenue where you could look out the window and see crackheads hiding in a shed having sex and shit, so I'm kind of wary of people banging on my door and ringing the bell all crazy. I look out the damn window and it's Floyd and Bradley and this white chick, Kyla. Ricca ain't like that. They were all in class with me. We were like a clique. A little circle. So tight, like a family. Kept everybody out. Meeting them was like falling in love. Powerful group chemistry, Walter. Sometimes you either feel like that with people or you don't. And it's rare. There was one other chick in our group, but I don't know where she was at that day. She was married even back then, so she didn't always hang. Was in that *I'm-married-and-marriage-is-the-greatest-shit-ever-and-you-should-be-married-too-so-you-can-be-as-happy-as-me!* phase. I think that's some face-saving desperation shit. Loved her, but I got tired of her telling me I need to marry Ricca or be alone for the rest of my life. Being alone is no crime. When they came in with their beers and chips and shit, that's what we talked about, Sonya and her lame marriage. I didn't like her husband. None of us did. And they didn't seem to like Ricca. I knew that's what they talked about when I wasn't around. Floyd, he's gay. We didn't like none of the dudes he brought around. Anyone on the border of the group was like an enemy. Kyla and Brad were kind of a couple, almost. Never called themselves a couple, but always flirting and off alone together. But here's the thing: Kyla wanted to have sex with me. She was on and off real aggressive about it, and when she fell back, I missed the attention and tried to get in her light again. I'm fucked up, Walter. We even made out once or twice and promised not to tell Brad. I see how you're looking at me, Walter, with your lids all low in judgment. You remember being in your twenties?

I'm not looking at you any kind of way, Rashid. Go ahead.

When they show up with their beer, I'm all dazed, but I'm happy to see them. If I could, I'd see them three or four nights out of seven even now that I don't see them at all. They pass out beers and we're laughing and shit and they barely even acknowledge Ricca, outside of offering her a beer they know she's not going to drink. I could tell she's pissed, and part of me was sad about that, but another part of me was having a great time. Listening to music. Making jokes. Talking about things that happened in class. Our professors. History shit. They hadn't graduated yet, so we were talking about the future too. Man, it's like this was a dream or something. Kyla's flirting with me, but trying to keep it discreet so Bradley and Ricca don't notice. Making these eyes, you know. Making all these comments only she and I would get. Inside jokes. Double entendres. She's really smart when it comes to wordplay. Brad's clueless. Ricca leaves the fucking room. I excuse myself to go after her, and she doesn't talk about Kyla, even though I know that's what bothers her; she's like, *What the hell is this? We're supposed to go and see my dad.*

I tell her that wasn't confirmed. We can go tomorrow, I say. She's like, *He's sick. There might not be a tomorrow.* Which makes me stop and think, but I decide she's being dramatic. I say, I don't want to be rude to my friends. She's like, *They're being rude by showing up unannounced. I wish we weren't here.* Then I said, Come back to the party. Dad will be there tomorrow. Single most insensitive thing I ever said, and you know what, I never even apologized for it. She put on some going-out clothes and went out the door, and I went back to the party and had another beer. My friends didn't even ask why Ricca left. They didn't care. I imagine they were relieved.

You put your friends above your girl? Walter asked. That's a classic young-boy mistake. Seems to me you were too old for that.

Probably.

Or were you just thinking about getting a piece of that white girl?

Maybe. I don't know. As soon as I sat down, she was back at it. I kept looking at Brad like, open your eyes. Brad's drunk and laughing with Floyd. As soon as Ricca left, though, I started feeling haunted. I heard

Ricca's dad in my ear. Dude was good to me. Almost like a father. Had a real gruff voice, and sometimes people thought he was mean, but really he was gentle and giving and shit. Then I thought about my own grandmother. Was supposed to spend the whole day with her in the rehabilitation center right before she passed. Stayed home and studied. Said she'd want me to do well. She had a stroke and died the next morning before I could see her. I was listening to my friends with one ear, but in the other ear Ricca's father was talking to his daughter, saying some shit like, *I'm glad you're here, but where is Rashid? What a shame. Told you the boy ain't shit.*

Kyla touched my elbow and was like, You look all dazed. Let's go downstairs. We can get some fresh air downstairs. Come, let's go downstairs.

Maybe her ancestors made up codes for the Underground Railroad or something. Her offer to give me head was brilliant. Like poetry, Walter. The repetition of *downstairs*. The well-placed use of the word *come*. Man, Walter, I'm ashamed to say I was aroused, watching her mouth. She had on this shiny-ass lipstick. Looked moist. Ready.

You're not ashamed to say that, Rashid. You don't have to lie about it to me. Throws your whole story into doubt.

You're right, Walter. I mean, Kyla has all the things I want. You know, all the things we're taught are superficial. Surface.

She got good geometry, huh?

What?

Shape, Rashid. You an expert on Cross River, got to know the talk. She got good geometry? She got that shape?

Man, like a playground of curves. Like a ski slope, Walter. And always down for some kind of adventure. First time we made out was when we broke into this park late at night. Me and Ricca share a religion, values, all that, but next to Kyla that shit seemed like the superficial stuff and Kyla's hips, her neck, her breasts, those shiny, painted-ass lips—all those things skinny Ricca can't compete with—man, Walter, those were the deepest most meaningful things in creation.

Walter chuckled. Not a man on earth who hasn't faced that, he said.

Really?

I don't know. I guess. Maybe I'm just saying it to make you feel better. It sounds true, doesn't it? Anyway, Rashid, what happened? You went ahead and got the blow job?

That's the funny thing. You couldn't tell me at that moment that my deepest desire wasn't to get head from Kyla, but I resisted. Told myself it was the honorable thing to do. Got up and got another beer and we all joked and laughed some more. If this were a movie, the audience would clap and smile, Walter. The triumph of love over simpleminded lust. And then you assume the main character is faithful to his wife forever. I don't think it was that sort of triumph. I don't know. I kept hearing my grand-mother's voice from when she was laid up in the rehab spot and I was like, *I'll be there tomorrow, Granny,* and how disappointed she sounded over the phone. My mother said she visited Granny early in the day and she kept asking, *Where's Rashid? Where's Rashid?* Even worse, Ricca's dad was at my other ear. Sounding more gruff than ever. *Boy, get your ass over here to this hospital!*

It was all a bit much, Walter. I excused myself and went to sit down in the bedroom. Granny at one ear. Ricca's dad at the next. Ricca in front of me. My dick crying out for Kyla. I was in a state. Only thing to do at a moment like that is go to sleep, so I did. But here's the thing. My dad has sleep apnea, and he passed it on to me. It's under control mostly, but espe-cially times of high stress like this one I snore like a monster.

I woke to Floyd and Kyla and Bradley standing over me with their faces all looking crumpled like some trash. Floyd said, If you wanted us to leave, then you should have just said so. Kyla and Brad were nodding. Man, I never seen them so pissed off. But how would I have explained the ghosts at my ears? Kyla's ghost lips on my dick? Huh? It's impossible to explain. They filed out of my place, and I tell you they were pissed at me for a while. Even Sonya, who wasn't there, was all distant after that. I know they got together and talked shit about me. Probably talk-ing shit about me right now. Only got the group chemistry back when I announced I was moving and we had a going-away brun—

At that moment Walter and Rashid turned at the sound of a key tum-bling in the lock. Walter began scrambling. These damn cans, he said. The front door swung open and in stepped Laura. Walter, with all six empty cans in his arms, froze beneath his wife's glare.

Just what is going on in here? she asked as the door slammed shut behind her.

Hello, Ms. Laura, Rashid said. Me and your husband was just having a man-to-man talk.

And drinking, huh? You're both drunk out of your minds. She sucked her teeth. That's the last thing either of you fools needs.

I just, Rashid said. I just—I mean, you know, thank you for saving my life. I can honestly say that I was trying to kill myself—

No shit, baby.

—and I wouldn't be here if it weren't for you two fine people. Walter let me pour my heart out—

I wish you both would have poured the beers out. I mean, really. Aren't you a Muslim?

Rashid hung his head in an exaggerated comical fashion. Well, he said. Yes, I guess. Sort of. Ricca's more of a Muslim than me.

Rashid, Laura said. I think it's time for you to go. Go up to your wife and sober up and I'll sober up my husband so the next time you see each other you'll be in your right states of mind. You're free to visit again. Next time, leave the alcohol and come in through the front door.

Yes, Ms. Laura, Rashid said as he made his way to the door.

Rashid, Walter called. Your friend, what's his name, Bert . . .

Brad.

Yeah, Brad. Brad and Kyla, they together now?

Fuck no, he replied. Uh, excuse me, Ms. Laura. They hardly talk. I think they only keep in touch by way of the group. Feel like I stood in the way of their happiness or something.

And your father-in-law, he died that day before you could see him, didn't he?

Rashid laughed. That would make the story very congruent, wouldn't it? Naw, I saw him the next day. Just me by myself. Ricca had yelled at me about not being there for her or being present in her life when she got home, so I went and spent the whole day with him. Saw him a few other times after that. He was all *Marry my daughter or else*. Feels like I did the old man a solid.

Rashid waved to Walter and Laura before fumbling with the lock and disappearing into the hallway.

What was that all about? Laura asked as Walter went into the kitchen to dispose of the beer cans.

That boy's all messed up, Walter said. He was just giving me his story.

All messed up?

Well, not *all* messed up. Young people today just don't know how to handle the burden they got.

He's just a baby.

Baby? That guy is at least thirty, Laura.

Thirty-year-olds are babies nowadays, Walter.

Whatever. Get this, that boy is some kind of brain. A real egghead.

Yeah?

Got a Ph.D. Teaches over at Freedman's University. An expert in Cross River history.

Impressive.

He didn't even know what a Riverbaby was.

Some expertise. And look at you, Walter. You haven't drank in thirty years. Why in the hell would you let that boy throw you off track?

I'm fine, baby. Walter wrapped his arms around his wife. The burning blast of beer-scented breath brought back memories of the days when they were young and poor and their bodies were the only entertainment they could afford.

The only good thing about when you were a drunk was that you brought out the monster, Laura said. I can't lie about that. I do miss Sid the Sex Machine. He coming back tonight?

You know it, Walter said with a growl as they flopped onto the couch.

Just tonight, though, she said as Walter kissed at her neck and chest. Just tonight and then Sid gotta go back where he came from.

III

The morning of Luce's third birthday party, Laura baked oatmeal cookies and Walter purchased a dancing Cookie Monster doll which they delivered before the party guests were due to arrive.

That's very nice of you, Ricca said. Luce, say thank you to these good people.

Luce bounded from his seat on the living room floor and first hugged Laura's legs and then Walter's. Tank you, he said, returning to his coloring book.

It's no problem at all, Laura replied. He's such a precious little baby. Rashid told us you'd be having a Cookie Monster party, and we're delighted to help you out.

Is Rashid—

Before Walter could finish his sentence, Rashid trudged from the back wearing a faded blue robe, slippers, and pajama pants. His eyes were ringed in black and his hair bushy and uncombed.

He was frowning when he came out, so the smile he feigned upon seeing his neighbors hung particularly false. Ms. Laura, he exclaimed. Walter! Thanks for showing love to my little guy. I know his screaming drives all the neighbors nuts. That's really nice of you. We'll talk soon, Walter.

Before either Walter or Laura could respond, Rashid turned and exited the room. That's when Walter noticed the state of the place. The half-hung decorations. The stuffed animals, colorful plastic toys, and newspapers strewn about the living room.

Ricca apologized for Rashid. It's okay, baby, Laura replied. When they got down to their apartment, Walter settled into his couch and turned on an episode of *Good Times*. Laura gathered her things to head to work. Just before Laura walked out the door, she asked, Isn't their party supposed to start in an hour?

Yep.

Good Lord.

It promised to be a nice afternoon for Walter. Three straight episodes of *Good Times* and a fourth about to begin. He went to the kitchen for a glass of water, but that throbbing on his tongue and in his throat— Yes. His body was crying out for a beer. A beer and another episode of *Good Times*, that's how to make a nice afternoon divine. He had only ever driven by the corner store, never giving it a second thought in all the years he lived in the neighborhood. But if he left now, he could be back just before JJ could shout his first *dyn-o-mite!* Besides, how many times had he seen this episode since it first aired in the 1970s? The 1970s. It was in those days he had learned that drink had the power to make all that bothered him fade into a soft and fuzzy haze. When he drank, it didn't matter that the vague image he had of himself as a bigshot never came into focus. He was a nobody like everyone else he knew. A nobody out in the world but a bigshot in his house, at least in the eyes of Laura and his daughter, Anna. A beer, he found, helped him accept their admiration. Allowed him to accept the world's ambivalence. Just a guy behind the counter at a store. One of thousands any given person encounters in a lifetime. That type of human being is designed to be forgotten. A beer. A beer or two upon walking in the door after work. A glass of expensive whiskey over dinner. Cheaper whisky before bed, maybe a glass of wine. Too many of those nights were now a bubbly haze. One day he realized he had no memories, not really, just a continuous blur. At the same time Laura asked him to put up the drink for good. No yelling or badgering. Stop so your daughter can see who you are, she said. And Walter stopped. But then he drank with Rashid and the only consequence was a night of youthful lovemaking. Walter put a beat-up brown hat on his head and was almost at the door when he heard a loud knocking. First he thought it was the neighbor's door, but then it got louder, vibrating even the floor beneath his feet. Walter peered through the peephole and all he could see was a fuzzy blue.

Walter, Rashid's voice called from outside. Walter, let me in. I got to talk. Walter!

When Walter opened the door, a smell like twenty pounds of garbage struck his nose and crept down his throat. And what a sight. Rashid, the Cookie Monster, pushed his way in, stepping awkwardly. He wore a fuzzy blue costume, though his head remained bare. He held the googly-eyed Cookie Monster headpiece in his hand and promptly tossed it to the floor.

Damn everything, Walter, he said. Fuck every little thing.

Rashid—Walter stammered. Just what—I mean, what is—what is it this time?

Why is every little thing always so fucked up?

Because that's how it—I can't even talk to you looking like that. And Rashid, that smell . . .

Close your mouth, Walter, this isn't the strangest entrance I've made into your apartment.

And that's the worst part of all this.

So after I tried to kill myself, that very night, I figured I needed a project to keep my mind off all the fucked-up-ness. Off Ricca and all the money I didn't have. I was like, I know: I can make my son's birthday party the best thing ever. The greatest of all time. Whose idea was it for a Cookie Monster party? Me. Who spent hours on the Internet downloading *Sesame Street* songs to play? And can you believe Ricca has the nerve to be angry with me, talking about I'm not participating? That she's the only one putting up decorations and she has to bake the cookies. Un—

Rashid, I'm not following any of this.

16

Right, so I'm thinking what would be the coup de grâce? A visit from the cookie man himself. I go onto the Internet and start looking at prices and shit. These people want an arm and three legs. Like five hundred bucks for a professional to show up. And renting wasn't any better at all. It seemed wasteful to rent a Cookie Monster costume for a hundred dollars an hour or three hundred for the entire day, especially since I barely had fifty in the bank and my bills were all overdue and shit. Ricca told me not to worry about it. Said we didn't need no damn Cookie Monster visit. That's what she said. She said *damn*. Said Luce would be happy without it. I wasn't buying that, of course. Just her saying that shit annoyed me, but I pretended like I agreed because I was tired of hearing her voice and I didn't want another fucking argument. Anyway, it was clear renting the thing wasn't the move. Besides, who would want to rent something like that? Why not own? Hang it there in the closet and break it out on any old day. Take the boy to the park dressed as the Cookie Monster. Drop him off at daycare all furry and blue. I'd be the most popular father who ever existed, showing up shaggy and blue with a tin full of snickerdoodles. That was the dream.

You have strange dreams, Walter said, returning to the couch. He let out a sigh as he removed his hat and settled himself into his seat. I'm not sure I want to hear the rest of this. Is this better than an episode of *Good Times?* Because I'm missing *Good Times* and you're missing your son's birthday party.

My brain was all cloudy and black before this, Rashid said, gesturing about with his furry, blue hands. I was all filled with goddamn anxiety, man. This gave me purpose. Now it's turned to shit.

I can smell that.

Are you just going to make jokes?

I'm sorry. It feels like the moment calls for some humor. You're ranting and dressed like Elmo.

The Cookie Monster.

Whatever, Rashid.

I spent every free hour rooting through the Internet, trying to find a deal on a Cookie Monster outfit. Got fat on sugar cookies and chocolate chips and on the creme-filled ones, clicking from site to site, chasing one dead end to another. Sometimes I'd be fucking red-eyed late at night at that computer, then I'd wake and do it all over again. This was all during my summer break when no one was paying me shit and I had to be home with Luce playing babysitter most days. Luce is running about and screaming and smelling like warm piss and shit and I'm searching, not even noticing my son is stinking until the mess starts growing stale. I figured if Luce doesn't care, why should I? Luce at some point would try to climb onto my lap. And I'd have to say, Kid, you stink. But he'd be crying and screaming and pushing his way up there to sit, like my lap's a throne and he's king, and I'd search until I couldn't take it anymore and then I'd go change him and search some more.

So . . . Luce shitted in your costume? Walter asked.

What? No. No, no. I found this one late, late at night just before school started in August. Did I tell you that I'm broke? I put off getting this costume so many times waiting for some money. Waiting for when I got a little left over, but it's mostly check to check for me, bruh. This one was on some auction site. An out-the-way one most people know nothing about. Bids started at five dollars and went up to fifteen and I bid thirty to get it going. But thirty dollars from where? Ricca had to cover the entire rent that month. If Ricca knew I was bidding on this costume . . . Fuck. You know, I had to shake my parents down for just enough to cover the cable and Internet. Cable's important. I watched *Sesame Street* three, four times a day on the kiddie channels to study Cookie's mannerisms and voice. No use being some generic monster; if you're going to do something, do it right. That's what my father used to say. He's probably upstairs now trying to figure what the hell is wrong with me. Trying to figure out why I'm not doing things the right way like he told me. Fuck, you think he'll recognize that I tried?

Rashid, every father says that bit about doing things right. I said that to my daughter and one day you'll say it to Luce.

Right. Anyway, to lose the Internet would have been tragic. A disruption in the costume search would mean a shitty party for my son. You ever bid in an Internet auction? That shit is a white heat. Checking back every few minutes. It's all about defeating all the other bidders and cheating the auctioneer. There go the bids. Forty dollars. Fifty-five. Higher. Seventy-five, ninety. Something was telling me to stop. I wouldn't have an extra ninety bucks for weeks. A hundred and fifty. All this tension throbbing at my throat, Walter. One fifty-five, one seventy-five. The other dude topped off at two fifty and, Walter, I'm at three fifty and thought that was it. No one bid for a while. In the last minutes someone bid four seventy-five and I hit back with five fifty. And then someone hit back and I hit back. When it all ended and I realized I'd won, everything was silent all around me and I heard my office chair creaking. And I'm sweating and grinning like a dumbass fool. All very exhilarating, right? Then I got the sudden awareness that I was on the hook for twelve hundred and fifty big ones that I didn't have.

Walter sat on the couch, leaning forward, his head in his hands. Man, Rashid, I seen some reckless things, but damn. If you were married to my daughter—

I'm not that reckless. I thought about the change jars I kept. Sometimes I could get like a hundred and fifty out of there, but they were empty. Then I remembered that Ricca had just dumped all of that into Luce's college fund.

Oh, God, Rashid.

God had nothing to do with any of this. Nothing. He's no help to me. So, yeah, I looted that college fund. Ain't tell Ricca shit about that. It's in my name, therefore it's my money. Went into our shared savings. Shared checking. Cleaned that shit out. I don't know how we're paying rent next month. Then there's our retirement fund. Thing is down to twenty-eight dollars and it's got a thirty-five-dollar maintenance fee every month. You know what I got for my troubles? A used, holey costume that smells like someone pulled it out the rankest dumpster in America. I bit my nails and waited two whole weeks to find out the world is a fucked-up place. Ad said it was brand new. Never worn. Look at me. This look like something that's never been worn? The thing came to the door after the damn party had started. I took that box to the back room quick, quick, quick.

Rashid's words became caught on the cracking of his voice, and tears poured down his cheeks.

Man, Walter, he said. I screamed and Ricca came in and I screamed again and she was like, There are twelve kids out there. I told her I spent a G, much more than a G—I don't want to even tell you how much—on a smelly maggot-covered Cookie Monster corpse. She was pissed, Walter. Ain't even mention the money; that's how I know she's pissed. I'm gonna hear about it later. Gonna have to tell her we have to start all over with Luce's college fund, with everything. She just looked at me with these dead eyes. Wasn't no more love in those things. She said, Rashid, get a grip. There are twelve kids out there trying to eat cookies and have a good time. Don't be a jerk. We'll deal with everything else later. She stormed out and I thought about it and was like, She's right. So I put on the costume and walked out singing about how C was for Cookie and you know what, all twelve of those kids started crying and the adults started coughing and waving their hands and one little girl grabbed her mother and said, Mommy, the Cookie Monster stinks. That's when I took off the head and ran out and came down here to you.

Walter breathed deeply, taking the garbage smell into his lungs, and then he sat silently with his eyes closed, hoping when he opened them there would be no absurdity, no insanity inside his apartment. Where was Laura when he needed a firm but patient hand? Walter opened his eyes and there was the Cookie Monster with the head of a man and a stench that grated at his throat.

God, Rashid, that's quite something, he said. I'm not sure—You young people. There are going to be rocks in your way and rocks on your backs. You're a man, you can't approach this like a baby would. It won't get any easier, Rashid. Not a lick easier. It's gonna be like this forever. Shit, it's going to get harder.

Forever, huh? I was going to name Luce forever, or rather, Samad, one of the ninety-nine names of Allah—Al-Samad, the eternal. But then I started to think about eternity, what a curse if you're not God, right? My man God doesn't have holy rent and holy bills to pay. Eternity means someone always digging into your pocket, forever being distracted from your deepest desires, spending all your time doing something you don't want to do in order to pay a petty light bill. So in that hospital room while Ricca was screaming and pushing Luce out, I changed my mind about wanting my son to be eternal. His little head looked sort of like a beam of light so I dropped my college Arabic for my high school Spanish. La Luz, the light. But light, it's beautiful and all, but it generates heat: heat burns. That's what this family shit does, it burns you. Sets you on fire. Burns you to a fucking crisp. All my sense is burned from me. Everything. I'm gutted like a burnt-out building. I'm burned. I can't stand. One day I'm gonna topple over, a pile of fucking burnt ash that'll burn forever.

And that, Rashid, is the good news. The sun burns and burns and burns and one day it'll burn out. Massive explosion, taking everything with it, kid. But while it burns, look how much flourishes. Go back to your family, Rashid. Make the day special for Luce. Let Ricca scream at you. You deserve it. And then tomorrow, continue to burn, it's all you can do.

Rashid stared at the old man and then he turned and slowly walked to the door. Yeah, he said with his hand on the knob. Yeah. You know something, Walter? I regret it all. Every single moment. Not getting head from Kyla. Ricca. Luce. This stinking-ass Cookie Monster costume. My job. Cross River. And if I had made any different choices in life, I'd regret those too. Catch you later, Walter.

Later, son. Oh, you might want to take off that smelly costume before you go back in there.

Right, Rashid said from the hallway. As he shimmied from the furry blue outfit, the door slammed itself shut. Walter heard Rashid's feet moving up the stairs and above him a door opened and slammed.

If there were a time to head to the corner store and get a pack of beer, it would be now, he thought. Why would he want to remember all this? This was the type of memory that one wants to fade into a fuzzy haze. Walter noticed the blue Cookie Monster head resting on the floor. From some angles, the smiling open mouth looked like an expression of abashed joy, from others it resembled horror. He rubbed his eyes and his forehead. He felt drunk, but it was a different drunk from the one the bottle would give him. Walter suddenly was struck by the image of one day coming in to see Rashid's legs dangling atop his balcony, all dead and furry and Cookie Monster blue.

But right now there was music and children's laughter from above and when he got close to the balcony, he could even hear Rashid laughing, to be sure. Walter placed the smiling, googly-eyed Cookie Monster head atop his bookshelf and rested himself on the couch. That afternoon he fell asleep watching the grinning puppet head and listening to the joy from above.

Everyone Lives in a Flood Zone

Walking with a hunched posture, shambling through a windy day, being pelted by cool dots of water. There was something inevitable about my bent gait. Somehow, somewhere deep down I really did believe it would protect me from the rain. Did no such thing, of course.

The day was breezy and cold, and I wore a thin jacket as I'd expected it to be warmer when I left the house in the morning. Cold wetness does much to clear the detritus from the mind and leave one focused only on the moment, and before long I had two thoughts: I'm soaked. I'm shivering.

I've never been one to watch weather reports. It's more honorable to take the weather as it comes.

Forgive me if I digress; you wanted to know what happened to my brother.

So it was raining that day, pretty heavily. The sky glowed an incandescent gray, shimmering overhead. I nervously smoked a cheap cigar, my lungs burning. I imagined them a flaming red, shining through my skin and through my clothes. Then I imagined them a crusty, charred black. But really they were likely still a fresh bright pink, like cooked salmon. I only smoke at times of distress.

The Cross River had again breached the Southside, at least part of it, the part that's always taking the brunt of the floodwaters—the part where all the poor folks live and where my little brother lived. First it was dry, and then it started to rain and just like that the water rushed in, a steady flow of dirty brown liquid. I have never understood why people live there. This is nearly a yearly occurrence and nobody seems to care. There's a trailer park down there that regularly becomes a scattered field of over-turned trailer homes, the flimsy material they make those pieces-of-shit with strewn all about the place. I see pictures, almost every year, on the front page of the *Days & Times*. And then they rebuild absurdly like a great flood never happened.

I told my brother not to move into that trailer park, but listening—not drugs—was his true problem. The bastard that owns that place calls it Riverview. What a fucker.

In the morning when they were threatening rain and promising a flood like this town hadn't seen in a hundred years, my mother called me up nearly in tears, telling me to go find Stephen, make him come home.

Mom, I told her, the last time I talked to him he said that trailer park was home. He cussed me out. He's not going to listen now.

Nobody had talked to him in weeks, since he didn't have a phone. Every once in a while he'd call, sounding distant and scratchy, just a dis-embodied voice offering a mumbled cry. Usually he requested cash, some emergency always on the horizon, and my mother would send me to Western Union with a fat envelope of her Social Security money. He'd pick up the cash across the bridge in Virginia—Port Yooga. It always galled me the lengths he'd go to avoid letting me or Mom see the desper-ate creature he'd become. Those times, I couldn't help but imagine the phone call I'd receive one day telling me they'd found his gaunt, lifeless body on a dirty floor.

This stormy day when I saw her, she put the money in my hand, clutched my free palm tightly, and stared at me soulfully with those big gray eyes. Go and get your brother, she said, and bring him home.

She tried to appear strong, but I knew she'd been crying for him as she'd never cry for me.

When I left her house it had already started getting chilly, but the rain hadn't begun for the day. I didn't believe it would rain, at least not as hard as it did. I needed to think about what I'd say to Stephen when I saw him, so I decided to walk. It would be a long walk, but it would give Stephen a chance to sober up for the day and me a chance to choose my words carefully.

Ever notice how the weather can turn your whole mood? As I walked, the sky became darker. I watched the churning clouds move. They seemed black with rage and so was I. How could Mom allow herself to be played over and over by this con man? I pulled a cigar from a package and lit it as I rehearsed my words, and they became more rage-filled and the rain fell harder. I had heard that tobacco can calm the disturbed soul and it only became a problem when modern man began using it as a crutch. At first it tickled the back of my throat, then it felt like pinpricks in my windpipe. Before long my lungs burned, and I started to think about my mission and I hunched over. Rain poured and the high wind blew my jacket about and made me stumble. The rain pellets stung as they sprayed the exposed flesh of my cheeks. My cigar grew soggy, the damp tobacco blotting out the glowing tip. I sheltered beneath a tree, but then the thunder clapped. It was a loud and deep rumbling, accompanied by a bright purple fork of lightning. I tossed the cigar and kept moving.

As I walked, I noticed two squirrels scurrying ahead of me. One chased the other, so I assumed they were a male and a female. The pooling rain would be a problem for them, I imagined, but instead of troubled, they looked carefree. It reminded me of the story my mother used to tell my brother and me when we were children about the boy who willed himself into a squirrel rather than live a difficult life. I really don't know what my mother was trying to get at with that story, but I loved it. Stephen loved it more than I did. I figured my speech to my brother would involve squirrels somehow. I tramped through deep, dirty puddles and the water collected inside my shoes and I thought I could hear my socks squishing beneath the weight of my steps.

I walked underneath awnings and beneath the eaves of houses. I stooped over like an old man. It was all so ridiculous, and I stopped preparing my speech to address the stupidity of my gait. I straightened my back and raised my head to the glowing gray. As soon as my walk was somewhat automatic, I took my mind from it and returned to thinking of what I would say to my brother. About a block or two down the road, a man in a black rain-beaded bowler hat and matching umbrella called my name. He looked hazy in the rain. I didn't at all recognize him.

The bowler-hatted man told me his name and it still didn't sound familiar, but he spoke as if we were friends.

Say, jack, where you heading to in this storm? he asked.

Going to see my brother, I replied.

Yeah? How's he doing?

Man, I haven't talked to him in like months. He lives his life, I live mine.

You have his face.

He has my face. We have our mother's face.

And your mannerisms. It's like you're the same person.

I assure you—

Let me ask you something, jack.

I really got to run.

It'll only take a second.

Okay, but make it quick.

Okay. He paused without saying a word. The rain rapidly splattered against his umbrella, making a clopping sound. I let out a frustrated sigh and he continued: So, would you like a ride to the Southside? It's pouring and it's a long walk. I haven't seen Stephen in a little while and I'd really like to see him.

Well, man, I appreciate it, but I need to clear my head and I got some real brotherly shit to say to him, I replied. It's kind of personal, so I'll need to talk to him alone. You understand, right?

He took a step toward me, in a way that was meant to be menacing, but it didn't really scare me. Some rain from his umbrella splashed into my eyes.

Listen, jack, said the bowler-hatted man as I snapped my eyes shut and wiped the water from my face. When I opened them, a woman wearing a black veil over her face and a black hijab that nearly covered even her feet strolled up to us and he stopped talking.

She held a bright yellow umbrella spread out overhead. The bottom of her garb was damp.

Do either of you have the time? she asked softly, and I became transfixed by the watery brown and green pools of her eyes. The rest of her body was totally covered, except for her hands with their soft, slender olive fingers. But her eyes were two celestial bodies. I wanted to ask her if her eyes were real. Instead I simply looked at my watch and, as coolly as possible, told her the time.

She chuckled. Mocking me, I thought. She said with a serious voice, You're not going into that mess, are you?

I have to. My brother . . .

Yeah, he's a superhero, the bowler-hatted man said.

She cut him a frowning glance—I could tell by her knotted brow—and turned her shoulder to him, cutting him from the conversation.

You should leave it to the professionals. Ordinary people get lost on the Southside on regular days. Just imagine a day like this. Your brother will be fine.

You know my brother?

Everyone knows your brother.

He's like a cold or something, the bowler-hatted man said. He comes around to aggravate everyone once in a while.

That's not how I'd describe him, she replied. Sometimes he's a good man. And then sometimes he's a good man high on drugs. He's helped enough people over the years that everyone knows where the real Stephen lies.

I wish I knew where he's lying right now, the bowler-hatted man said. Shit, wherever the fucker is lying, you know he's lying.

Listen, she moved closer and whispered and I thought she whispered my name. Be safe. Keep your brother safe. Don't let anyone take advantage of him. You know what I mean, right?

I nodded, though I wasn't sure what she meant. She smiled. Of course, I can't be certain, but I knew then that she had smiled. She thanked me and walked off.

The bowler-hatted man and I watched her disappear into the pouring rain. The curtain of water made her look wavy as she strolled into the distance, holding herself upright instead of hunched over like me.

Damn A-rabs, the bowler-hatted man said. He looked at me knowingly, preparing for me to share his sneering disgust, but I remained stone-faced.

Where were we? he asked.

I was leaving, I said.

I walked from him and he called after me. Better get under this umbrella, he said. It's raining. Don't be an asshole. You'll regret not riding with me.

Some blocks from where I had seen the bowler-hatted man, I noticed the woman's yellow umbrella just ahead of me. She strolled all alone in the rainstorm. So unreal. Mythical somewhat. Had to remind myself that she's no myth. Just a woman like any other. Which made her more mythical.

After the twin towers fell, back when my brother drove a taxi, he stuffed a bunch of them into his cab and drove them home for free. Groups of guys from some of the projects, and even folks from the college and Uptown, yelled filthy things and threw rocks and even brandished weapons, but Stephen never backed down. Drove every inch of every street in Cross River for free on this mission. He did that for a couple weeks until it seemed like the coast was clear. That was the one time he made me proud. I spent those weeks drunk.

I wondered if my new obsession was one of those Muslims he helped during that time.

She crossed the street; I needed to go straight, but I crossed with her. She took me down a narrow road. She knew I was there behind her, but she didn't look back. And the day became like any other day because I forgot about my brother. She walked slowly, and when she came to her door, she lowered the bright yellow umbrella and with a bump of her shoulder stumbled inside.

I spent a great deal of time deciding whether to knock or to just go. The rain didn't matter to me, as I could get no wetter. Nearly an hour passed, and I came up with a compromise: a quick look and then I'd go. A light was on in a room on the east side of her house. I remembered my brother, and I moved to get one last glance at the woman before going on my way.

I crept to the window and peered over a bush. What I saw startled me, and I gasped. She had removed her head covering and her face veil. The woman's gorgeous black curls rested on her shoulders. She began removing the rest of her clothes, and part of me, deep in my animal heart, wanted to stay, but we weren't ready to be that intimate, so I eased away from the window. Too late: she turned. Perhaps my vision had burrowed into her flesh; perhaps our connection on the level at which all human minds are connected deepened at this precise moment.

It occurred to me that I wasn't myself. Not in her eyes. In those eyes, I was a creep. A common Peeping Tom. A flash of fear pulsed in my chest.

I eased backward and dashed through the puddles. When I looked back, she was at the door. Robed. Face uncovered. Out of respect, I looked away. She called my name. It was unreal. And if it was truly real, then it was all wrong and I wanted no part in making this woman violate herself in this vulgar way. I'm like Stephen with his touch that turns all to shit.

I'm scared to admit that it's a family trait, and I wanted—and still want—no part of it. So I ran, splashing rainwater on my legs, chest, and back as her calls faded behind me.

The showers slowed to a drizzle, and when I reached the Southside, the rain that had fallen for most of the day had stopped. The river that once knew its place now escaped its bounds. Part of the Southside, the lowest part of the Southside, was gone, replaced with a putrid brown lake. I waded in up to my calves. A dead squirrel floated by. In the distance: a drowned shaggy black dog. My brother's out there in the muck, alive or dead, I thought. I stood in awe of the brown waters, shaking my head at the enormity of it all. A black Jeep with a canoe strapped to the top pulled up, and two men hopped out and walked toward me. I recognized one of them as the bowler-hatted man that I had spoken to earlier. The other man wore a black leather jacket and had beads of sweat or rainwater dotting his bald head. When he got close, I had to look up to gaze at him.

A third man, a squat man with dark glasses, hung back untying the canoe from the top of the Jeep.

You ready? the bowler-hatted man asked.

Thinking of no better response, I nodded. We set out into the water, the two goons paddling—the squat man in front and the tall man in the back—and the bowler-hatted man and I in the middle locked in an awkward silence. The tops of street signs peeking from the water, partially submerged houses, and neighborhood landmarks guided us toward my brother. The statue of the town founder, Ol' Cigar, on his horse stood as a heroic presence on normal days. This day, however, it looked as if the horse was struggling in a pathetic attempt to keep his nose above the water.

Your brother is a good guy, the bowler-hatted man said, he's just made some bad, bad choices.

I didn't say anything at first, but then I said this: He came down here to help these people and became one of them.

The tall bald man gave me a sharp glance. I don't know why I said what I did. It was a half-thought-out comment. But there was nevertheless some truth in it. Down here is where people hop out with guns and take your money, and then for sport they take your life as if whatever thrill they get from murder is more important than any plans you had for the next day. I don't regret what I said. People live like animals on the South-side. There is such a breach I often can't understand the language of the people here no matter how hard I listen. The two goons talked, but I only nodded and pretended I was listening intently, as I had no understanding of their words. Even when the bowler-hatted man spoke to them, I listened, but it made no sense to me.

What had my brother gotten into? What had he gotten me into? There were rumors that he'd run afoul of the Jackson Crime Family. But I never believed that. Most of those guys had been rounded up by the cops or wasted in family rivalries with the Johnsons or the Washingtons or with themselves. There wasn't much money in gambling or protection to be made in Cross River. The most reliable drug customers were dying off. The Jacksons that remained had crossed the bridge to do business with the Italians. All of that was probably bullshit, however. What the hell did I know about organized crime? Just what I heard from know-nothing know-it-alls or half read in newsmagazines or what I saw in movies and heard in rap songs. I was out of my depth, and I imagined my brother was too.

People waved and shouted from rooftops. I wished we could stop and rescue them all. Bring food or water. We ignored them as if their cries were silence. We passed the bodies of floating cats and dogs, mostly cats. Dead insects floated by, and dead rats and pigeons, but they all deserved to be dead. I imagined myself shot and tossed overboard, floating next to them. The men were paddling in the direction of my brother's place. A human body floated face-down in the distance, his white T-shirted back an island.

Maybe that's your brother, the bowler-hatted man said. The fucker had a smile in his voice, sounded excited. I scowled at him. It might have been my brother, though; I couldn't deny that. The body was the right size. The right shape. The right color. I wanted to jump from the canoe and swim to the floating man. We got close enough to flip the corpse. The nose looked like a smashed mushroom sitting there on his face. His eyes filled with redness. Face puffed out, all bloated and cracked. A sad case, but not my brother.

We passed the next several minutes in silence. The light crept out of the sky, making it a darkening gray. I spotted my brother first on the top of a roof with two other men. I didn't dare say anything. Didn't want to alert the bowler-hatted man and his goons to Stephen's existence. He waved his arms and jumped, calling out to me. Expressionless, the men turned their heads toward him and paddled in his direction.

Stephen's face had become gaunt and pockmarked with scars. He had a bulge in his pocket that I took for drugs but could have been anything. My brother, a mass of bones and baggy flesh and hair and eyes that were too big for their sockets. A mess of parts that didn't quite fit. His garments were too big for him. Dirt-caked jeans drooped and bunched at his ankles. A flannel shirt lay askew at the shoulders. He looked like a boy wearing his father's clothes. I told myself I had never seen him looking so bad, but that's untrue. This was his natural state. I always looked the other way, but now I couldn't turn from him.

He smoked a cigarette, looking again like a child doing an adult thing.

Big brother, he said, all this water and I'm thirsty as shit. Didn't God promise he wouldn't flood the earth again?

When have you ever known God to keep a promise, the bowler-hatted man replied.

What are you doing with that asshole? my brother said sharply, pointing with his smoking hand.

I stood to cross from the canoe to the rooftop and felt a hand on my shoulder. I stumbled and tripped onto the roof. The goons yelled and cursed. The two men sitting behind my brother pointed and laughed at my clumsiness.

What the hell are you doing? the bowler-hatted man screamed from the canoe. You almost capsized this shit. You are as dumb as your brother. Don't share his fate, motherfucker.

Threats always put steel in my spine. There is something about an asshole trying to make himself bigger by acting like a tough guy that brings out the thug in me.

Look, I don't have time for your fucking nonsense, I said. I need to talk to my br—

Thug-me disappeared the second the goons crossed from the canoe to the rooftop, holding pistols and wearing the flat emotionless faces of killers.

Maaaaan, my brother said. What kind of shit is this? I spend months ducking these clueless fuckers only to get sold out by my own family. Thanks, bruh.

Fucked up, said one of the dirty men, the one with the lopsided Afro, as he rested his hand on the shoulder of his friend, a balding man with gray and black dreadlocks sprouting from the sides of his head.

I've said it before and I'm gonna say it now, the man with the dreadlocks said. Family will sell you out quicker than your enemies. Fucking family, man.

I . . . we . . . they had a boat, I said. All I had thought to tell my brother sputtered from my head. Mom sent me, I said.

At that he scowled. The dirty men both smiled broadly and chuckled back and forth. Mommy, the man with the dreadlocks called, and I shot him a look. He shot me one right back.

Your brother loves you, the bowler-hatted man said. I, on the other hand, don't. Stephen, you made us look like fools. Running around town searching for you. And for what, a few thousand bucks?

Look, man, I got robbed by some big gorilla-looking pig. He be shaking down every nig—

What makes you think I want to hear your bullshit?

I've been working to get you your money. You can kill me and get nothing, or you can work with me and get paid back.

The bowler-hatted man and his squat goon walked toward my brother. The time for talking was done. Perhaps it had finished weeks ago, but I couldn't help screaming like my voice would be able to make up for all the times I ignored my brother's existence, all the phone calls I didn't return, emails, old-fashioned letters I read briefly and tossed into the trash; eventually he realized I'd never respond, and all contact ceased. When my voice mattered, all Stephen heard from me was silence.

I'll pay you triple, dog, I screamed. You're throwing away a fortune. Don't be a f—

I felt something seize my throat from behind. I reached for it and thrashed around, but that only made it tighter. The heft of another human being weighed heavy on my back. I swayed side to side to shake him. We toppled from the roof into the dirty water. Free from whatever choked me, I thrashed like a bucking beast trying to tread water. The dirty liquid soaked into my clothes, making me heavy. Pressure to the back of my head and my shoulders prevented me from rising. The more I thrashed about, the more nasty brown water spilled into my mouth and swam down my throat. My head bobbed above the surface and I gasped, taking in a mouthful of water and a lungful of air. A hand shoved me back under. Everything went black.

The world around me turned emerald. Those eyes. They hung above me like twin suns. She blinked every few moments and the world became black again and then emerald again and then black and then emerald and on and on. The woman whispered to me in a broken Arabic. She struggled with it as if it weren't her native language. Amina. Khadijah. What could her name be? I heard a voice like my own voice raining down upon me. *She's here to watch over you.* It was as if I had died and returned to become my own spirit guide. Magical, mysterious, mystery muslimeena. Madam, my muslimah, make me more than a mark who's made my brother mortuary bound. My brother. I'd forgotten about him through this meaningless obsession. My own voice cascaded down upon me again. *How do I return?*

I awoke face down on the roof, shivering and coughing. My brother was gone and so were the two goons and their leader. I hacked up thick brown phlegm and a bubble pressed against the inside of my stomach. It seemed that sometime during my unconsciousness I had vomited and shat myself.

He's alive, I heard the man with the lopsided Afro say.

What happened? Where is my brother?

Yes, your brother was a good man, the balding man with the dreadlocks said.

May he be blessed with long life, the man with the lopsided Afro replied.

They both wore flat, creased faces that looked like abused rubbery masks.

How long was I out? I asked, sitting up.

Hours, the balding man with the dreadlocks said. I would say it's the middle of the night, but them dudes took our watches. You was mumbling. Kept going ma-ma-ma-ma, like you was sucking on a tit. Mama. Mama. That's what it sound like you was trying to say while you was out.

There hung a big moon that cast a white light over the slow-moving water. The sky was a navy blue. I glanced at my wrist and my watch was indeed gone. I reached for my pocket. My phone was gone too, along with the money my mother gave me for my brother.

I asked again: Where's my brother?

He's paying some of his debts, the man with the lopsided Afro said.

I'm gonna miss the little guy, the balding man with the dreadlocks said.

Yeah, the man with the lopsided Afro said. That guy always had a story. Say, jackson, you remember the one about the squirrel?

The balding man with the dreadlocks laughed.

Yeah, the man with the lopsided Afro said. That dude in the story went through all kinds of shit and then zap, he plum turns himself into a squirrel and don't have to deal with none of that shit no more. I wish I was a squirrel. That's how I'm gonna remember your brother, as a squirrel. Yeah, man, it would be cool to be a squirrel. Call me Buck Buck Squirrel.

You a damn fool, Buck Buck, the balding man with the dreadlocks said. How being a squirrel gon' get you out this mess?

I guess it wouldn't, he replied. Maybe if I was a flying squirrel. They say it's gonna rain again.

Who say that? the balding man with the dreadlocks asked. It's only the three of us here. You got the Weather Channel beamed into your knotty head?

You think anyone's coming for us?

Naw, man, don't nobody give a fuck about us down here.

Can you believe it? That nigga Stephen used to be my social worker. Then he was my taxi driver. Then my drug dealer. Ha!

And you was gonna sell him out for a few dollars?

Can't trust nobody these days, right?

The men started laughing and then they shut their mouths, but the laughter wouldn't stop. What a sound. A deep full-throated open-mouthed laughter. Though they looked silent and stoic like wood carvings, they weren't silent or stoic. They were laughing.

Say, jackson, the man with the dreadlocks said to me, you all right? You looking all fucked up.

Even as he spoke, he competed with his own laughter. His words and the laughter were a chorus simultaneously singing different parts of the same composition. I turned onto my side and vomited. I shivered. Sweat poured down my skin, though a cool breeze kept blowing. This must have been how it was for Stephen every blessed time he tried to kick the stuff.

I lay on my back, coughing up the saliva and bile that had caught in my throat. The men stood over me. I heard them through the persistent laughter.

He not looking good.

I'd be surprised if he make it through the night.

Shit, he ain't no good no more.

What you think we can get for him?

I said he ain't no good no more.

But he look enough like his brother; we could still get some money.

He ain't no good. He spoiled. Rotten. Won't no one pay us nothing for that. Help me with him.

Man, I ain't touching this dude. I'm not letting no sickness jump from him to me.

You don't want him to make you sick? Then help me flip him into the water.

I tried to scream out, but the only sound I could make was a donkey-like neighing, which just made the men's laughter more pronounced. Water touched my skin. Soaked into my clothes.

Again everything turned black.

I awoke to the rocking of a boat and the watery sound of oars thrusting through the water. The putrid sulfur smell of the filthy muck below filled my nostrils. I coughed. A voice called my name. It sounded like my brother. I glanced upward at the figure who stroked the oars back and forth. The person was hunched and cloaked in all black. I became convinced that it was my brother; he had survived and, in turn, had come to rescue me.

It's nearly morning, a voice said. You were out for some time.

The voice was a feminine one. I wanted to respond, but still I couldn't speak. It took all my strength to pull myself up. What I saw, though it was not my brother, filled me with joy. First, the dazzling eyes, two burning brown and green sparks dancing on her face. Then the veil.

She told me to lean back, to relax. Still unable to speak, I muttered a horrible sound over and over until I became frustrated.

You were out there clinging to a piece of wood, she said. I don't know if you remember. But you're safe now. We gotta get you to a hospital.

I started to mutter again, but it was no use. My face hurt and I could form no words. I tried to ask her all the pertinent questions. Tried to tell her about my brother, who I knew I would never see again, but my brain felt tired. I couldn't even remember his name, though I could see his face, which brought such shame welling up in my heart that I nearly began to cry. I wanted to tell her about myself, about my mother who would soon be bawling. I wanted to tell this mythical woman that I loved her, that she was beautiful.

She reached her slender arm back to me and took my right hand in hers, telling me to rest. The woman reassured me that everything would be okay. And it was only then that I noticed how warm it had become and how the light from the expanding sun had taken over the whole sky and how it made the ripples in the dirty water shimmer.

A Friendly Game

I

Every day, twice a day, Joan Santi bathed her son in lavender, from the soft spot on his head with its wispy hairs to his tiny light brown toes. You could always smell it emanating from every crevice of baby Phil. Consequently, Joan's hands carried the smell. This was back in the eighties when she was a new mother. That's what she became known for. That beautiful purple smell. This pudgy woman, occasionally with slight acne and neatly pressed hair or carefully chosen wigs. Who didn't gravitate toward her in those days?

II

It was only after the boys had played their last game of basketball that Casey noticed the woman. He was a bit lightheaded from the workout, and he breathed briskly through his mouth. He bent forward, rested his hands on his knees, and looked up. She was in the distance at first, appearing very briefly like a hallucination, walking round and round, speaking gibberish to herself loudly and animatedly.

Her shirt was dirt-caked and dotted with black smudges. It stopped just above her navel so that her belly flopped over her waistband and hung low. The woman paused and watched Casey and his three friends for a few minutes before moving again in a circle round the perimeter of the ball court.

At first they ignored her, making small talk and jokes, and then Casey said, What she want?

A new shirt, Richard replied.

She ain't bothering us, Wayne said.

When she strode closer, Casey noticed a bulbous pus-filled sac just above the right corner of her upper lip. Curly whiskers grew out of it. Wild crabgrass patches of hair dotted her chin and cheeks. She parted her lips and the boys watched the gray and black strays that surrounded her mouth.

Fillafil. Fillafil . . . Fillafil . . . Fillafil, she called. Then she walked.

The boys screwed their faces in disgust, chuckling between short breaths. Kwayku was the first to get a hold of his breathing and in a husky, wheezy growl he said: Look, Casey, there go your mother.

Everyone laughed except Casey, who twisted his brow. If only he had taken more shots instead of listening to Wayne and passing the ball, he could've shut Kwayku up by gloating over a victory, but after a loss, or a series of them, there is very little the loser can tell the victor.

The conversation moved along to girls in general, then it turned specific, the boys tossing off names of girls they'd sleep with if ever given the chance—or, in Kwayku's case, boasting of girls he slept with or came damn close. Casey, through everything, stayed fixed on the woman; he studied her as she passed. The boys swatted at gnats and dabbed sweat from their foreheads while they discussed female body parts, particular body parts they were all familiar with and had glimpsed through clothing at one time or another: a left breast, a thigh, a few particularly thick butt cheeks, some puffy cleavage that recurred day after day. Marcy's breasts. More to the point, her ass. It was an outsize thing. An impressive thing. A jutting-outward-and-still-rounded thing. A disproportionate thing when compared to the rest of her. A special and jean-warping thing. Twin planets divided by a crack of slender outer space. And much to the pleasure of boys everywhere, it was unable to be hidden beneath sweaters tied round her waist or any other type of thick clothing no matter how she tried.

Man, Kwayku said. If I could be the wallet in them back pockets.

Times like this, Casey wanted to punch Kwayku right in his wolf smile. Then he remembered that it was all jealousy. Marcy belonged to him, ass and all.

A white girl with ass, Kwayku said. It's fucking unheard of.

The bearded woman danced through Casey's peripheral vision, and he was happy to take his mind off Kwayku's nonsense.

There that bitch go again, Casey said.

Calling your mother a bitch? Have some respect.

That woman, that bearded freak, looks nothing like my mother, Casey thought, rubbing the slick sheet of sweat that covered the back of his neck.

She moved purposefully. Staring forward, her head tilted. Casey had seen her before in one of her lucid moments, sheepishly approaching passersby and requesting change. He had seen her angry and belligerent, but most often she was just babbling and confused. Always she was an irritating and bothersome creature, like the stray dogs of the Southside who roamed at night in packs.

Fillafil . . . Fillafil, she said as she made another pass.

What she saying? Falafel? Why she keep circling the playground, why don't she go somewhere? Casey asked. I bet you she gonna ask for money any minute now.

Well, damn, Casey, she your mother, you should give her some money, Kwayku said. At least pay for a shave.

She was nearly out of sight when Casey picked up a rock, medium-sized and irregularly shaped. Had some heft to it. He didn't mean to strike her when he threw it, only to scare her, but he did hit her, square in her head. She covered the bleeding spot with her hand.

Kwayku howled sharply, unable to contain his shock. Wayne gasped and Rich followed. Everyone silently watched one another. The woman's eyes widened as blood ran down her face. Kwayku snickered and then doubled over in laughter.

The woman stood frozen, and then she was in motion, running off into the street, and then she was gone. The boys spent a half hour replaying the event, changing it until it became a myth.

Man, that was fucked up, Wayne said.

Shut up, nigga, Kwayku said. You was laughing the hardest.

At the end of the half hour, they remembered the rock striking as a light thing, an inconvenience to the woman. They forgot the terror on her face. The sinking feeling of fear that wound through their chests. The blood. It became a scene in a slapstick comedy. They renamed her Lady MacBeard. Instead of shocked silence, the boys recalled laughter being stuck in their throats. It was all a kind of nothing, and in brief moments they remembered what they forgot.

When they were all done and Casey versus Lady MacBeard became little more than an elaborate story, they walked down the hill to Marcy's house to watch the Spice Channel as was their custom.

III

When she returned to work after maternity leave, Joan's scent would light up every corner of the library. She glowed lavender and purple and fuchsia and plum. Maybe it was from baby Phil. That's what her husband said as he stood and watched his wife and son from behind his ever-present cloud of smoke. There was no one at the time who didn't also radiate their own colors when they saw Joan. The librarians she assisted grinned when they spoke about her. The children in the reading room crowded around once a week as she sang songs and read them picture books. They cooed when she showed them the images and giggled at the different voices she put on for each character.

It was one of those facts lost between childhood memories, but Casey used to be there sometimes, infrequently really, sitting in the front row. Each time she read, she daydreamed one of the children was her Phil watching his mother read from a favorite storybook. One or two times Casey was Phil. And Wayne once was Phil. Every week a new Phil.

Joan loved that place. The smell of the books, for a time, gave her just the highest feeling.

IV

A week of heavy rains kept the boys from venturing from their homes after school. The basketball court up the street from Marcy's house at Wildlands Forest Elementary sat beneath several inches of water. And even Marcy's basement, where Casey and his friends went to see naked people writhe about on the television screen, hosted a shallow pool of floodwater. Nothing major, just an irritation, but enough to keep guests out for a while. Then all that passed away and the boys went back to the basketball court.

The day of their return, a Tuesday, the court was dotted with puddles, and when the ball rolled into the grass, it became coated in muddy water. To clean it, Kwayku rolled it off his long black fingers high into the open air, and droplets of brown water went shooting off in all directions.

The atmosphere was damp and heavy with unfallen rain. Wispy gray clouds hung low in the sky. Kwayku spent most of the day telling and retelling the tale of Casey's triumph, adding a flourish here, a detail there. Casey kept a grin on his face all day until Kwayku said: Man, why you want to do your mother like that?

She does look like his mom, doesn't she? Richard said.

The grin melted from Casey's face. She looks nothing like my mother, he thought.

When the four boys finished their basketball game, Kwayku and Richard found themselves victorious again, and Kwayku began his taunts by offering to do Marcy in various positions. Casey noticed Lady Mac-Beard circling the perimeter, her head bandaged. She walked slowly and ignored the boys, mumbling to herself and occasionally waving her arms for emphasis.

Kwayku pointed and said: Casey, your momma is looking for you.

Casey felt his thoughts darken. He threw a rock. It slapped the ground behind the woman with a thud, splashing onto the muddy earth. She walked on as if it never happened. Casey dug another from the dirt and lobbed it. It whizzed by her. He threw another and another and another until one slammed into her back. She stumbled forward and then stood still, her face frozen in confusion and horror. And then she ran.

Yeah, run, bitch, Kwayku said as he curled back his arm and hurled a stone at Lady MacBeard. It fell far short, as if he never meant to hit her at all.

Richard timidly collected a handful of rocks and tossed them at the fleeing woman, all of them flying far wide or far short. Wayne sighed and shook his head in disgust at his friend—really a neighbor his mother asked him to watch out for—before grabbing Richard and ordering him to cease. And like that, Richard stopped and looked up at his older friends as if waiting on directions.

Casey scratched at his neck, where sparse patches of hairs had started growing in. The boys threw the ball toward the hoop and, tiring of that, walked off to watch pornography at Marcy's house, speaking of the thing that was her ass the whole time.

The next day, just as Kwayku drained a perfect three-point shot past Casey's outstretched hand, Marcy showed up, points of sunlight shimmering against some of her stray blonde hairs. Casey smiled and waved at his girlfriend. Sweat covered his face. She smiled back, standing at the edge of the court where the blacktop met the grass, swaying, saying nothing. She greeted Richard and Wayne and ignored Kwayku. He nodded at her as he threw the basketball at Casey's chest. It smacked into his torso. He gasped, letting the ball drop to the ground.

Your ball, Kwayku said with a growl.

Let me show you how to play, Casey said, tearing his shirt from his sweaty back and slapping the ball against the hard black playground court.

This fool want to take off his shirt when his girl show up, Kwayku said. Put the bird back in the cage.

Casey charged the basket, leaping off the ground and letting the ball rise from his fingers into the air. With little movement, Kwayku reached his ropy arm to the sky and slapped the ball to the earth.

Get that shit out of here, boy, Kwayku said. What you think this is?

Stop showing off and pass that shit! Wayne screamed.

Casey looked over at his girlfriend. Their eyes met and she grinned and shrugged. He looked away, pretending Marcy wasn't there even as he felt her eyes on him. She clapped and shouted Casey's name, which made him more conscious of his own existence, the physical space his body occupied.

Whatever, Kwayku, Casey said. Let's see you do that again.

Kwayku slapped down Casey's shots three more times. Richard, after each block, snatched the ball and tossed it into Kwakyu's waiting hands. In a single swift motion, Kwayku pulled up and each time released a perfectly placed shot that would have swished in the net had there been a net. And just as he released the ball, he dedicated each shot to Marcy, who accepted the honor by playfully blowing kisses in his direction. Before long, it was over for Casey and Wayne. Kwayku snatched his baseball cap from the ground and slapped it onto his head, declaring it his crown.

I'm the king of basketball! Kwayku shouted. And Richard is my deputy. Everybody address me as *Your Highness*. Forget that sucker, Marcy, you could be my queen.

No thanks, *Your Highness*, Marcy replied.

Casey strode to the edge of the court, ignoring Kwayku and Richard's trash talk, and put his arm around Marcy.

I don't need your sweat all over me, she said, pulling from him. Shoot, she mumbled. When I ask you to touch me . . . She sucked her teeth. Casey shot her a glance that was supposed to look angry but only appeared wounded and weak.

Kwayku bawled and clapped his hands. The massive things slapping together sounded like hooves clopping along the road. Yeah, Kwayku said, you stink. He laughed louder. Richard and Wayne joined him.

Damn, your girl dissed you, Kwayku said, his words riding waves of laughter.

Whatever, Casey mumbled.

Marcy, you know you don't really want to be with him, Kwayku said. Come holler at me.

Casey frowned. Marcy said nothing. She smiled, though.

You got a donkey, girl, he continued. Casey don't know how to ride that.

Shut up, Kwayku, Marcy said. Stop talking about my ass. You're just jealous 'cause Casey got this *donkey* and what you got?

Then there was quiet until Kwayku said: Hey, Rich, she told that nigga he stink. She said: *Get the hell off me, nigga! You stink!*

She ain't say that, Casey said.

Man, everybody heard her, Richard said.

You and Richard, y'all need to stop instigating, Marcy replied. Casey know I said nothing like that.

The back-and-forth went on for several minutes. Lady MacBeard circled the playground slowly as if on a mission, though no one noticed.

Watch, Marcy gonna be laying up with me today, Kwayku said. Ain't that right, Marcy?

Whatever, she replied.

Can't stop talking shit, huh? Wayne asked.

What? I'm just saying, she know she want to, Kwayku replied.

Man, Kwayku, that's enough, Casey said.

Kwayku walked over to Casey, standing so close to him they traded body heat. He had nearly a foot on Casey. Kwayku's voice rumbled where everyone else's squeaked.

Who you talking to like that, boy? When Casey didn't respond, he said: Dog, I'll smack the shit out of your little ass. He paused. Just 'cause you can play some ball don't mean I won't smack you.

Casey looked down at the rocks on the ground. In the distance, Lady MacBeard made another circuit and Casey noticed her for the first time.

Watch, man, I'm gonna fuck your girl. What you think about that?

Again Casey didn't respond.

Man, that ain't a rhetorical question. I'm gonna stick my dick in that ass. What you gonna do?

Marcy was as still as a plastic doll, or rather a mannequin from a department store window. Richard and Wayne chuckled, yet they didn't smile.

Casey looked around at each eye. They were fixed on him, hungering for his reaction. He opened his mouth, but nothing came out.

Huh? You forget how to talk?

Man, Casey said slowly and quietly. I don't care. Do what you want.

Kwayku, man, why don't you leave him alone? Wayne said.

Casey's my nigga. Kwayku smiled and put his arm around Casey. He know I'm just playing.

In the distance came an animal-like bleating. Fillafil Fillafil Fillafil, Lady MacBeard cried. Her voice echoed throughout the neighborhood.

Marcy and the boys looked at her. Kwayku's smile broadened, and he looked toward Casey.

Man, he said. I ain't even gonna say it.

The group walked slowly to Marcy's house, with only awkward asides cutting into the silence. Marcy was in front, her arms wrapped around her torso, speaking only when addressed and then replying with just one or two words.

She was on display as usual—one of the only white girls at District Central Senior High School, a member of one of the only completely lily white families in Cross River. And sometimes, she had told Casey on the Saturday after the heavy rains had passed, she hated being a star, hated the older guys speaking to her with unsaid words hidden behind their words, hated all the mistaken assumptions about who she was. Casey, timid and understated, was a change of pace from the world she, as an oddity, a display piece, was expected to inhabit. She told Casey this, except that when she said it she said: Casey, I like you 'cause you're so laid back, you're a thinker. Sometimes I want you to take action, though—be more assertive like, you know, those guys who be hanging out in the afternoon by the bus stop.

What do you mean? Casey asked. They were alone in her basement, yet they sat on opposite sides of the room. You want me to yell about how much I want to *hit that* when you walk by?

Grow up, Casey. You know that's not what I mean. But, you know, you could grab my ass sometimes instead of waiting for me to make a move. Don't you want to do that? she asked, walking over to him. She pressed Casey's left hand to the soft cushion behind her.

They kissed and fondled for a while, and then he climbed the stairs with a dull ache burning beneath his waist. Casey described his pain to Marcy as the two made small talk by her front door, and she responded: It's your own fault. Then there hung a blank, lingering and torturous silence that he was learning to get used to.

Marcy, he felt, was slipping from him.

V

Three out of the four Christmases when Joan was employed by the Downtown Branch Library, she played Joan Santi Claus, handing out slim paperback picture books to smiling children who had spaces where their baby teeth once were. Casey, even as a teenager, still had his book. It was about an Italian witch with a magical cauldron that produced end-less pasta. That's how everyone regarded Joan, as magical. Unruly hel-lions became docile and sweet in her presence. Even when she began to miss work and generally faded into her own world, children and librarians and parents all regarded her as the good witch. They couldn't help it; she inspired smiles and conversation. The good witch from *over there* on the Southside of Cross River. It's a shame what's happening to those neigh-borhoods *over there*, her coworkers would say. She just nodded when they said that. Nodded as if to a beat. Not like how her uncle and his friends nodded. She used to watch them and they'd make her promise to never lose control that way. That herr-on, Joan, her uncle would say and then shake his head and rub his swollen, scabby hands.

That September—on the second Thursday of the month, before her last Christmas at the library—was the first time since maternity leave that she had to cancel story time. Phil was nearly a year old. She called that morning, as she would many times after that, following a long night in her Southside townhouse. She felt so sick, she told her boss. In those days, it was always a party. Passed bottles and joints. Her husband one night laid out a line of white powder and made it disappear inside his vac-uum-cleaner nose. Joan observed him like a scientist day after day, and he was the same man going off to his job at the Public Works Department and coming home to play with Phil before welcoming the neighbors for drinks and a card game. One night she closed her eyes, blocked her right nostril, and disappeared a coke line that burned the space inside her face just beneath her eyes.

All those books, she thought the next morning, debating whether to go to work or to stay home. How could I possibly stand the scent of all those books?

VI

In Marcy's basement, they crowded around the glowing television set. Marcy sat on Casey's lap for a bit before moving to the floor. Naked body parts and nondescript faces writhed about the screen. Soon, though, the sound of fucking smothered all speaking, except the words Kwayku dashed off as he sat on a beanbag chair in the corner laughing a raspy laugh and slapping his thigh. The group barely heard him, engrossed as they were in the sweaty gyrations on the television screen. Kwayku took his hat from his head, leaned forward, and placed it on Marcy's. She clutched the brim and pulled it down.

This looks good on me, she said. Don't you guys think so? Everyone responded with mumbled, distracted affirmatives. There was a figure on the screen who was more penis than man.

He call that little thing a dick? Kwayku said, pointing at the screen. He unfastened his belt. The metal buckle jangled. That ain't a dick. He unbuttoned his pants and clawed at his zipper, pulling it down slowly. Marcy stared, her mouth open. Casey leaned forward. Wayne frowned. This is a dick. He shoved his hand into the opening at his crotch.

Kwayku! Wayne yelled.

Kwayku eased his hand out of the opening, leaving his penis inside. He laughed and pulled his zipper up. It sounded as if he was barking.

Man, he said in a gruff growl, I was just joking.

Kwayku boy, Marcy said, shaking her head and smirking a bit. You're out of control.

Wayne stood. Man, I'm getting the fuck out of here before I see some shit I don't want to see.

Casey also rose. Yeah, man, I'm out of here.

Kwayku nodded at them. Peace out.

Rich, you coming? Wayne asked.

Man, we watching the show, Kwayku said.

Yeah, we watching the show, Richard mimicked.

My parents aren't gonna be home for a couple hours, Marcy said.

I gotta get home, Wayne said. What are y'all staying here for?

Aww, these niggas want to ruin our good time, Kwayku said, rising from the beanbag. Richard rose too. The group ascended the staircase, making their way to the front door, Marcy at their backs.

You guys don't have to leave, Marcy said again as the boys stood outside her front door.

So, um, yeah, uh, I'll see you in school tomorrow, Ms. . . . um . . . What's-her-name's class, Casey said.

Behind him Kwayku and Richard mumbled to each other. Richard bounced the basketball against the concrete before throwing a mock shot to an imaginary basket.

Bye Casey, Marcy said, leaning toward him. The edges of their lips collided. She hugged Wayne, Richard, and Kwayku, and the group walked off.

Somewhere during the silent stroll, Kwayku noticed that his head was bare, and he let out a howl.

Damn, I forgot my hat at Marcy's house.

Get the shit tomorrow, Wayne said.

Naw, dog, I need my hat. Rich, come back up the street with me.

Why don't you call her and have her bring it to school? Wayne asked. But it seemed Kwayku and Richard were halfway up the street by the time Wayne had finished his sentence.

Rich, Wayne yelled. You better get your ass home. When your mother calls, I ain't lying for you.

See y'all tomorrow, Kwayku said. The sound of the basketball tapping against the ground became lighter and lighter before it faded.

Casey thought of Marcy's face and realized that instead of the kiss he had received, he would have preferred the hug his friends got. Her hugs were deep and soulful. That's simply the way she hugged, solidly with her entire body pressed tightly against the other person. It was a nice hug.

Soon Casey and Wayne passed the playground.

Ain't that your mother? Wayne asked Casey as they cut across the Wildlands Forest Elementary playground. Casey looked up expecting to see his mother, but instead Lady MacBeard strolled slowly by. Casey dropped his backpack in a rage, scrounging through the dirt at the edge of the blacktop for the perfect rock.

Lady MacBeard sidled up to the boys, swaying back and forth, one side of her old face drooping. Casey rose, his hands empty. He scowled at her, watching the yellowish bump on her lip and the long wavy hairs that curled into her mouth.

The woman's head was still bandaged, and there was a brown spot where she had bled through the gauze. She emitted a scent like rotting cheese.

Y'all know where Sycamore Lane is? she asked. I'm trying to find Sycamore Lane.

No ma'am, Wayne said. I'm sorry. Sycamore Lane ain't around here. That's closer to the library downtown, right?

Casey shrugged.

Fillafil . . .

This bitch want a falafel? Casey said to Wayne.

Shut up, Wayne replied.

There's no need to be rude, the woman said. I'm looking for my boy Philly Phil. Have you seen Philly Phil? Philly Phil. Fillafil Fillafil Fillafil Fillafil . . .

Can't say that I've seen him, ma'am, Wayne said.

Bless your hearts, she said, walking off. Y'all look just like my Philly Phil.

When she was again in the distance looking something like a specter, Casey bent and snatched a smooth, heavy stone from the ground.

Bet I can hit that crackhead right in that brown spot on the bandage.

Man, Casey, Wayne said as he walked. Stop being stupid. Ain't no one here to show off for.

Casey stood upright, dropping the rock, and followed his friend.

VII

Everyone, including Joan, blamed her decline on what happened to Phil. His baby heart stopping suddenly in the middle of the night as if he were an old man with a poor diet and a pack-a-day habit. That was in the October before her last Christmas at the Cross River Downtown Branch Library. Really it started before that—long before—in the basement of her Southside house. The place was always in motion. What times those were. The people that came in and out. The jokes. The drinks. The music. That smoky basement. Just as the party started getting old, Joan's husband came one day with tiny white rocks, a butane lighter, and a glass pipe. What a brief intense dizzying derangement. Slipping from yourself for a few moments. That's how she described it and little by little, each time, less and less of her returned.

After Phil left, her husband disappeared into the wilderness of the Southside. He'd be gone for days at a time. The parties ceased, and the people who had once come in and out passed the house without so much as a glance. Once in a while Joan would spot them when she peered out the window, and they would just shuffle by.

But mostly, Joan sat for hours in her favorite spot on their old living room couch where she once breastfed Phil. It felt sometimes like he was resting in the crook of her arm. Other times, her breasts would drip milk and she'd sit with a throbbing ache in her chest. Her husband went away and returned, a different person each time, as if trying on new identities: laughing, angry, sedate, violent, arms swinging, stoic. Sometimes he brought the rocks home with him. Sometimes Joan would have to go out looking for rocks of her own.

Joan returned to work and seemed normal until one day she no longer glowed lavender.

Bit by bit, her husband stripped the house of everything from the copper wires to the front door. There's a market for anything if you look hard enough.

At work, Joan heard the librarians whisper. Not like their normal whispers, these whispers were sharp hisses. The whispers were ice picks at Joan's eardrums. Why didn't they just pull her aside, grab her, shake her, say what they had to say? Instead they whispered until whispering would no longer do.

Why don't you take some time? said the gray-haired librarian who managed the branch. Phil just—I don't think you're ready.

Joan's wig sat crooked on her head and her eyes burned with a fiery haze. She didn't smell like lavender; she smelled like a rough Southside night. She wanted to say that she was Joan Santi Claus and the kids needed books from Santi Claus to live, but it seemed like a silly thing to say. Who needs books to live? Even those kids didn't really believe Joan Santi Claus was the real thing. Joan Santi felt like a mythical being. Like she always had been just that, unreal.

Joan wanted to speak her thoughts or at least acknowledge them in some way, but she found she couldn't. She spoke in a knotted bullfrog croak and could only mutter her son's name.

VIII

Casey had thought all night and most of the next day about the previous afternoon at Marcy's. The hat. Kwayku's grin. Marcy's flirtation with him. Kwayku's back as he walked up the street to Marcy's house. It all provided motivation for him as he gripped the orange sphere and breezed past Kwayku's bony form.

Watch, Casey, I'm gonna fuck your bitch, Kwayku said as Casey eased a layup into the waiting hoop.

That's game, Casey said through short breaths.

Wow, you won one. It don't matter. I'm still gonna fuck Marcy. I'm gonna flip her white ass over, and next time you fucking her, you gonna see pink fingerprints on that ass. That's me. Remember that.

Casey ignored him, tossing the basketball against the backboard. It clanged over and over as the ball struck the orange square in the center.

Have you even fucked her yet? Been with her how long and you ain't even hit that? You must be gay, man. You the only one that ain't hit it. He a virgin, that's why he be throwing rocks at people.

Man, that don't even make no sense, Casey said.

It's from the Bible, Kwayku replied. *He who is without sin can cast the first stone.*

Kwayku's friends erupted in laughter, and even Casey chuckled. Kwayku stood waiting for the laughter to die down before he continued: Dog, I fucked your bitch.

Check the scoreboard, Casey said. I was raining jumpers all over your ass.

What you expect? I'm still tired from raining all over Marcy's ass. He paused. Rich hit it too.

He stopped talking for a moment to make sure his audience paid rapt attention. They were silent, eyes widened, waiting for the next word.

Yeah, Richard fucked her too. Ain't you, Rich?

Richard nodded.

She let us run a train, Kwayku said. He stopped speaking for a moment, pausing for effect, letting the silence hang heavy. Dog, I was hitting that shit doggie-style. I was watching that shit bounce and shake.

She ain't a girl, she's a receptacle. All I could see was these two round globes. He paused again. With ripples all on them. I love that shit, man. Sexy ass ripples.

Casey frowned. The thick flesh back there did have ripples. He had seen the ripples a few times—kissed them even—before something invariably stopped the proceedings. He remembered pulling down her panties for the first time and marveling that the meat of her ass wasn't smooth like the asses in the magazines but was choppy and dimpled. The truth of her flesh was pleasantly disquieting and arousing. And this knowledge, he felt, let him into a secret club.

Game's over, Wayne said. Y'all lost. Could y'all stop the trash talk? You do this every damn game.

It ain't trash talk, it's reality, Kwayku said. Me and Rich was rocking that shit like ungh-ungh.

Kwayku did a little dance, closing his eyes and twisting his face into a tortured expression; he clenched his fists and thrust his hips back and forth. As he danced, like clockwork, Lady MacBeard strolled by, crying her son's name loudly, wistfully.

Your mother's here, Kwayku said.

For a long moment Casey closed his eyes in frustration.

She don't never learn her lesson, he said. He cupped his hands around his mouth. Hey, Lady MacBeard, go somewhere. Don't nobody want you here.

She continued walking as if she didn't hear him. Swaying, swaying, though stepping methodically; the stroll for her became a mission.

Missus-Casey's-mama, you're looking mighty dirty today, Kwayku said.

Casey frowned. Even on his mother's worst days, this woman looked nothing like her. He dug a rock from the loose dirt and lobbed it, striking the woman in the head just as he had so many days before, and then he picked up another and another. The woman covered her head with her hands as stones rained down upon her.

Casey had rocks in both hands when Kwyaku started pelting stones in her direction. Go on, get! Kwayku said, lobbing a handful at the woman. All flew far past her. Get on back to your sideshow!

Wayne threw one, and so did Richard. A barrage of rocks flew in her direction, plapping against her body and the soft earth.

She simply stood there, holding up her arms as if calling on divine intervention. Blood streamed down her face. Wayne dropped his rocks and took off, jerking Richard's arm. Richard followed, speeding down the hill and away from the playground. Casey reached for another rock.

Stop! Kwayku yelled. Stop!

Casey cupped his hand around a large one with curved lumps. He cocked his arm back. Kwayku reached for his friend, throwing his entire body into Casey's path and tackling him to the ground. It didn't matter, though. Casey had already released the rock into the air. The stone landed in between Joan's open hands, striking the top of her forehead.

The woman collapsed. She lay on the ground unmoving, a wet spot expanding outward from her crotch.

Casey looked into Kwayku's face, hoping to see something other than what he saw: a stare of revulsion and pain. It looked like a fright mask, forever molded into an expression of rubbery distress. And Casey couldn't help it, or even explain it, but it brought him laughter. He laughed like hell until burning water spilled from his eyes onto his cheeks.

Boxing Day

Daddy's pissed. I can tell 'cause I can hear his gloved fists slapping the punching bag downstairs. It's a flat plapping noise. The louder the sound, the more pissed he's become. He says every day he punches the bag is boxing day, but today is actually Boxing Day.

I would stay out of the basement, away from my punch-drunk father and every delusion he's used to sew himself together, but my mother's sent me to descend into his Hades to deliver a message.

He notices me and begins to speak as he punches the bag, breathing hard between phrases.

My father, he says, used to always tell me about the day after Christmas. How he and Grandma and Grandpappy and all the kids would head out to the beach. Can you believe that?

He stops to catch his heavy breath and then starts punching and talking again.

We suffering in arctic weather—the goddamn river's frozen and shit—and I bet your grandfather is swimming with tropical fish right now. When I was a kid, all he did was tell me about it. *Look, kid, the days before you got here was the best, and now all we do is watch our breath steam.* Now he's back where he wants to be. Happy fucking Boxing Day!

Daddy is in one of his moods, that steady persistent low-level blue. Every word is a bomb filled with cynicism. I'm always surprised by the burn of his napalm.

That morning I woke early to catch some cartoons in the basement. My father says I'm too old for cartoons, so I didn't want him to see me slink downstairs. As I rounded the corner and approached the stairhead,

53

I saw Daddy with his gloves hanging about his neck from a set of black strings.

Stay up here, kid, he said. I'm about to beat that thing till it cries. Yep, gonna be down there a while.

He doesn't need to say, *I don't want you around.* His shrug, the curt dance of his eyes, they speak for him.

Daddy's blue moods never care about anyone. Every minute when he's like this I'm in a four-dimensional world made of endless time: hours lain next to hours, hours stacked atop hours into the sky. This broken man, reeling from daily compromise. Sarcasm and boxing the only things keeping him together. As for me, I'm one of many chains round his neck that hold him in a cold, tiny basement of mediocrity.

My father is shirtless and slick with sweat, swaying before the punching bag. He leans into his maroon opponent, clinging to the thing like he needs it in order to stand. Ref, he shouts. Ref! This motherfucker tried to bite my ear.

Dad.

Say hello to Tyson, kid.

Dad, Mom said there is not enough tofu for all of us, and it's your turn to cook and wash the dishes.

I'm the heavyweight champion of the goddamn world and that woman wants me to eat bean sprouts? I need some red meat. A steak or something. *I'll eat your children.*

He bares his teeth and shakes his head and lays rapid-fire blows into the punching bag.

It's vegetarian day, Dad.

Seriously, kid, tell your mother to go jump in a lake.

I can't tell my mother to jump in a lake. When I'm back upstairs, I tell her he's on his way.

Later when my mother sends me back down into the dim, cold basement, Daddy is Muhammad Ali standing over Sonny Liston. He's Mike Tyson coming into the ring like a vicious animal. Then he's Tyson whimpering after losing to Buster Douglas.

His whimpering stops being a joke and crosses over into real tears, his face a rain-slicked street at midnight. He leans into the bag like Tyson leaned into Don King after his loss to Douglas. I rarely saw my dad embrace my mother the way he's hugging that bag. I don't know whether to turn and tiptoe back upstairs or to go to him, hug him in the way he says men are not to hug.

Dad, I say.

When our eyes meet, he squares his slumped shoulders and throws a weak set of punches at the bag.

Tyson in 'ninety-one, he says. Good impression, huh? He wipes his tears with his forearm and punches the bag again and again and again.

The Slapsmith

Nicolette fingered the cuts above her eye and the tender spots along the side of her face. Her shoulder ached, as did her back, which had absorbed the shock.

The train pushed away, clanging along the tracks. She thought she could still hear voices hooting at her.

The baby was okay, though. Cried some, but he was okay. There were rips in his yellow blanket and smudges of black dirt and grease splotched all over it. She had fashioned the blanket into a sling to hold the baby. There was dirt about his face, which she brushed off. The river lay just down the slope. She washed her hands in it and cleaned off her son—making sure to get the dirt out of every little crevice and crack—and then she tended to her wounds.

Nicolette grumbled as she washed, shaking her head, thinking angry things and spitting them from her mouth. Nothing could be done now, but in the future she'd heed what her mother had said about trusting strange men. He looked so honest, she thought, as she shook dust from her sweater and jeans.

What's a girl like you doing out here on these rails alone? he had said after lifting her onto the slow-moving train through the open train door. I'm not going to bust you. Let me help you out.

He was nice at first, offering her a private corner in the dusty car. The gentle rocking of the train lulled her into a peacefulness she hadn't felt for some time. But soon he was grabbing at her sweater, his friendly smile turning wide and sinister. Sounds rising all around her, the baby whining, men laughing and hollering, calling her filthy names. Strange hands reaching for her. As she rolled away from the rails, the men chuckled and screamed.

She again touched the raw wounds with her free hand and wondered what they looked like, whether they would leave scars. Nicolette could still hear the hollering and laughing tumbling about in her ears. Men having fun could sure sound menacing sometimes.

Nicolette walked along the track, looking out at the dark waters. The jagged rocks squeaked loudly beneath her feet. She had left her bag, which held almost her entire world, with the men on that southbound train. Her stuff would soon be in Port Yooga and she'd be here.

Just down the embankment was Cross River, a town she had hoped to bypass. She looked up. Overgrown branches like groping arms reached for her. She looked to her back. No one would ever take advantage of her again. They'd get theirs one day, she thought. All of them.

The baby bawled, wailing punctuated by staccato stabs. She bounced him gently in her arms and spoke soothingly, which only seemed to agitate him.

Her face ached as the chilly wind blew against it, and her shoulder ached and her feet ached. The cold stabbed pinpricks through her sweater. Nicolette thought of the baby's delicate flesh and pulled him closer. The temperature could only drop at this time of night. The pain in her back made her stop. Why did the men have to act the way they did? She wrapped the blanket more tightly around her torso and kept hiking, trying not to think of the miles of track in front of her or the miles of track in back of her.

Down the hill, beyond the brush, Nicolette spotted a fire. She walked toward the light as if a voice inside it called her. The baby had quieted, his bright eyes staring up at her. Twigs cracked beneath her feet. She crouched behind a bush and peered into the flames. Watching fires burn had always soothed her, but never more so than now. Her limbs needed rest. Her mouth needed water. Her fingers needed heat.

A man sat alone by the flame. The baby waved his brown limbs and struck a high note. The man looked up.

Who's out there?

Nicolette moved toward him. Hello, she said. There was a tremble in her voice; she hoped he hadn't noticed.

Girl, you're all beat up, he said, looking at her sadly. I been there.

I fell.

The man winced. Look like you been hit, he said.

She shook her head. I fell.

Them bruises ain't from no fall; a man did that to you. Boy, they getting more savage along these rails. You lucky they didn't do worse. I heard some stories.

Can I sit? she asked. I'm tired.

Sure. You look like a tough girl—

I am.

But ain't no girl tough enough to be out here all alone with a baby. Don't you have a man?

Just this little one here.

Nicolette felt uneasy. Foolish. Saying too much had gotten her hemmed up so many times. She lied: I'm meeting some people in town.

Water? He passed Nicolette a large jug and she took a long swig followed by another long swig.

Thirsty, huh? Bet you hungry too, mama?

She smiled at the man. The firelight flickered across his face, casting shadows and orange light. His nose was twisted and his upper lip slashed; his eyelids looked puffy and his skin lay thick and leathery. He touched his face, trying to obscure the ruddy splotches on his swollen cheeks.

Gotta be careful out here. Every nigga you meet ain't on the up and up. I'm only telling you this 'cause you're young. Girls trust niggas too much when they young. I may not look like it, but I used to be a tough guy. Greatest slapsmith the Southside ever saw. Used to brawl with the best.

The man showed off his red, thick, scarred hands. Nicolette looked down at her son. He had turned toward her chest and fallen sleep.

Look at these. Ever seen this, huh? That comes from twenty years of slapboxing. I won the World Brawl four years running. Got knocked slapdrunk in the fifth match. Ain't never recover. They call me Slapfest. Heard of me, huh?

Nicolette shook her head, still eyeing his hands. Once upon a time, a man's hands flew toward her face. Slaps and punches. They looked nothing like the slapsmith's hands. Those hands were soft and thin. A manly vein bisected the backs of both of them, but the nails always stayed bright and clear, neatly and obsessively polished, rounded and filed. Sometimes

59

grabbing hold of the baby was the only thing that could make those hands stop swinging, and then later when he was onto her, even that couldn't stop him. What kind of woman am I, she would think, using a baby for a shield?

Girl, you never heard of Slapfest? Know what the World Brawl is? No? Well, I guess that makes sense. You on the train, so I guess you coming from out of town. It's okay, you don't have to tell me where you coming from or nothing about you if you don't want. I ain't nosy.

Yeah, I'm a tough guy. Only lost the World Brawl that one time 'cause the nigga cheated. He punched me! Punched me four times in the face and nearly knocked me the fuck out. Ref said he ain't see it. Can you believe that? You not supposed to be punching nobody when you slapboxing! In the papers they called it some win-at-all-costs shit. Said any professional woulda done the same thing, but to me it's a matter of integrity. Who you is is shown by what you do when you desperate. I was getting him. He only punched me 'cause he was desperate than a mu'fucker. Pardon my language.

He stood and swung his arms wildly, ducking his face from a rain of imaginary blows. Blap! Smack! Blap! I slapped that nigga like, Smack! Blap! Blap!

The child turned and cried in his sleep. Nicolette bounced and shushed him to make sure he didn't wake to see all this.

A man approached. An even older man. He had friendly features, and his cheeks and chin were dotted with scraggly gray hairs. The slapsmith paused. Then he held up a frying pan. Like my pan?

It looked old and gritty, flaky and burnt, a veteran of many fires, cast-iron heavy. Nicolette nodded again and looked around for an out. She eyed the approaching man cautiously. He was tall and skinny like one of the men from the train. Perhaps she could break for it. Up the grade and back to the tracks. But with tired limbs and a baby? There was no cause to run yet, anyway.

Hey Daf, the slapsmith called to the man, who sat and rested a cloth bag next to the fire.

Hey there, Daf replied. And who is the lovely lady?

Why, I never got her name, the slapsmith replied.

Nicolette. And this little guy's Gabriel. I say Gabby, though.

Gabby's eyes opened slowly and he blinked and blinked and yawned and blinked. The baby stretched and watched everyone with suspicion, which made Daf and his friend smile. Gabby's eyes shut—slowly like little falling curtains—and he settled into a shallow sleep.

Gabby's a nice name, Daf said. Real nice. Hello Gabby and Nicolette. My man isn't bothering you guys, is he? No? That's good. You guys hungry?

As ever, Nicolette said.

Daf rested the cast-iron pan atop the fire and began laying out bacon strips. Nicolette said she would feed Gabby while Daf prepared the food. She walked off to get some privacy, lifted her sweater, and pressed the drowsy baby to her nipple.

What a pleasant surprise, she heard Daf say. He cracked an egg atop the sizzling meat. How often do we get to entertain guests?

Remember that guy who knocked me down in the fourth match during the last World Brawl and I couldn't get up again? She and that guy share features, don't you think, huh?

That was a long time ago, 'Fest. Those days are gone.

She felt the men watching her as they chattered back and forth. She shut her eyes and sucked in a wisp of air. Fully in the moment, just her and Gabby. She imagined herself and the baby as the shadows that exist for only an instant near a flickering flame. But then the men's chattering threw her from the moment. Daf's friend made little sense. Nicolette looked about at the menacing trees. Peacefulness, she realized, was synonymous with vulnerability. She became sad and then scared. And she asked herself why again she had failed to heed her mother's words.

Though Gabby wasn't finished feeding, she removed him from her nipple, lowered her sweater, and returned to the fire. Gabby whined and Nicolette shushed him. The men had begun eating. Nicolette dipped bread into the bacon grease and chewed slowly. The three of them sat in the quiet of stirring insects, flickering flames, labored breaths, and smacking lips. She noticed for the first time a chorus of crickets and, in the distance, the lapping of the river.

Nicolette asked for another slice of bread. Daf reached into the bag.

The Breadsman, the slapsmith said. That was his name. Owned a bakery in Cleveland and slapsmithed on the side. I was good at talking shit. I said to them cameras that any fight between me and him would be *The Death of a Breadsman*. That pissed him off, so that's why he punched me.

The World Brawl. One day, twenty-five matches. Like a tournament and shit. Lots of money riding on me. But that don't matter when you up there in the moment fighting. When you in that ring it's just you and another warrior. That's all that matters, and eventually when you start slapping, it's just you. Everything else disappear. And then you disappear. And that's when I'm most alive, when I disappear. People come from all around to fight. They got slapsmiths everywhere, but mostly here. We invented that shit. Tournament of emperors, not kings. They give you a purple cape and a crown when you win. Fuck a belt. Who need a belt? I want the damn crown! Four years in a row I'm the champion. And the only way I get taken out is when they cheat me. You about as slapdrunk as a mu'fucker when you get to the end of that thing. I done seen people start it a genius and they fucking retards by the end of the day.

Now, Slapfest, Daf said. I don't know if our guest wants to hear all that.

The slapsmith started yelling. The Breadsman, he cheated. He punched me. You a slapsmith or a bitch?

Slapfest stood, bounced on the balls of his feet. Again he dipped and ducked from imagined blows. Slapping and backslapping the air. Emitting a soft hissing sound with every slap he threw. He glared at Nicolette. Come on. Come on.

His eyes turned to glass. He was staring at an invisible enemy and everything else disappeared. Shadows danced to the rhythm of the fire. Nicolette imagined an audience, lusting and crying for violence.

She flinched each time the slapsmith swung his hands. The baby cried with a new rhythm. The sounds echoed through the night.

You'll have to forgive our friend, Daf said. He's off in a zone. A part of him is permanently slapdrunk. There's no rousing him when he's like this. Give him a minute and he'll calm. Look at him. You, me, that baby, even his own body. It's all disappeared. He might not look it, but he's at peace now. He's lucky really that he has a place to go and just be. Most people don't even have anywhere like that to go. That sort of peacefulness is what it's all about, isn't it, Nicolette? Nicolette?

Nicolette trembled, and tears beaded at her eyes. She didn't hear Daf's words; she only saw the slapsmith's menacing taunts. I'm Slapking Of The World and who the fuck are you?

Nicolette remembered the train and the men snatching at her, baby be damned. She grabbed a cloth from the ground and wrapped it around her free hand.

I'm not down for the count, uh-uh, the slapsmith bawled, slapping at shadows. I can go another round. Another two. Uh-uh. That bitch nigga punched me! That bitch nigga punched me! Let me at him!

Nicolette sprung to her feet, snatched the skillet from the fire, and slammed it to the side of the slapsmith's head. Bacon strips flew through the air. The baby roared as if cheering. The slapsmith dropped to the ground, out cold.

Daf rushed toward his friend. His movements reminded Nicolette of the men on the train. Before Daf could reach the slapsmith, she rammed her foot square into his testicles. Daf stumbled, holding his crotch. He fell, groaning and wheezing. As he tried to rise, Nicolette tossed the skillet toward him, striking him in the mouth. She could hear the clack of the metal against his teeth. He fell back onto the dusty ground. One hand cradled his crotch, the other his bloody mouth.

Nicolette bounded up the embankment and walked swiftly along the track, listening to the music the rocks made beneath her feet. She shushed her son and bounced him, and finally he fell asleep peacefully against her chest. Every so often she'd stop to adjust the sling and to glance at the flickering fire at her back. Soon she could no longer see the injured men, and then even the flame was no longer visible.

What a long walk it would be that night, and an even longer journey across that twinkling river to wherever she'd eventually rest her head. She paused again to shift the sleeping baby. She looked down. At her foot lay a rock, big and smooth, heavy to the touch. Nicolette rested it in the sling, a good luck charm, sitting right where the tightness in her chest met the untroubled child.

202 Checkmates

In my eleventh year, my father taught me defeat.

I sat with my back pressed on that old, scratchy brown couch. Tom chased Jerry across the television screen and then the image dissolved into a white dot in the center. I turned to see my father holding the remote control in one hand and a crumpled cloth cradled in the crook of his other arm.

What are you doing with that rag, Daddy? I asked.

It's not a rag, girl, he said. It's a mat.

He unfurled the dirty checkered mat onto the coffee table and dropped a handful of chipped and faded black chess pieces in front of me. He started setting up the white ones without looking at me. I tilted my head, watching my father curiously.

I tentatively set up mine, following his lead. Each piece looked like a veteran of many battles, with nicks and gashes exposing the wood beneath the paint.

Your queen always starts off on her own color square, he said. She's a woman like you and your mother. She likes to match. He reversed the positions of my king and queen.

When my father explained the rules, I thought I'd never be able to keep them straight, especially the rules about the horse, because he moved like a ballerina, jumping to far-off squares, or rather he galloped. I grabbed hold of a horse and moved him to a vacant square.

Now hold on, little girl, my father said. Chess is like real life. The white pieces go first so they got an advantage over the black pieces.

With that I removed my horse and he inched a pawn one square forward. I was on my way to being checkmated for the first time.

He was the god of chess each time he spread the crumpled mat and set up the pieces with his haggard, dark brown hands. I used to look at the grime beneath his fingernails and the scars on his knuckles, wondering why his hands looked older than him.

And my father's voice crackled when we played chess. Daddy often sounded like a kung-fu master in one of those movies me and my brother watched on Saturday mornings. He didn't speak like that all the time, but he always spoke like that when we played chess.

Once, I was so deep in concentration that I didn't look up when my father broke our silence. Instead I chose to imagine one of my horses speaking.

I used to play this game with your grandfather when I was your age, he said sitting hunched over the board, moving around the pieces he had captured, waiting for me to make a move. Pop was good, he said. I never beat him.

How come?

'Cause he was good. Naw, really, I could have beat him had I had the chance. He got real sick. Couldn't even finish the game we had going 'cause we took him to the hospital. He told me to bring the game with me when I went to see him. Your grandmother wouldn't let me take it to the hospital, though. *Don't bother your father with that foolishness now.* Daddy's impression of my grandmother was a high-pitched shriek that sounded like her only in spirit, and even then it was Granny as a cartoon character. You know how your grandmother is, he continued. Every time we went, he used to ask me about the set and—

My father paused as I moved my queen to a middle square. He swooped in swiftly and tapped it from the board with the base of a knight. It bounced once it hit the carpet.

Thought you had something, huh? Let that be a lesson, little girl.

With my queen gone, I made my moves lazily, waiting for the twentieth checkmate, and then my father said this: You playing like the game's done. The game ain't over until that king is pinned down and can't go nowhere.

If a pawn makes it to the other side, he told me, it becomes a queen. I imagined a little pawn magically blossoming into royalty on that last square.

It became something I longed to see. Sometimes when all was lost, I'd just inch a pawn forward, but the piece would never make it. The fifty-seventh checkmate was one of those games.

We woke early in the morning before I went off to school to continue a game carried over from the night before.

While we played, my father told me that when he was my age he imagined he'd be the first black grandmaster. He was the best chess player in school, winning casual games as easily as drinking a glass of water. He became king of the tournaments.

Yeah, figured one day everyone would call me Grandmaster Rob.

What happened?

Just didn't work out that way, I guess. After a while, I wasn't worrying about being no grandmaster or nothing like that. You stop thinking about these things at a certain age.

I'm going to be a grandmaster, I said.

My father stared hard at the board.

You know, Daddy, it's never too late.

He chuckled, and in less than two minutes my king stood pinned by a bishop, a rook, and a pawn.

Checkmate!

He jumped and shuffled across the floor like the Holy Ghost had slithered up his pant leg.

Robert, she's eleven years old, my mother said, passing by.

The girl ain't too young to learn, he replied. Then he turned to me. Ain't that right?

I nodded, thinking about my loss rather than whatever I was nodding about. My impotent pieces stood meekly, no longer any use.

He stuck his hand out for a victory shake.

You cheated me, I said, raising my voice a little, ignoring his hand and frowning, damning him for phantom moves I was sure he had made in my absence. Daddy, you cheated.

Don't blame me because I'm better than you. You gotta start thinking two, three moves ahead. Then you can challenge me. Don't worry about me. Worry about your game.

My mother called out from the next room. Said I was going to miss the bus. My little brother had walked off to wait without me. My mother stood before us talking fast and loud. She got this way sometimes. My father placed his hand softly on my head.

Come on, baby girl, stop pouting and get your stuff together. I'll walk you to the bus stop.

My father never walked me to the bus stop in the mornings. Most days he'd leave for work early before I even got out of bed. He'd return late in the evening long after I had come home from school, his clothes and skin covered in black grease. After a half hour he'd walk out of his room looking immaculate, his face clean and smooth, each hair lined up waiting on my inspection. His hands, though, were always stained with traces of thick oil and dirt that rested beneath his fingernails. He'd sit on the couch with his scarred hands wrapped around a green beer bottle that rested on his thigh.

As I stood from the game, Daddy took my hand in his, and there sat the grease, nesting beneath his nails, as much a part of his hands as the creases and veins.

Even though in my little girl mind he had cheated me, the thought of walking with him filled me with pride, making me the happiest girl in all of Cross River.

Dammit, Robert! my mother said. You made her miss the bus.

I peered out the window to see its yellow tail pulling off.

Well, baby girl, we're going to have to take the L9 downtown to Ol' Cigar Station, my father said. But we got to leave right now, because I'm sure the buses are behind schedule.

We stepped out the door and I forgot to wonder why he wasn't at work.

That was my fifty-seventh checkmate at my father's hands. I refused to play with him after that and instead taught my little brother the game. He was six at the time and had a short attention span. I got tired of beating him, though. He never figured out how I could mate him in three moves.

Soon my father and I returned to the board. Around this time it became clear that my mother didn't much like chess. She used to say things like, Chess ain't gonna get your homework done. One night when she thought I was asleep I heard her tell my father, Chess ain't gonna get you work. That was in the middle of a bunch of hollering from both of them. Then the front door slammed. My father was back in the morning to finish up the previous night's game.

Sometime around the hundred-and-first checkmate, I cut through the park on my way home from a friend's house late in the afternoon. There hung a sharp chill in the air. Around a picnic table stood a silent crowd looking severe and intense. Everybody pulled their jackets closer when the cold breeze blew in, but even as the heat left their bodies the people's eyes stayed fixed on the game. Two guys—an older man with a white Afro and yellowish-brown tobacco stains soiling his white mustache and a younger man with smooth dark skin and thin, trimmed black hairs neatly resting on his upper lip—sat at the picnic table with its black graffiti on flaking maroon paint. The men were face to face, staring at a crumpled board more tattered than my father's. A pale brown time clock sat near them, and after each move one of the men slapped a button atop the timepiece. The elder man had a grizzled face that looked as if it had been punched too many times, while his opponent's was young, strong, and handsome, dimples passing over his cheeks when he flashed a transient smile.

Brilliant, a tall guy whispered loudly after the older man moved a pawn one square forward. Then a few minutes later: Man, fuck a Bobby Fischer. We got two Bobby Fischers right here. And these Bobby Fischers ain't crazy.

From the chatter I learned that the younger man was Manny, his opponent was Chester, and nobody had ever seen anyone defeat either of them.

Eventually Chester pinned Manny's king. He didn't get up and dance. Manny didn't rip the black hairs from his upper lip and storm off in anger. The two slapped hands, complimented each other, and left in opposite directions.

When I reached home, I told my father all about the match. Speaking breathlessly, I mixed up parts of the story and corrected myself into an incoherence I knew only my father could understand. And he did make sense of it, even if he had to ask me to slow down a few times.

I heard about them dudes, my father said.

We should go out to the park, Daddy. You can beat Chester.

Baby girl, chess ain't about who can beat who; it's about life. He unrolled the board and set up the pieces. Now come let me beat up on you.

It wasn't until checkmate one hundred twenty-one, or perhaps one hundred twenty-two, that I convinced my father to come watch the men in the park play. It was a mild day, coming off a string of cold ones, and he agreed that it would be a shame to waste the shining sun and pleasant warmth by playing indoors.

When we got to the park, Chester sat blindfolded at a picnic table. He had three games going at once. He'd make a move and then a woman would guide him to the next table to make another move. The crowd looked on silently.

He's just showing off, my father said.

You can beat him, can't you, Daddy?

He's a showboat, my father said as if he didn't hear me. Chester vanquished an opponent and walked slowly to a different picnic table to make a move as another challenger set up a board for defeat. My father said, He a good showboat, though.

You can beat him, right?

My father grabbed my hand and we walked downhill, away from the action, to a maroon picnic table of our own. He unrolled the crumpled mat and set up the chipped pieces. I played with the black ones as usual. He said I could be white when I beat him. My father took one of my knights and taunted me.

Now, little girl, you know you can do better than that. You gotta protect them pieces, girl.

I took his queen and laughed at him. He clenched his jaw, and his whole face became tight. Playing my father was no longer as hard as it had once been. I was getting used to his rhythms and seeing weaknesses in the creaky stiffness of his gameplay.

Now where did you learn a move like that? he asked.

Don't worry about me, worry about your game, I replied, which made him laugh.

We both hunched over the board. There was no world outside the both of us, outside of this game.

Hey, little lady, you missed a chance to take back the game from your old man, a voice called out. My father looked up and frowned. It was Manny. He sat on a nearby bench studying our board, his right hand rubbing against his smooth dark chin.

Move your queenside knight—

Come on, man, let me and my daughter play in peace.

All right, brotherman, I'm just saying that if I was her, I'd move that queenside knight so I could castle and set up some opportunities to put you in check, otherwise the game is over in three.

Whatever, man, worry about yourself, my father said. I hear Chester did you like that computer did that Russian.

Aw man, fuck Chester—

Could you have some respect for my little girl?

Sorry, man. I ain't mean to disrespect the little lady. Let me play winner, Manny said, and then he winked at me. I smiled.

Staring at the board, I could see Manny was right. My father knew it. His annoyance showed in his stiff brow and the nests of wrinkles at the corner of his eyes. There was only one way out. But winning wasn't as important as doing so gracefully and on my own. The knight stayed in his position and I moved a pawn instead, hoping to get it to the other side of the board before the game ended.

Aw, little lady, you just signed your death warrant, Manny said. Let me play winner.

Man, my father said, let the girl play. With a quick maneuver of his fingers he trapped my king. It stood there lonely and helpless, cut off from all its allies.

Checkmate! my father called with the drunken excitement of a midnight partygoer. You're getting better, but you're still not good enough to beat your old man.

My father gathered the pieces, snorting and grunting in a way that let me know he was pleased.

Come on, man, let's go a round, Manny said with a dimpled smile.

Naw, man, I got to take my little girl home.

What you scared of? he asked.

My father barely even bothered looking up at Manny as he rolled his board and cradled it in the crook of his arm.

My dad's not scared of you.

Looks like he is, Manny replied.

Come on, Daddy, you can play one game.

Naw, girl, we got to go.

Yeah, little lady. Y'all gotta go, Manny said. The way your pop plays, I'll have him mated in two. He doesn't want to embarrass himself in front of you.

My father unrolled the crumpled board and set up his pieces.

Manny removed a cigarette from the right breast pocket of his black leather jacket and made a ceremony of lighting it. Then he took a long pull and blew out a cloud of formless gray smoke.

I'll even let you be white, he said.

It's my board, boy. I'm the defending champion. You can't *let* me be anything.

Turn your head, little lady. I'm 'bout to beat your daddy like he stole something.

They didn't just play one game. They played three, my father staring into the crumpled board as if that vinyl square held an opening to the abyss and the chipped pieces were Satan's own demons flying out to wreak havoc. He was so still at times it was as if he had become one of his chessmen. But his face tightened with each falling of his queen, his bishops, his knights; and it dropped each time Manny calmly said, Checkmate, and blew another plume of smoke.

Manny smiled in my direction after the last game, dimples sitting again on his cheeks. Then he winked. I looked away.

My father clutched my hand as we walked home in silence. I replayed each of his three games, mostly the endgames, in my head, still not believing what I had witnessed. All I could see walking up the streets were my father's scarred thick hands clumsily moving pieces and Manny's smooth brown hands, with their feminine fingers and strong snake veins, nimbly moving in confident counterattack. I couldn't beat either of them, but I could see just where my father had gone wrong. For all his talk of thinking ahead, Daddy didn't do it very well. And he couldn't adapt to changing circumstances, always protecting his queen while his king stood exposed. Why did I never see his sloppiness when he was my opponent? As the image of my father's leathery hand laying his king flat in surrender played in my head, my father spoke:

Sometimes you lose. A lot of times you lose. Sometimes you lose more than you win. That's all.

My mind now drifted during our games, thinking about my father pushing over his king while Manny folded his arms across his broad chest and nodded in satisfaction. It was that slight nod, more than anything, that drew me back to the park day after day to watch the neighborhood chess heroes inch pieces forward and stare at their boards as if the world depended on each of their moves.

Manny sat before a board every time I wandered through Ol' Cigar Park. He was as much a part of the place as the maroon wooden benches, the crumbly blacktop of the basketball court, and the dark green weather-beaten statue of the serious-faced man atop a galloping horse—sword in one hand, reins in the other, and a cigar between his lips—that sat in the center of things and watched over the whole area. Sometimes Manny would look up from a game while waiting on an opponent's move. He'd smile or wink and then return his gaze to the board before I could respond with a smile or a wave of my own.

Manny checkmated a man once just as I showed up to watch the afternoon's matches.

Little lady, he called, and waved a raised hand as his opponent slinked away. He returned the chessmen to their starting positions and offered me the white pieces. His board was vinyl like my father's but smooth and new. When I made my first move, he told me it was all wrong. Manny had a comment after each of my turns. I clutched the head of a knight. He guided my hand instead to a pawn I hadn't considered. When he removed his hand from mine, I slowly eased my arm back, knocking over my king and queen, and felt myself blushing. Manny laughed and placed them back on their squares. Chess had never made more sense; the game had never been more beautiful. I watched his smooth hands dance as they conducted the lesson. He took his eyes off the board to look up at me when I spoke and complimented me each time I did something unexpected.

As I moved my queen, a woman, tall and brown-skinned, holding a silver purse over her shoulder, walked up behind him and placed her hand on his back. He greeted her without turning from our game. Just after her arrival, he took my queen. The woman smiled at me. I kept a serious face and stared at the fallen piece. He mated me with his next move.

Manny placed an unlit cigarette at the corner of his mouth, lit a match, and cupped his hand around the flame to protect it from the wind.

Good game, little lady. He stood from the table, scooping up a handful of pieces and dropping them into the woman's purse. He rolled the floppy vinyl board, and the woman stuffed that too into her purse. You're going to be real good one day. Go home and show your daddy what I taught you.

Manny winked at me over his shoulder as he walked off with the tall woman. A board sat empty on an adjacent table. In my mind I filled it with pieces, reliving the game I had just played, trying to make all I had learned a part of me.

My twelfth birthday neared. It landed on a Sunday, so my father let me stay home with him on the Friday before the day. I floated between sleep and wake as my little brother rustled around, packing his stuff for school.

How come she gets to stay home? he asked. It's not fair.

Life's not fair, my father replied. Hurry up, boy, and get your stuff together before you miss your bus.

The two-hundred-and-first checkmate came that morning after my father made breakfast. The doughy scent of pancakes mixed with the sticky, sweet smell of maple syrup and filled every inch of our apartment. My king lay flat on the crumpled mat as my father jumped up and shuffled across the floor in celebration. He called it his James Brown dance.

What? Did you think I was going to go easy on you because it's your birthday?

Watch out, Daddy, your dancing days are going to be over soon. Just wait.

It wasn't idle talk for me. His game was weak and strained, and I could see his king toppled and defeated, lying at the feet of my queen.

He cooked us hamburgers for lunch, and while I ate I heard him on the phone arguing with my mother.

He disappeared for a long stretch in the afternoon while I watched Woody Woodpecker and Droopy and Bugs Bunny, and when he came back his eyes burned fiery red and puffy folds of dark loose skin bunched beneath them. His breath burned with the harsh-sweet scent of alcohol. He moved slowly, as if his joints had stiffened with weariness and pain.

He sat on the couch next to me and we watched the Roadrunner outsmart Wile E. Coyote.

This used to be so funny when I was your age, he said.

It's still funny, Daddy.

I got something for you, baby.

He pointed to a rectangular box on the dining room table. It lay wrapped in two different types of paper that puffed out and wrinkled at the edges. My father had wound several strips of black electrical tape around the box. Daddy's wrapping job was so pathetically cute I almost didn't want to open the gift.

I know your birthday isn't until Sunday, but you played such a good game this morning.

When I ripped the paper from the box, I could do nothing but stare at my gift. It was a green marble chessboard. I ran my fingers along the clear glass that covered the thick emerald base. The white pieces were a shiny crystal, the dark pieces a frosted gray. It was heavy. My father grunted as he moved it to the center of the table for us to play.

When my mother came home we were on our way to the two-hundred-and-second checkmate.

Look what Daddy got me, I said as she closed the door.

That's nice, baby, she replied evenly and blandly, and her lack of enthusiasm irritated me.

My father and I played a long game, neither of us dominating. I had just taken his second rook when my mother made me go to bed. It was early. I frowned and sighed loudly in frustration, but I dared not talk back. There was no checkmating my mother.

The walls in our apartment were as thin as bedsheets. It didn't appear as if my parents cared that night. It was long after I was supposed to have gone to sleep, but I lay awake thinking of my next moves. This time I was sure I'd defeat my father. An army of pawns would become queens on the far side of the board.

The soft drone of my parents' conversation grew into muffled screams. I held myself still so the creaking of the bed wouldn't obscure their bickering, and I even took shallow breaths so as not to miss a word. My brother slept in a bed across the room, not stirring a bit even when the shouting grew so loud it seemed as if we had no wall to filter the sound.

How the hell can we afford that? my mother screamed. It's not even her birthday yet. I thought we talked about this. I told you we couldn't afford it. You don't think.

My father's response sounded like muffled grumbling, forever lost between the paint and plaster of the walls.

We haven't even paid the rent this month, my mother yelled. I got to go grocery shopping this week. Robert, you don't think.

Why is everything such a big deal for you? I didn't do anything wrong. I got the girl a nice gift.

You didn't get that for her. You got it for yourself. When are you ever thinking about anybody but yourself?

We always pull through. You're always predicting the worst and we always pull through. It's never as bad as you say it is.

You don't even know how we pull through.

Silence.

You want me to take it back? Fine, I'll take it back.

It's too late; you can't take it back now. You already gave it to her like a fool. You'll just be disappointing her. God, Robert, you apply for two jobs and then give up; got the nerve to spend the money I make on expensive gifts. I don't understand you. It's just like the garage. You never think anything through. All you had to do was apolo—

Could we not talk about that? I'm done talking about that.

Silence.

I don't know how we're going to get out of this one. We can't live on that chessboard, Robert. Did you even try to think this through? I'll tell you this, Robert, you're not going to have Bobby out of school on his birthday so he can grow up to be like you.

Whatever—

You're not a man, Robert. You don't. . . .

Think.

At least, I believe she said *think*, but I can't be sure because the door slammed on that word.

A moment later my door cracked and a sliver of light expanded into the room.

Baby, I heard my father's voice say. The gentle tinkling of wooden chess pieces bouncing against one another accompanied his voice. Baby, are you awake? Want to play chess with Daddy?

I pretended to be asleep. My bed shifted and creaked. My father sat on the edge by my feet. He said nothing for a while, sitting still. He sighed. He whispered something angrily. Before long he was taking short, tortured breaths and whimpering like an infant or a wounded horse. I cracked open my eyes and peered at him through slits. A glint of hallway light landed on half his face; the other half sat draped in darkness. A dampness slicked his cheeks. I burrowed my head between pillow and sheet and tightly shut my eyes.

Neither of us said anything about that night as the days passed. The marble chess set sat in the living room, our last game frozen on its face. Both my father and I barely acknowledged its presence most of the time. Every week, though, he removed the pieces, cleaned the dust from the board, and set them back just as we had left them that night.

One day it sparkled under the ugly yellow apartment lights while I sat across from it doubled over by an aching in my belly. My mother had cooked spicy wings for dinner; maybe that was the cause. I tried to ignore the pain by sitting on the scratchy brown couch and writing in my journal. As I wrote, I felt a new wetness between my legs. And there it was, a streak of brownish-red blood staining my underwear.

My mother knelt over the bathtub washing my underpants in warm soapy water, talking to me about babies and blood and all the ways my world would change. Most of it passed over me, disappearing into the universe.

A few days later I went to the park by myself, though my mother now forbid it and my father sided with her, saying, What are you looking at me for? You heard your mother. I slid into a seat across from Manny. He slowly took my pieces, finally checkmating me after the tall brown-skinned woman showed up. Manny walked off with her, leaving me with a dimpled smile and a wink as he had done before. I shrugged, sitting there by myself wondering if all that talk of my world changing was just another one of those empty things adults say to children.

My father barely spoke during this time. He usually disappeared after dinner, and I would hear him return late at night, taking heavy steps, loudly banging into furniture and cursing in pain. In the darkness I stared up at the ceiling, thinking about games I watched in the park or something else entirely. He would be gone again in the morning when I awoke for school. In the afternoon there was my father, sitting on the couch, red-eyed with a green bottle of beer in his hand.

The day we returned to the board was an unusual one. It must have been a school holiday, because my brother and I were both home, but my mother wasn't there. I remember my father's coarse hands gripping a folded newspaper to his face as I ate soggy cereal. His hands made me think of his loss in the park.

After I had cleared the table and washed the dishes, I spread the crumpled chess mat on the table next to the marble board. Without saying a word to my father, I set up the pieces, both black and white. My father put down the newspaper and approached the table cautiously. He suggested I be white and started to take a seat before the black pieces, but I shook my head and spun the mat so that the white pieces sat before him.

We stared at the evolving board, barely speaking, feeling for the fallen pieces almost as if they were dead family. My father made a mistake and grunted angrily. One of his bishops went down, and his king stood exposed.

Who taught you a move like that? my father asked. I was too deep in concentration to respond.

He made a helpless move and hid a crestfallen brow behind a false smile.

I imagined my father's mind racing, cataloging everything that had ever tumbled down around him. I put my hand on a bishop, my would-be assassin, and thought of my father's heights when he won, how he galloped around. The depths of his despair at losing, I expected, would be equal to the peaks. He'd mope about, his face fallen and miserable, his posture stooped as if his back ached. I took my hand from the piece and leaned back in deliberation. He ran his left hand over his cheek and his upper lip as a sort of nervous gesture.

My bishop moved to an out-of-the-way square where it died at the hands of one of my father's pawns, and my father chastised me for missing an opportunity to take the game.

It's not over, I said. That's all part of the plan.

His tight jaw eased. His eyes danced with life, and his down-turned mouth became a straight line.

I inched a pawn forward, anticipating that moment when it would reach the other side and take the rank of queen. We went back and forth trading pieces. My queen fell. The pawn I had been grooming fell, and I inched another one forward a single square at a time. My father's moves were now of little interest to me as I eyed that determined black pawn. If it became a queen, I could still pin his king in three or four moves. I watched his spare pieces as he studied the board. He angled them into position, maneuvering his bishop and a pawn to kill my king. Doubling back, I blocked him. He made another move, and I focused again on my pawn.

It danced to the last square, transforming into royalty, that most powerful lady of the board.

And as I smiled at the pawn's triumph, my father used a knight and a rook to seal my king's fate. He slapped his hands together and rocketed to his feet, announcing his checkmate with a shriek while he paraded around the table laughing and applauding. I gave the victor the slightest nod and tipped over my dead king.

Juba

The man walking toward me stretched his hand out as we crossed the street. I shook it and kept walking, as I had never seen him before.

Juba, he said. Boy, Juba, I ain't seen you in a long time. Juba woo-wee.

Because my name is not Juba, I was content to keep moving. The man stopped right in the middle of busy Carroll Street, still gripping my hand. A money green Acura turned sharply in front of us. I dipped and jerked to avoid being struck.

Are you crazy? I asked as we made it to the sidewalk.

Sorry, Juba, man. It's just that I ain't seen you in so long. It's good to see you, man. You still up to your old tricks?

I had an idea what sort of tricks he might be talking about. The man looked old, but it was an artificial old. The kind of old that seizes a person who abuses himself. That sort of old comes from too many late nights. The old of hard liquor and worse. He was scarred in the face and on the arms, but also on his wrinkled hands. He wasn't the sort of man you saw around here very often.

I'm sorry, buddy, I said, but I'm not Juba.

Stop messing around, Juba. You always was a trickster. Stop playing games, man. You still hustling?

Sir, I'm hustling to catch this bus. Other than that I don't hustle, and I really have to go.

I really did have to go. I had a job interview at an accounting firm downtown in an hour, and I had timed everything perfectly. If I caught the 12:45 p.m. B58, I would make it there exactly fifteen minutes early. I had performed a test run the day before and another one a day before that. This was my second interview, and I could tell the woman who ran the office liked me. All I had to do was show up. Since the layoff I had been out of work for several months. In another couple weeks my unemployment checks would be at an end.

There was something odd in this man's smile, perhaps something in the webs of wrinkles at his cheeks.

Juba, you something else, boy. The man let out a wheezy, whining squeal. Man, I'm trying to buy a dub. Can you help me out with that?

A dub?

Yeah, a dub. Remember when you used to be selling nicks down by Riverhall? But then one day you said since times is hard it's dubs or better.

I have no idea what you're talking about, I said. I think you have the wrong person.

I reached into my pocket and pulled out a $5 bill. Here, buddy, I said. Go get yourself a sandwich or coffee.

The man stared at my hand, curling his lip in disgust. Man, I don't need your money, he said. I'm tryna buy some green.

I turned and started to walk when the man grabbed at my elbow.

Hey, Juba, man, he said. Stop playing games, all right?

I thought I heard his voice change. I snatched my arm from him and nearly tumbled backward, but I caught myself. I hadn't been in a fistfight since I was a young man at District Central mixing it up with guys from the Southside who thought I was a punk because I lived on the Northside. I wondered if I even remembered how to fight. I balled my fists and stepped backward a bit. He was big guy, and his hands seemed built for strangulation. I used to be so skinny back then, nearly frail. In college I lifted weights to give myself some definition, but it didn't work, so I stopped. It was important not to get wrapped in his massive arms, because then I'd never break free. I had to strike first, and then strike again and keep moving if I had any chance. All that was jumping the gun, though. I had no intention of getting into a fight.

He appeared to be looking over my shoulder. I glanced back to see three men approaching me with guns drawn. Confused, I raised my hands over my head. They wore badges around their necks and light black jackets. There was one to my left with a puffy pink face and a brown mustache. He appeared tense. I looked from man to man quickly, disoriented by their shouting. I put my hands out in front of me, but I wasn't sure if

82

that's what I was supposed to do. They kept calling me Juba. All I had to do was explain that I didn't know this man and that our very conversation was a simple misunderstanding. If only they would stop shouting.

Juba, get down on your knees and put your hands to your head, the man with the puffy pink face said.

I . . . Am . . . Not . . . Juba! I screamed it as loudly as I could. You can check my ID. My name is not Juba.

I became aware of each and every one of my movements, each individual heartbeat and blink. I slowly moved my arms to reach for my pocket where my IDs were, but that seemed to make them more agitated. They screamed at me, and I could barely understand them. I looked over at the man who had started all this confusion. They didn't seem to be troubling him. It dawned on me that he was with them, perhaps an undercover or a neighborhood snitch.

I fell to my knees as they asked. The officer with the brown mustache shoved me face down so that my cheek pressed flat against the sidewalk. One of them wrenched my arms together behind my back and pinched cuffs tightly around my wrists.

For some reason, even with all my attention on my movements—both involuntary and otherwise—I didn't realize that I had been yelling, screaming all along: *I am not Juba! I am not Juba! I am not Juba!* They had been telling me to shut up, but I kept screaming, *I am not Juba!* as I lay there on the ground. I suppose I had said it so much that it lost all meaning. It was the truth, though. I am not Juba.

They didn't release me from the police station until after midnight. All I got was a halfhearted apology from some detective who remained unconvinced that I wasn't Juba. They showed me photographs of myself leaving my condo, driving, going to catch the bus, and meeting with family members on the Southside. One officer slid me a cup of coffee after it was established that I wasn't Juba. He told me to watch my back because Juba is still out there. I had only a vague sense of what he meant. But they had to let me go, as there was no evidence that I was Juba.

Still, no one told me who Juba was or what Juba was supposed to have done. For all I knew, I was uncomfortably close to lying strapped to a gurney with chemicals streaming into my veins.

I called the accounting firm in the morning to explain my absence.

The office manager told me she was sorry, but they filled the position when I didn't show. She asked why I didn't call, and I couldn't make up something fast enough. I turned off the telephone and threw it across the living room of my condo. It slapped against the wall and nicked it.

I thought about suing. I invited my cousin over for a drink that night. He was a few years older than me and ran a private law firm downtown. I would have offered to go to dinner, or at the very least a happy hour or something, but thanks to the CRPD I was still unemployed.

My cousin always made an impression. He stood tall as a professional basketball player and had the sturdy build of one. Women seemed to like him. Guys wanted to hang around him. I wanted to hang around him, but I was always too broke to keep up. When he came to my door, he wore a sports jacket over a white shirt with thin brown vertical lines and a stiff, stiff collar.

He slapped my hand and held it firmly, pulling me into him and embracing me tightly. My cousin often went overboard with his handshakes and hugs. It was like something out of the seventies.

Cousin, he said sitting on my couch. I haven't been here in such a long time. I been meaning to come see you.

Yeah, I replied. Man, you look like you're here for a job interview.

Just trying to look as fly as my cousin. Speaking of job interviews, what happened to the one you were supposed to have by the place near my office?

Man, I said, and paused briefly. We'll get to that one.

He nodded, peering down at me quizzically. I didn't want to seem as if I'd just called him to do me a favor, so I led the discussion to any number of things from politics to his cases to family—the normal topics people usually talked round and round.

Listen, jack, I said. You'll never guess what happened to me. I got arrested, man.

What? I told you to stop going to those grimy Southside Row clubs, man. Don't nobody go to The Garden no more, anyway. I got some clients trying to get some of them dirty buildings torn down so we can get some condos up—

These fools cost me a job, I said, cutting off my cousin's ramble. Kept me locked up all day. I missed my damn interview.

That's terrible, my cousin said.

I wasn't doing anything.

You know how often I hear people say that? You had to be doing something.

I was walking down the street and then I get accused of being someone named Juba.

Juba? I heard a hint of fear in my cousin's voice. They actually called you Juba?

Yes.

Did you have any marijuana on you?

What?

Weed, cousin. When they busted you, did you have any weed on you?

Of course not. What are you getting at?

Did they charge you with anything?

No. But I'm thinking about suing. They cost me a great job. This damn condo's not cheap.

Look, I think you should drop this whole thing. You're free. No one thinks you're Juba, thank God. Let it go.

I'm not letting shit go.

I didn't realize it, but I had raised my voice. My cousin jerked back, somewhat rattled, I think. I softened a bit.

I had everything planned to the second, I said. I was going to arrive early and make small talk with the secretary, so I could look all witty and charming and shit. Then I was going to spend my wait time reading, so I could look sophisticated when the executives passed. After that I was going to sail right into the position. Now all that is ruined, man.

Blame Juba.

Who's Juba, anyway?

You sounded like him for a minute, yelling like a crazy man, my cousin said. Juba is bad news. Bad news.

Yeah, he has been for me.

Well, cuz, he's a phantom. A convenient explanation. Juba may not exist, but the cops in Cross River are convinced he does, and they plan on locking his ass up. They been prowling the city for a while looking for this dude. I'm starting to think he's an underworld myth. An urban legend. Juba.

What did he do?

He's sold enough weed to keep half the country high. The war on drugs is just a war on Juba. My cousin slapped his knee when he said this. He's Tony Montana, my cousin continued. The Medellin Cartel, John Gotti, and Black Caesar in one. It's hell up in Cross River, boy. Juba is one bad nigga. He supplies the Washington, Johnson, and Jackson crime families, and he got them all going to war over his product. You know how many folks are dead behind Juba?

And they think I'm this dude?

They've thought a lot of people were Juba. One of my clients, they initially thought he was Juba. Turns out he was a little punk from the Northside who went to Cross River Community College and sold a little herb to look cool. He's at Freedman's University now. Probably pretending he's tough and slinging nicks. One of my dummy clients. Clown.

I've never even smoked a joint before.

Not even in college?

Nope.

What the hell have you been doing with your life, cousin?

I didn't respond to that, just shook my head, thinking of Juba.

We talked for a few hours, had some more drinks, and then my cousin left. Before leaving, though, he told me again to forget about Juba. I hadn't made up my mind whether or not I would leave it alone, but I told him I would. There was so much on my mind, and most of it involved Juba.

Every day I sat at home without a job I thought about what had happened. I awoke from nightmares where winged beasts with guns swooped in and slammed me to the ground. I felt so weak and powerless and foolish, and still so unemployed.

I kept hearing the name, folks mentioning him in idle conversation. Juba's name seemed to pass from every lip. I wondered if people had always talked about Juba this much or if something new had seized the consciousness of the town.

In between submitting job applications, I went from person to person telling them about my ordeal. To a man, all knew of Juba. Some said I was lucky I still had a life. Others tied Juba to a police slaying so many months ago. A good number of people described Juba as a happy-go-lucky guy, the Santa Claus of marijuana peddlers, a grandfatherly guy with good advice and a sack of chronic. Only I, it seemed, had never heard of Juba. One cousin, one I rarely spoke to, said: Juba ain't shit. That nigga sells nicks and dimes, but he smokes most of it himself. I used to buy weed from him. High off his own supply every damn time I seen him. He ain't no throat-slitter. He a joke.

Where can I find Juba? I asked.

Fuck if I know. I ain't seen him in a long, long time.

And that was what most people said. No one knew where Juba stayed. Most had never even seen him. I couldn't be sure he even existed.

My cousin the attorney checked up on me from time to time. He kept telling me to drop it. I grew sick of hearing from him, so eventually when his number flashed across my phone, I didn't answer. One time he called, I let it ring, and when it finished ringing, I thought to call a reporter friend of mine. I figured if anyone had the resources to find out more about Juba, it was him. He sounded rushed. Told me he had never heard of Juba and apologized about what had happened to me. Before I could say anything more, he said he had to go and hung up abruptly. I sat in my living room smoking a cigarette right down to the filter, hoping to forget about Juba.

I decided I wouldn't obsess about Juba anymore or think about that day the police shoved me to the ground. But two things happened to make it impossible to forget.

Each week, I volunteered at K.I.D.S. Community Center in the McCoy neighborhood on the Southside. I forget what the letters stood for, but it could have been Khaotic, Ineffective, and Detrimental Supervision. I taught math skills to children who were behind in school, but mostly I told them to shut up, as the brats were forever talking out of turn and fighting with each other.

Before class one week, an adorable girl with big eyes, brown skin, and hair plaited into one thick braid hugged me as I came in the door. I smiled at her embrace. Most times she was the loudest, most unruly of the bunch, forever threatening to punch one of the other kids, including boys older than her.

Are you going to be boring today? she asked.

I felt my smile wither, and immediately I wanted to go home. I watched the kids scurrying about, finding places to hide from me. I looked down.

Are *you* going to be boring today? I said, and she jumped back as if I had burned her. Even I was surprised by the heat of my words.

I got through about half of the lesson before I became frustrated with their interruptions and walked off to talk to a pretty counselor with red-dish brown eyes and long hair that I later learned was a weave. In the past she had seemed unimpressed with my condo and my watch. I kept telling her about them, hoping to wear her down.

The counselors ignored the children who now ran through the place tossing things about. Occasionally a counselor would shout at a student, but for the most part the adults and the children didn't at all interact. To make conversation, I told the pretty counselor the story of my confrontation with the police. When I said the name Juba, her eyes widened. She pointed to the cute little girl who had accosted me. The girl, the counselor said, was Juba's niece.

The little girl raised her head when she heard her uncle's name and looked over at us, meeting our gazes and the counselor's pointing finger.

You guys talking about my Uncle Juba? she asked.

No, no, sweetie, the counselor said. No. We're not talking about your Uncle Juba. No.

Sweetie, I said. Tell me about your Uncle Juba.

My Uncle Juba is tall and his hair is black and gray. And he's smart. Smarter than you. I bet he knows more about math than you.

I bet he does.

He taught me how to count and he taught me how to spell. And he's always reading the Bible. His eyes are big like my mother's, but they're always red.

Red like a sunset?

Red like when I get cut. My mother said that's 'cause Uncle Juba never sleeps. He stays up all night and all day long. I seen Uncle Juba asleep before, but mostly he don't sleep.

Where's your Uncle Juba now, sweetie?

She shrugged. I haven't seen Uncle Juba in a long, long, long, long time, she said. He calls me. Sends me e-mails too. Says I'm the prettiest little girl he has ever seen, and Uncle Juba is right. I'm the prettiest little girl in all of Cross River and the whole world.

Juba Franklin. That was his name. That's what the little girl told me. I didn't ask any more questions because I didn't want to let on that I was looking for Juba.

The second thing that happened to keep Juba on my mind was that my reporter friend called back that night. He was just as brusque as he had been the day before, but he had found something from talking to his sources. There was a Juba Franklin who hung out in a bar in Port Yooga, Virginia. He was there every night. Why the police didn't know, my friend wasn't sure. Juba had moved his shady business from Cross River to Port Yooga, hiding in plain sight, and the fools couldn't figure out how to find him. Get me a nickel bag, he said before hanging up.

I've never been a religious man. My mother says that's why I had such a hard time finding a job. Still, I took the turn of events as a sign. Maybe to find a job, I needed to track Juba down. I needed to see his face to understand all that had happened to me. Perhaps I could even say a word or two to him.

I brushed that idea out of my head. There were so many incarnations of him. He could have easily been a cold-blooded killer, but it was just as likely that he was a friendly neighborhood pot peddler. I figured the truth of him rested somewhere in the middle. I called a few people to ask their advice, but I only called those who shared my curiosity and thought Juba was probably not a dangerous guy. Sitting at home all alone, watching daytime television, I had a lot of time to think about things. Such a man, one who knew everyone at all levels from the dirtiest dealer on Angela Street to the well-heeled people on the Hilltop, could explain so much that I, with my limited experience, had never understood. In all honesty, I had made up my mind after I got off the phone with my reporter friend, but it took me a few days to realize it.

I sat in a bar in Port Yooga in the middle of the day drinking a beer called Purple Haze in honor of my potential meeting with the weed dealer, Juba Franklin. I felt preposterous, but less preposterous than I had felt with my cheek to the pavement and my hands cuffed behind my back.

I glanced around, trying to figure which of these men was Juba. It was an easy question to answer, as I was the only black man in the bar. I chomped on peanuts to pass the time and at one point ordered chicken wings. I felt foolish with the grease from the wings on my fingers and asked for a knife and fork. The bartender looked at me strangely and then handed me the utensils. Eating the wings with a knife and fork made me feel like more of a fool, and I stopped, letting the wings grow cold. At about six I realized the ridiculousness of the whole enterprise and planned to leave, but before I could summon the will to walk away, two men strode into the bar. The shorter man had an ashy bald head shaped like the peanuts I ate. The other was tall and dark with black, lightly salted hair. His eyes were bloodred, nearly glowing in his face. Juba. There was a part of me that said, just turn and go home, but I could still feel those metal bracelets pinching at my wrists. I walked over to the man's table. Nearly called the man Uncle Juba when I opened my mouth, but I caught myself.

I'm new in town, I said. I don't trust these crackers. They don't seem too cool. You know where I can get some pot?

Uh-uh, Juba replied. I really don't know nothing about that.

You Juba?

Sorry, jackson, don't know nobody by that name.

I twisted my brow, giving him a puzzled look. He blinked a lot, so I wondered if that had some sort of meaning. He shook peanuts from their shell and crunched them in his teeth. It seemed like he was making fun of me.

The other man tried his hand at looking menacing. He gave me a flat look of irritation. It said he was unafraid and would destroy me if I bothered him for too long. His intimidation was a moderate success. I could see myself turning and running, but I held firm.

Well, I said. I guess it's for the best that you're not Juba, because I was going to tell that guy that his weed isn't shit. He's trying to pass off dirt as the chronic.

The bald man cracked a smirk, his head a flaky white under the dull glow from above. Juba's face remained flat and expressionless, but he bowed his head and shook it side to side as if lost in prayer.

Boy, why you want to mess around with your life, huh? Juba asked. Don't even ride yourself like that, my nig-nig. Everybody from Cross River to Port Yooga and all spots in the middle know that Juba got them fire tea leaves, chief.

So you do know Juba?

You police?

If I was, you know I could lie if I wanted to, I said. It's a myth that I legally have to tell you the truth if I'm a cop. And I'm not a cop. But if I was one, I'd just lie.

Ain't you a reg duboishead? he replied.

A what?

A regular genius, jack. Keep up, my nig-nig.

You speak fast. It's hard to follow sometimes.

The bald man's eyes danced in disbelief.

I'm not rapping fast, Juba said. I'm just talking a different language than you. When two niggas from El Salvador get together and talk, neither one of them complain that the other is all flashy speaking or whatever. It's just the squares, the outsiders like you—not me, I know Spanish—like you that complain. You a Riverbaby?

I prefer Cross Riverian.

Course you do, he said. Bougie niggas always prefer Cross Riverian.

It's better than being a baby, I replied. The problem is we always infantilize our people. Folks don't want to grow up and be men and women. The world would finally respect us if we'd just be men.

Blah, blah, blah; right and sure. Tell me, if y'all niggas got money and houses and things over there on the Northside, and I can already tell you a Northside nigga, then why y'all so cross? Cross Riverian literally means angry river person, you know that, right?

Looks to me like Southside folks are more angry. That's where people get robbed and shot and stuff like that.

Checkmate. I tell you what. You look like a true. I'll griff you some of that Starr Product if you give me a fumi.

Huh?

Juba sighed. The bald man grunted and crunched peanuts between his teeth.

Riverbabies don't even own their own tongue no more. Nigga, give me a cigarette and I'll sell you some weed. Shit, may even have a story to tell you too.

I handed him a cigarette and he asked me to follow him. Juba and I left the bar; the bald man stayed behind.

Juba took me into a basement apartment so small it seemed like a cell—a spacious cell, but still a cell. A few beams of natural light came in from the streets above. Juba's bed took up most of the space. He had a bookshelf filled with holy books and books about the holy books. In the corner sat a little desk and atop it a thick raggedy Bible with torn pages and Post-It notes sticking out from the edges. It was opened to the first page of the Book of Revelation. Juba had several sentences underlined and notes running up and down the margins in a graphomaniacal frenzy.

Juba rolled a joint, lit it, and offered it to me, but I passed. He sat it at the right corner of his mouth and blew smoke out of the left. Then he spoke rapidly about the flow of the Cross River for minutes on end, the way a man might speak about a lover he missed.

I got a sale on that Starr Product, he said. Chronic's always a crowd pleaser. I got 'Dro, Purple Haze, but I recommend the Starr Product. Cross Riv's finest. They don't grow that shit nowhere else. Only find that shit in and around Cross River. I'm smoking it now for your sampling pleasure.

I looked around at his cramped apartment.

You don't make a lot off of this, do you? I asked.

Enough to afford this mansion and to keep me in these fancy Armani linens, he said, running his hand along his jeans and long-sleeved T-shirt, both torn and faded from frequent washing. Naw, my man, it's all shorty-cool. Don't need to make a lot. Just enough for rent and books.

I—I heard you were a kingpin.

Yeah, there are competing versions of me out in the world. Damn near heard I popped a Kennedy one day in November.

His words were slightly amusing, but as I watched him, something shocked me so much that my skin tingled. I noticed that he and I did share a slight resemblance. He too had drawn cheeks and big eyes that looked as if they were floating in his head.

Hear the police tell it, I got tons flying in on planes every afternoon. They scared of me 'cause they think I'm getting their little daughters hooked on my jungle weed. He paused. I guess I am. I sell dubs and half-centuries and centuries and sometimes I might sell an LB, but that's as much as I griff. I ain't trying to be their monkey in a cage. That's why I had to come down here until things ain't so radioactive. I found out they were after me. Accused me of doing some apocalyptic shit, of being behind all the tea in Cross River, jackson. You know how many niggas be selling grass? They looking for me back home, they can't even imagine I'm over here. They know how much I love Cross River. They figure I'd never leave my home. Shit, I never thought I'd leave The Riv, myself. Things'll calm down eventually and I'll be back. I don't even like this job.

You don't?

Fuck no, my nig-nig. Been doing this too long. You look cool, so I'll tell you this.

Juba walked over to his desk and picked up a notebook. He flipped through the pages before putting it into my hands. See that? That's my real job. I'm just doing this weed dealer biz until I can finish up this project.

There were strange markings on each page, words I didn't understand, beautiful sketches that had an unfinished quality.

What is this?

Man, can't you read? See, Cross River folks so busy talking like white people, they done lost their tongue. Every strange word you hear in Cross River, every little piece of slang, probably sprang from me. Like seventy-five to eighty-seven percent. I come from a long line . . .

Of weed dealers?

Don't get smart, my nig-nig. You knew I wasn't gonna say that. My dad was an engineer, but that wasn't his main thing. I capture and create the language we speak in Cross River. Just like my daddy before me and my grandfather before that and my great-grandfather who was in the Great Insurrection before there even was a town called Cross River in Maryland. We done lost our tongue. Some shit I got to say to you, I won't even try to say 'cause there ain't no words for it. I got to use more words than I would have to use if we had our language back. I got to speak slowly so you understand me, even though we from the same place. Ridiculous, but it ain't your fault. I'm trying to complete the Cross River tongue.

I flipped through the book. The words started to make sense a little, but there were huge canyons of language I couldn't understand. It's probably the way, with my high school Spanish, I'd look at a book written in that language.

So what is this, a dictionary? I asked.

A dictionary? You niggas in Cross River are more lost than I ever thought. Shit. He stopped speaking for a moment. Naw . . . naw . . . hell naw, this ain't no damn dictionary. The people ain't ready for that. For like twenty years, I been translating the Bible into Cross Riverian, as you bougie niggas like to say. Naw, y'all wouldn't even call it that. Y'all don't think the way we talk is nothing special. At least not special enough to have a name. Y'all spend a lot of time translating from English to Cross Riverian and back in y'all heads. Y'all just don't know it. Niggas ain't slow, they just translating.

I'm gonna do the Koran next, and then the Bhagavad Gita. I already did the Heart Sutra. Did that shit to warm me up. I got a rack of other sutras to do, but that's a ways off. I got a lot of books to translate. It's gonna take a while, though. Once I finish the Bible, everything else should move quickly. I need to capture the language first. It's triply hard now that I ain't in Cross River no more. Got folks mailing me new words in exchange for 'Dro. The police might catch up to me before I'm done.

As he spoke, it was like a spirit moved over the void of the words on the pages, and I started to understand completely what Juba had written. I came to the end of the story of the Great Flood and it was like one of my cousins from the Southside had whispered it into my ear.

I tell you what, brotherman. I've enjoyed this convo with you, Juba said. Take a dub of that Starr Product for the road.

I shook my head. I-I-I can't—

Naw man, you don't know how good this has been for me. I like meeting Riverbabies. I don't hardly get a chance no more since I'm in Port Yooga. Not that I don't like Port Yooga in its own way, but it ain't Cross River.

I pocketed the bag of weed. It was nearly black, and it smelled like all outdoors. One whiff was enough to intoxicate me for precisely fifteen seconds, at least that's what Juba said. I never did smoke it, though. I put it in my basement in a briefcase where I kept things I wanted no one to find. After a while I forgot the code and couldn't even get back into the briefcase if I wanted to. Juba and I stayed in touch, but I never saw him again. I offered him words, phrases, and critiques on his translation of the Bible by mail. Sometimes he'd send me weed as payment, and I always threw it away. As I walked from his house that evening, I had no idea what to make of the afternoon.

When I got onto the bus to Cross River, I sat next to a man from the Southside who spoke to me about his life. His accent was thick, so at times I got lost, but when I was engaged I felt transported to his childhood. As the bus crossed the bridge from Port Yooga into Cross River he said, I know who you are.

Who am I?

He leaned in and whispered, You that dude they call Juba.

I shook my head and smirked a bit. I'm not Juba, I said. I'm not him at all.

It's okay, he said. I ain't a yauper. I can keep it to myself, my nig-nig.

The man pulled out a piece of paper and wrote down some words and phrases. They were things a Cross Riverian might say. He nodded and crinkled the paper into my palm and I accepted it, folding it away in my left breast pocket.

The Legend of Ezekiel Marcus

I

A month after school opened—when the most coveted boys had paired off with the most coveted girls and, for the majority of us, our affections were going tragically unreturned—Mr. Coles, the new art teacher, decided he hated Ezekiel Marcus. It was in the way he shied from addressing Zeke whenever he could, the upturned curve of his lip when he was unable to avoid talking to him, and his clear relief during Zeke's frequent absences. Mr. Coles wasn't like most of the other teachers at Alfred McCoy Middle School; he was essentially a good and decent man, so he would have never admitted what was plain to me. Even to this day—wherever he is, certainly no longer a teacher—I bet if I were to ask him about these old times, he'd deflect with his signature joke, *I hated you all equally*. Then, thinking twice, he'd take the edge off and add, *I loved you all equally, too.*

We called him Mr. Cold. A name, I think, Zeke made up. Anyway, Zeke was the first one I heard say it during third-period art one day, and my laughter turned from tittering to inconsolable, if laughter can be called inconsolable. Mr. Coles had a young, elfin face with tidily groomed hair on his cheeks and chin, none on his upper lip. He was handsome. Impossibly, even freakishly, handsome—strong cheekbones and a smooth dark complexion—a fact I had to reluctantly admit and one that most of the girls never let anyone forget. Hair all black while most of his peers sported grays and bad dye jobs. And Mr. Coles always smiled, even when angry and trying to be stern, especially when angry and trying to be stern.

All of this is why we treated him poorly and why he overcompensated, first attempting to come across as a pal, a trustworthy big brother, and when that failed turning into a hard-ass for a time, though he was a phony hard-ass, one we could see clear through. Rarely, if ever, did we tremble in fear at his silly yelling and stiff pointing finger. Marshall, Mr. Coles called to me as I choked on laughter after he grew upset from Zeke's taunting. Marshall, it's funny, but that's enough. This just caused us to laugh more. The warmest man in the school, Mr. Cold, then sent Ezekiel into the hallway as his mentor, Mr. Drayton, probably advised him to do. Damn, that's cold-blooded, Mr. Cold, a proud and smiling Zeke said on his way out to another rise in laughter.

The next time we saw Mr. Coles, he was stiff and stern. Even his movements changed to reflect the new him. We talked through the roll as usual, and by the fifth name he stopped and looked up. In spite of his contrived scowl, he still managed to appear somehow smiling. He stared at Zeke, though we were all speaking. There were always five of us at the front table: me, Zeke, a Puerto Rican girl with curly hair named Jana, and two jokers named Ernesto and Tommy.

Hey, Zeke, you want to go stand in the hallway again? Mr. Coles asked.

I didn't do nothing, Zeke said. I'm not the only one talking. Why don't you pick on Tommy and Ernesto?

Either you be quiet or go stand in the hall. Those are your two options. I'm not here to argue with you, Ezekiel.

When Zeke kept talking to us, Mr. Coles ordered him into the hallway. Zeke stood swiftly so that his metal stool toppled to the floor. On his way out he said, Man, we were going to stop calling you Mr. Cold, too, but you keep showing us how cold-blooded you are, so you're gonna be Mr. Cold from now until whenever.

Zeke, be quiet or it's the office instead of the hall.

Zeke spent most of the class in the hallway rapping the uncensored version of a dirty song that played every few minutes on the radio stations we all listened to. *Shake that ass buck naked, bitch / don't you fake it, bitch / Shake that ass buck naked, bitch* . . . Mr. Coles pretended not to hear him, and that's how we all knew that this new Mr. Cold was a put-on. His demeanor was a lie, a desperate one. I could understand, Mr. Coles's true self earned him zero respect, but still, a lie was destined to fail. It was no wonder he was so adrift in the classroom. Much of his behavior was straight from the manual of so many of our educators, but particularly Mr. Drayton, who was old and stiff and smelled vaguely of urine. I'd often see Mr. Coles sitting in the cafeteria joking with this crumpled old white man. Chatting in the parking lot outside their cars. In each other's classrooms between classes. Mr. Drayton needed an ego stroke and Mr. Cold needed a clue.

Near the end of class, Mr. Coles called Zeke back into the room and asked us all to pay quiet attention.

You may have noticed that I am not as open as I once was, Mr. Coles said. Less apt to listen to excuses. More likely to punish. I never wanted to be this kind of teacher. I figure you've all had enough hard-ass drill sergeants, but you guys have been so damaged by that kind of teaching that you don't respect anything else. Not your fault. And it's not all of you, but enough that I'm forced to change my approach. From now on, if you are not in your seat by the time the bell rings, I am marking you tardy. Too many tardies means you lose credit for the semester. You talk when I am talking, I'm sending your ass out of the classroom. Not to the hallway, but to the office. You don't work on your art, I'm sending you out of class. We can have a good time, but it's something you have to earn now.

Damn, he's Mr. Cold for real, someone in the back said, and Mr. Coles shot Zeke a stone look.

And, Mr. Coles said as the bell rang signaling the end of class, my name is Mr. Coles. Please address me as that and nothing else.

That afternoon during gym class, while the sixth-graders were having lunch, me and Zeke placed bets on how long Mr. Coles would keep up his hard-ass persona. It was a soccer week, and we competed to show the girls who could keep the ball in the air the longest using just our feet, heads, thighs, and chests. Zeke was already a soccer star and could out-dribble even the best of the high school students. As we kicked the ball around, we compared notes with others, and it seemed Mr. Coles had given similar speeches in his other classes, but thanks to the presence of Zeke in our class, third period got the harshest lecture.

It's because of that fucking Mr. Drayton, Zeke said. I know he got in Mr. Cold's ear and turned him against us. I bet ol' piss-breath was like, *You got to break Zeke's spirit.* I hate going to Mr. Drayton's fucking class.

Yeah, I said, and now we're going to hate art class too.

Zeke pointed to Mr. Drayton overseeing the sixth-graders' post-lunch recreation time and said, I bet I could hit him right in the nose with this soccer ball from here.

You think you Pelé, I replied.

He tapped the ball gently ahead of him. Just strike it in the right spot, you can place it wherever you want. That's what my coach says. What would you give me if I knocked the shit out of him with this ball?

I had no doubt that Zeke could make the ball sail from the top of the hill down to Mr. Drayton's face—I had seen him score some impossible goals—but I pretended I didn't hear him so he'd drop it, and he did.

For the first week of Mr. Cold's new persona we worked in silent misery most of the time. In history class we learned about the Soviet work camps, and during third period I imagined we were in one, fashioning cheap, meaningless trinkets out of wire and then out of clay or papier-mâché. Mr. Coles taught us to make animals out of newspaper, paint, and lacquer. Zeke chose to work with wire, bending it into a little man on a little bicycle, while most of the rest of our table continued to work with clay. I think that was the most peaceful I had ever seen Zeke, and Mr. Coles complimented him more than once for his demeanor, but to me it was all wrong. Zeke was happiest when he was causing chaos. I made a human out of newspaper and painted it brown and joked that I was creating an Ezekiel Marcus doll.

He took it in good spirits at first, and then one class—I made the joke over and over to a rising chorus of giggles—he unwound a piece of wire from his bicycle and wrapped it around the neck of my Zeke doll. I'm gonna kill that motherfucker, he said. He tried to make us feel as if he was kidding, but I could tell the conformity and silence weighed heavily on him.

Mr. Coles frowned.

Marshall is working really hard, and here you come to disrupt things, Mr. Coles said. I just don't know what gets into you, Zeke. You haven't caused any trouble lately, and now this. Go stand in the hallway.

Zeke stormed out as Mr. Coles continued to rant: Lucky I'm not sending you to the principal. The only reason you're not going to the office is because you've been good the past few days. Think about that while you stand there.

That day during gym class a bunch of us ignored the soccer game at the other end of the field. Every few minutes Zeke spied Mr. Drayton down the hill looking stiff and severe.

I hate that nigga, Zeke said.

Why you worried about him? I said. You let Mr. Cold turn you into Meek Zeke.

Jana and Ernesto stood nearby along with about a half dozen other students too cool to play soccer. Hey, Weak Zeke, I said too loudly. I looked around at the people next to us, pathetically, hoping their reactions, their approval, would suddenly make me three or four inches taller. Without warning, he shoved me to the ground and kicked dirt in my face while people pointed and laughed. Ernesto pulled Zeke back, and I stood and cursed at him, but I didn't lunge. Zeke was bigger than me. Even more than looking to avoid a beat-down, I certainly couldn't afford a beat-down in front of Jana. I watched Zeke angrily as if poised to swing. Zeke shoved past me, pushing his way through a group of fight-gawkers. Jana asked me if I was okay, and while I nodded and preened for sympathy, Zeke was deftly removing the soccer ball from the feet of the clumsier players at the other end of the field. He came barreling toward us while slower players trailed, a cloud of dust in his wake. He waved his right arm like a windmill and pulled his leg back so far I thought he was going to flip, but he didn't flip, instead he kicked the ball, and I ducked, though there was no need to do so. It sailed over the goal in a magnificent rainbow arch until it struck the unsuspecting Mr. Drayton right in the nose, breaking his glasses and dashing them and him to the ground. Mr. Drayton cradled his face. I could see blood stains forming continents on his white shirt.

The principal, Mrs. Badwell, called me and Zeke to her office during fifth-period pre-algebra. Some snitch said they heard us joking about hitting Mr. Drayton with a ball. Mrs. Badwell questioned us separately, but I feigned ignorance and righteous anger. How could a young boy kick a ball from on top of the field all the way down the hill with the precision of Diego Maradona? I asked the principal, though I said it with much less eloquence, and eventually she chalked it up to an accident.

The Legend of Ezekiel Marcus grew that day. To us he became The Bad Nigga No One Could Touch. Unfortunately, to the teachers he became That Bad Nigger No One Could Touch. Some days I could literally see the target burning red on his back.

Ezekiel's ascension from badass kid to rebel coincided with us learning about the civil rights movement in history class. During lunchtime on Tuesday he gathered me, Ernesto, Jana, and Tommy near the soccer field and began speaking in a hushed, nervous tone.

Look, he said. We got to take back that art class. It was the only fun we had all day, and now the thing is all somber and shit. Cold's gone fucking crazy.

Well, it's your fault, Zeke, Jana said. He was just trying to be our friend and you decided to act like an asshole.

It's not time to be blaming nobody, Zeke said. I want old Mr. Coles back. Everybody want him back. We need to do what Martin Luther King did and act as bad as can be. Civil disobedience. Don't nobody call him Mr. Coles. He's Mr. Cold. When he tries to talk, cut his ass off. And we take the consequences. He can't send the whole class to the office. Watch, in a week we'll have nice Mr. Coles back and it'll be because we took a stand.

That's stupid, Jana said.

If it's so stupid, why Martin Luther King do it like that, huh? Zeke said. Why Gandhi do it like that, huh? Didn't they win? They hit them with some hoses and made dogs bite them, but they won. I'm from Cross River, I ain't afraid of no fucking water. And ain't no one in Cross River afraid of some angry dogs. We got angry dogs up in the Wildlands. Who here hasn't stared down an angry dog or two?

We all nodded, except for Jana.

What I'm saying is, they can't do nothing to us if we stand together.

I think he's onto something, Ernesto chimed in.

Y'all dumb, Jana said. Mr. Coles fine as shit. I'm not getting on his bad side for y'all childish nigs. Jana walked away while the rest of us made plans for our revolution. I watched her behind swish and thought seriously about following it, but the moment was so electric I couldn't bear to walk away. We slapped five on our conspiracy and proposed various disruptive actions. I felt like we were witnessing the birth of the Rev. Dr. Ezekiel Marcus Luther King Jr.

For a week, when Mr. Cold lectured on art history or on some technique, we cut him off to discuss something inane. Zeke would loudly chant his favorite parts of his favorite song, "Shake It Buck Naked, Bitch": *You ain't really do nothing / I'ma make it do something / Twerk that thing baby now / Let me see ya shake something.* We threw clay around the class. Zeke harassed and shamed those who wouldn't get with the program. Me, Zeke, or Ernesto usually got sent out in the first few minutes. Jana would sit there working on a clay mask, shaking her head. The last straw was the day Zeke gathered a lump of clay, big as his head, and dropped it out the second-story class window onto the shiny red hood of Mr. Drayton's convertible.

As soon as that metallic thud struck, we could hear Mr. Drayton in his downstairs classroom emitting a sound like the final wails of a wounded wolf. He dashed up the stairs, leaving his class baffled and teacherless. Me and Zeke sat in the corner suppressing our laughter while Mr. Drayton screamed at us all.

By the next week it seemed something had shifted. Mr. Coles arrived to class looking not broken but hopeful for once. Like it was again the first day of school. Like we were all eager learners and not the assholes we had become. He was fresh-faced. Shaved all that hair off his cheeks. The man looked less like an authority figure, more like a boy. He no longer fought the losing battle to suppress his smile. When someone called him Mr. Cold, he chuckled and said, Now, now. We were confused at first. Thrown way off guard. We still talked over him, and flashes of annoyance still passed over his face, but he shrugged and took the discussion in the direction of whatever interested us, which is how we spent much of one class discussing "Shake It Buck Naked, Bitch."

You know you be listening to Dem Freak Boyz N Motion, Mr. Cold, Zeke said to our amusement.

You mean, Dem Zeke Boyz, Mr. Coles replied. I'm tired of seeing Dem Zeke Boyz in motion. You should sit your *ass* down sometimes. No, just kidding. I know the song. What? You guys think I'm too old to listen to what's out there? Not my thing, though. I do like how some of those rappers take that George Clinton and James Brown stuff I grew up on and recreate it. Yeah, as a collagist, I can certainly appreciate that. I tell you what, class: on Mondays, Tuesdays. and Wednesdays I'll bring in some of those songs your rappers sample, and if I don't have to send anyone out of the class those first three days, you can bring in your music to play the rest of the week.

There were some cheers. Applause from the back. If we were confused before, at that moment Zeke and I and everybody else understood that our plan had worked. We declared total victory. Mr. Coles gave us a sorry what-have-I-done? look. Jana winced at our excitement, but she also smiled. How could she not be happy about taking our class back? We sat through Parliament on Monday and James Brown on Tuesday, but by Wednesday we had commandeered Mr. Coles's boombox, and for three days straight we danced in our seats and played little else but "Shake It Buck Naked, Bitch."

Silly kids. We could never see that we were causing the breaking of a man's spirit. Brutally unraveling him. That when he went home to relax, to watch a television show, to drink a beer, to make love to a woman, he would hear our shrill voices and see our smirking, rude faces. Perhaps I say this to elevate myself. To give meaning to times that have faded from everyone's memory. Maybe I just want to justify my obsession with bygone days. And why do I keep up this obsession, huh? Why do I carry this memory like cross wood on my back? Maybe it's because I saw a homeless man beneath layers of dirty blankets on Alan Street and he had the face of Mr. Coles and I couldn't bear getting closer to find out if it was him; to find out if I had helped to fatally wound not just a man's career but all of his life. Maybe this vision was a symptom of the obsession—in other words, I saw Mr. Coles's face because I am crazy about the past, not because it was actually him. What are the chances that it was him, huh?

Sometimes I see Ernesto and he's dressed in a suit, looking respectable. A lawyer now, brokering deals. And only if you know how to look can you see the rowdy preteen's face upon his. I only see him on my lunch break at the bookstore or at a fast food joint—we work two blocks from one another—and we only talk in five-minute bursts. Though we mention meeting up on the weekend, we both know such a meeting will never happen. When I bring up Mr. Cold or Ezekiel or Mr. Drayton, he says, You still remembering all that shit? It is what it is, man. Let it rest.

One time I mentioned Mr. Cold, and he said, remember Kelli? That was crazy, right? Shit was funny back then, but . . . Hey, he said changing the subject. Did I tell you my wife is about to have a little girl?

That's great, Ernesto. The world can't have enough little black girls.

I'm one and done, boy, Ernesto continued proudly. Wife want another one, a boy, but the world got enough men, right?

Right.

II

Kelli showed up in that art class like some kind of illusion. I thought I was a period early or something and I checked the clock, and then I lost interest in time. Even the most basic words fled from me, and I stood in the middle of the class staring at her. It was as if one of the fertility dolls we fashioned out of clay in the beginning of the school year had come to life.

Certain things stay with you. Certain things cause rivers of shame to well up in your chest whenever you recall them, and no matter where you go or what you do, there's little chance of escaping those poisonous thoughts, little chance of not having to relive them from time to time. But there you go, trying to fill up your head with enough noise to drown out the insistent hum of shame. Standing there staring at Kelli is such a moment. Even in my memories, her face is obscured by her chest, as if she was made of breast meat and nothing more. The thing that made Kelli different than all the other girls was that while their chests bore nubs—good starts, at best—Kelli's sported round fleshy bulbs. It was as if God the artist was working on a line of clay figures and He had finished shaping and smoothing and baking this one sculpture—and He had sculpted it to perfection—while the others needed years of fashioning before they'd be ready.

Kelli's breasts. What was it about them that caused such derangement? Commonplace, pedestrian, ordinary things, even when beautiful. Utilitarian chunks of flesh. How we diminished her and in turn ourselves. Turned parts of her body into heavy burdens to carry. Watching. Tittering (we no longer laughed, from then on it was just tittering). Commenting. Losing our composure. Falling in love, developing obsessions, and growing resentful when our shallow affections were ignored. Zeke was the only one who treated Kelli like a real person, and even that was a put-on. Whenever she wasn't around, he'd remake his favorite Dem Freak Boyz song, chanting, *Bounce them big things, Kelli.* And we'd titter and we'd titter and we'd titter . . .

She was usually wrapped in her own solitude. Arms folded as she walked, elbows pointed outward like spears. A trail of whispers followed her always. She had done this and that with so and so. She was removed from her last school for so on and so forth. She carried something inside her womb and a flood of milk had swelled her breasts. No, she had killed the thing inside her womb and the milk wouldn't go away and every day during sixth period she disappeared deep into the guts of the girls' locker room to spill her milk down the shower drain. The most coveted girls clutched more tightly to the most coveted guys, and the most coveted guys all pulled close to Kelli in the moments when their girlfriends looked away.

Only Jana offered Kelli friendship, and only in the art room. Sometimes they'd spend lunch in Mr. Coles's room and I'd swing by and watch Kelli and leave wondering why neither she nor Jana had ever fallen for me.

I pretended to work on my papier-mâché Ezekiel Marcus in a back corner of the class while I watched Kelli's clay-covered hands as she kneaded the material, searching for little pockets of air.

Why are people at this school so strange, Mr. Coles? Kelli asked, not looking up from her artwork.

What do you mean? he replied.

I mean, some of these bitches act so funny. They won't even talk to me, but they decided already that I'm the devil. Like I'm pressed to talk to them.

Some of them act so immature, Jana chimed in. I don't like this school either. I'm about to go to private school next year. Watch. My dad said give it one more year and then I can go to St. Joseph's over in Port Yooga.

I'm gonna try to go with you, Jana. I'ma talk to my dad about it.

Give it some time, girls, Mr. Coles said. Especially you, Kelli. People don't like change. They see something new and it challenges them. You are going to go through all kinds of things, and then it'll get much better. You'll probably even forget that the first few months here were rocky. Trust me.

I hope so, Kelli said. The only class I like is art. You're the only teacher who doesn't treat me like I'm some alien. Mr. Drayton'll go down the line asking people questions and skip over me. I don't even think he's ever made eye contact with me. I swear, Mr. Coles, it's like even the teachers are immature here. Can I use the wheel?

I haven't taught that yet, Mr. Coles said. No one's allowed to use it until I show you how.

I learned at my old school, Kelli said. It's not hard. Please.

Yeah, please, Jana said.

It didn't take much begging for Mr. Coles to start the motor and get the wheel to spinning. As Kelli sat there sculpting, flecks of clay flew up onto her clothes and onto her face and into her hair. Wearing an apron so dirty it appeared to be made of dried clay, she looked happy for once, no longer out of place. Outside the art room, though, a storm brewed all around us, and I was too busy staring at Kelli's breasts to even take notice.

These bitches gon' riot, Zeke told me one day during gym class.

Huh?

You ain't notice some of them Hatefield hoes ready to fuck Kelli up? And not in the way we want to fuck Kelli up. Vanessa, Carol, Isis, all of them say Kelli trying to fuck with their dudes. Ain't nothing else but to take it to the fists. Say they gonna rip her weave out, boy.

Zeke delivered the news with the excitement of a sports announcer, waving his fists as if the girlmob was advancing on him. And I have to admit, my veins throbbed with excitement. The last fight I saw was two sixth-grade boys smacking each other and then wrestling to the ground where they held the same position for five minutes until security came to cart them away.

When Kelli walked the halls, arms wrapped around her torso, girls cursed at her. Sometimes they threw things that missed. They drew nasty pictures and posted them around the school. The drawings didn't feature Kelli's name—just big cartoonish circles in front of a stick figure. We all knew what was up, but the teachers seemed oblivious.

When it all went down, me and Ernesto and Jana were near the cafeteria talking shit. I was awkwardly trying to get Jana to ride my bus in the afternoon, even though that meant a twenty-minute walk home from my neighborhood to her apartment in McCoy, the neighborhood we all called Hatefield.

I'll walk with you, I said. Besides, you need the exercise.

Go somewhere, Marshall, I don't know why you bothering me. Don't you like Kelli?

Where is everybody? Ernesto asked, and we ignored him to continue our banter while most everyone else had migrated outside and up the hill to the soccer field where, unbeknownst to us, ordinary girls had become gladiators. The Hatefield girls had finally grown tired of Kelli and her tits sauntering around the school as if it belonged to her. That's what I imagined they said before they punched her and kicked her and grabbed at her hair. Tommy and Zeke's accounts clashed on the minor details, but they matched perfectly when it came to the big picture. Four on one.

Kelli never stood a chance. Though to hear Zeke tell it, she put up a fight like a wild animal for a little while. Punching and scratching, keeping the four from getting close. What stopped her momentum was when Isis (or was it Carol? does it matter?) snatched at her shirt, ripping the buttons, releasing all that we dreamed about for the whole world to see. At that point Kelli could only fight with one hand. The other one she dedicated to covering her nakedness.

It all ended when Mr. Coles rushed into the fray to pull the girls off Kelli until security could arrive to take them to the office.

The next day in art class Kelli wasn't there. We did no work; instead we spent the whole time listening to Zeke give us the rundown. He and Tommy performed the fight blow by blow, second by second. When it came time for the big reveal, Zeke snatched at Tommy's shirt and yelled, Wump!

That's the sound they made coming out, Zeke said. They actually made a sound. I'll never forget it.

Damn, I said. I miss every fight. Every damn time.

And then when it was all done, Zeke said, the bitches started to chant, Hatefield, Hatefield is where we're from! Hatefield, Hatefield is where we're from!

Long ago, before even my parents were born, the people of McCoy named themselves Hatfields. Their poverty, it was said, put them in opposition to the very ground they walked upon. More recently, younger Hatfields renamed their neighborhood Hatefield because the hard gravel and weed and trash-scarred empty lots made the name feel truer.

Guys, Mr. Coles said. Stop it. I don't even know why you want to call your neighborhood that. Hate's not a good thing. We shouldn't be glorifying people getting beat up. Let's not be ignorant. Okay?

When Mr. Coles said this he had that smile, that smirk, that grin that destroyed the seriousness of anything he had to say. Zeke howled and pointed.

Come on, Mr. Coles, you know you were entertained, he said. I saw you, boy. This nigga only rushed in after them titties popped out. He was like—at this Zeke grasped at Tommy's chest, groping while pretending to hold him back—*come on now, stop fighting. Ooh, that's so soft.*

Leave Mr. Coles alone, Zeke, Jana said. You always starting stuff. Just ignore him, Mr. Coles.

Mr. Coles's face looked as if it was about to explode in laughter. He rubbed his closely cropped head and chuckled some.

We didn't need music that day. Whenever there was a break in the action we chanted: Hatefield, Hatefield is where we're from!

Man, Mr. Coles, Zeke said. Be for real. You know you was thinking about our song.

Our song? Mr. Coles asked. That Hatefield thing y'all chant?

Naw, you know what I'm talking about, "Shake It Buck Naked, Bitch." You the main one who be playing it in class. Man, Mr. Coles, you took one look at Kelli and was like, *I'ma make it do something / Twerk for me bitch now / Let me see ya shake something.* You know that's what you were thinking, Mr. Coles. Stop faking. Stop faking.

Mr. Coles shook his head and rubbed the short hair on his cheeks. His smile grew alligator-like. In a soft growl, he said: *Come on and bounce them big things, baby.*

Mr. Coles! Jana screamed, stepping away from her clay pot. Just as swiftly, she stepped back to the table and returned to massaging her artwork. I don't think she looked up for the rest of the class period. Ernesto hollered in delight. Me and Zeke slapped five. Tommy did a dance while Jana shook her head, massaged her clay, and turned up her lips.

And as soon as the words came from him, Mr. Coles's face became sheepish. His eyes darted upward. He passed his hand over his head. When I reached to give him a high five, he backed slowly away shaking his head from side to side.

All right, he said. All right. We had our fun. Let's get back to work.

There was no returning to work. Not that day. Not even in the days after. We never saw Mr. Coles again. No one told us anything. All we knew was that he was gone and a stern old woman with a wrinkled mask face would be our long-term sub. We relied on the trail of whispers for news. Folks said Mr. Coles had lost his mind and ended up in an insane asylum. But he had looked perfectly healthy to me.

Just a man. That's all. A regular man like anyone else. Years later I heard rumors of him packing his belongings after school while Mrs. Badwell screamed at him. So stupid, she was supposed to have said. What did we learn from all this? Let me answer for you, Dennis: Even if they look like women, they are not women!

Zeke said Jana had snitched on Mr. Coles, and when he accused her in front of everybody, she denied it with a stammer, but it was too late. We all turned on her, and she too became cloaked in a blanket of solitude. She moved on to the high school with us, but I don't remember even having two conversations with her after we determined she was the snitch. Kelli finished out the year, even navigating the glares and the stares to make a friend or two, but when we started high school, she was gone.

The weeks of turmoil made Zeke volatile, a volcano, and I could feel the rumble of his eruption at hand. He became consumed with the injustice of Mr. Coles's removal, speaking on it loud enough for adults to hear whenever he could.

He stopped the fight, Zeke said. He's a hero. This how they treat heroes around here? He ain't say nothing I wouldn't have said. Kelli got some big ass titties. Ain't no secret.

It came to a head one day in science class. Mr. Drayton brought his dog, Iggy, in for a lecture on mammal life. He did it every year, one of the few things he looked forward to. A white and black thing that looked everything like a wolf, except it had a friendly domesticated vibe. Not an ounce of aggression on most days. Still, Mr. Drayton kept Iggy behind a cardboard barrier that the dog could have toppled with his breath.

As Mr. Drayton tried to start his lecture, Zeke kept riding him. Speaking out of turn. You were supposed to be dude's friend! You sold the nigga out. Y'all always sell niggas out. Selling niggas down the river like you own them. Why is that thing even here? You lost your dog Mr. Cold, so you brought in another dog to replace him with? You foul, Mr. Drayton.

Nothing could settle Zeke. Mr. Drayton stepped from the room to summon security, and Zeke strode to the barrier that separated Iggy from the class and began barking loudly. Iggy stood and barked back, his hackles raised as if about to strike. Mr. Drayton dashed into the room and grabbed at Zeke, shoving him as hard as he could.

Don't you ever touch my dog, Mr. Drayton screamed. Don't you dare. Don't you dare. Don't you—

Ezekiel swung wildly, punching Mr. Drayton twice in his forehead. His head snapped back with each blow. Mr. Drayton fell fast, and even bounced when he hit the hard classroom floor. There he was, our Mr. Drayton, out cold during fourth-period science.

And after that, no more Ezekiel. No one was sure what happened to

Zeke. Yeah, I could have dropped by his house, it was only a half-hour walk from where I lived, but I'm not sure that ever crossed my mind. Those we think of as friends, how easily they can be disposed of when it takes even the slightest effort to see them. I learned that over and over after Zeke, sometimes painfully.

When Mr. Drayton returned several weeks later, he wasn't the same man. It's as if the already old man had aged two decades. He walked with a limp that had never been present before. The urine smell now sometimes stung my eyes. We weren't sure if he had always worn orthopedic shoes. One class he didn't even bother to talk science. He just told us that he wasn't mad at Zeke. It's not his fault, he said. Your people are naturally scared of dogs. It's because of what they put you through when you were slaves. Making dogs hunt you down. Then with the civil rights movement, how they sicced their dogs on you. Real cruelty. It got into your genes. Evolution, you know. Not Zeke's fault at all.

Last I heard, Zeke had murdered a pretty big drug dealer and fled the country before the law or the streets could catch up with him. I don't know if there's any truth in all that, but I wonder after him a lot. I get on the computer sometimes and search his name, but nothing ever turns up. Once in a while I hear that a member of Dem Freak Boyz N Motion is trying to make a comeback, and I check to see if Zeke is in his entourage. Ridiculous, I know. But wasn't he destined to become a soccer star? There are days I search through the roster of the European teams. Maybe he's a benchwarmer, maybe some sort of coach, a towel boy. Anything but a fugitive. What becomes of the children destined to be broken by their saviors?

I know where Ezekiel is. He's on a beach—in the Caribbean or Europe, somewhere where's there's no chance he'll be snatched and brought back to face his problems. He's looking calm, but yet still troubled. There on that beach, Zeke sips beer after beer as the waves crash. And he cocks his ear toward the whispering foam, hoping it will tell him how things went so wrong.

Confirmation

My father, dead now, but back then standing in that Episcopal church. Oak brown like the benches and tall like the sturdy tree out front that I often thought of when I thought of him. In fact, this Sunday I imagined him as that tree bursting from the ground beneath the undercroft, shattering the floor of the nave, the leaves of his head scraping the church ceiling. My father swayed, standing there, clean-shaven with a strong chin he used to hide beneath stubble or overgrowth. A shining knight among pawns, king to me and my mother and my sister (but in the church Jesus Christ is King and it's wrong to say otherwise). Impeccably dressed. Thin knot in a tie lain slightly askew, just enough so we all remembered who he was and how far he'd come.

This was our happily ever after. Dad had stopped drinking. He and my mother were now getting along. My sister was in her first year of college at Freedman's University. She lived on campus and didn't often attend church with us anymore. My father told anyone who would listen and even those who wouldn't that she had made the dean's list. We had even moved north from our Southside apartment to a house my parents purchased near the far end of the park. Dad now worked steady and worked well. At least once per week he'd speak of the virtues of being one's own boss. And each Sunday he said it was our duty to give it up to God, and I didn't mind much.

On this particular Sunday, just after the rector made a point during the sermon, the scent of my father's heavy cologne mingled with my mother's perfume, causing me to release a sneeze that echoed through the cavernous church building. It was as if I shouted an Amen. The pastor responded with the same joke he told whenever anyone sneezed—*Amens, achoos*, I'll take what I can get. I looked up at my father expecting to see anger bubbling behind his eyes. In the old days he would often scream about self-control when I shot forth a thunderous sneeze. Once, he waited until we got home from church and slapped me, a lesson he called it. That was long ago. So much had shifted within the man. He looked down, put his hand to my head, and smiled. He gave my spongy naps a squeeze. I took it as I took all his actions in those days: as parts of an extended apology for the rough times.

Sometimes he'd catch me gazing up at him while he sang Jesus songs—his voice lithe and bouncy—and he'd tap my hymnal, an order for me to serenade the Lord. But my voice embarrassed me. Croaky and cracky. Struggling to change from one non-tuneful state to another. God gave you that voice so you could praise him in any and every way you can, my father told me. Still, I rarely sang along.

I never did understand how my father so smoothly held notes for the delight of all around him. Even in the hard days when my father's voice was liquor-stained, he could still sound like Paul Robeson's little brother.

There was a moment that Sunday that I had looked toward for most of my short life. It came after a soaring Jesus number, and when the organist trailed off, the congregation sat with a thump. The wood whined beneath our weight. There was a silence punctuated by coughs and clearing throats. The rector started with the announcements. This was the announcement of a lifetime. Crafted specifically for me. The announcement that separated this boyhood from that manhood. Next week, confirmation class would begin. Twelve- and thirteen-year-olds and all other teens who had not yet been confirmed in Christ were to sign up for classes leading to the spring Sunday when we were to affirm our dedication to the Lord. My heart leapt. I nearly jumped from my seat and broke into open applause. With a class and a few simple words I would be a man in Christ's eyes. I suppressed my smile as well as the urge to race to the narthex to sign up for classes. Instead, I prayed solemnly.

No, that's not what happened. I remember it that way often, but the truth leaks through sometimes. At the moment of the big announcement, the rector had lulled me to sleep, and my head was back and my mouth open. My mother popped me on the cheek, lightly, but strong enough to send a message.

Open your eyes you lazy—, she whispered. You hear what the rector said? Don't forget to sign up for confirmation class when the service is over.

Confirmation? Was it really time? The service couldn't end soon enough, and after the final acolyte in the recessional passed, I raced to the narthex to find the list. Mine became the second name after Alana Spencer, intriguing because I was relatively new and didn't know any of the other children in the parish. I wondered just whom I would be stepping into adulthood with.

Bobby! my mother called. It was Sunday in the late afternoon on the week confirmation class was to begin. I was in the back shooting a ball at the hoop my father had installed shortly after we moved in. The chilly air caused my nose to run as I jogged about the concrete, dribbling the ball and stopping short to pull awkward jump shots. Bobby! She raised her voice, still refusing to call me Bob or Rob or anything with any sort of dignity. My father had dibs on Robert, which was understandable. Even years later when I had grown into adulthood and my father was gone, she refused to call me Robert.

Goddamn it, Bobby, she called through the window. What goes through your big head when you ignore me? Don't make me call your father for you.

I stilled the bouncing basketball and ambled over to the window. Huh? What did you say, Ma? I couldn't hear you, I lied, speaking loudly as if there was a din to rise above. I wanted the act to be effective. My father could be a cold and ruthless disciplinarian, at least with me; the rod in my sister's life had mostly been spared. He was probably in the basement working on repairing and restoring an old table—a beloved table left to him by my grandmother after she passed—that he said would make its debut at my confirmation party. It was missing a leg and covered in dust and scratches. He had started spending most of his free time sweating over the thing. When he was down there I heard the drone of power tools, the pounding of his hammer, and the stray screamed expletive.

Go take a shower, she said. It's time to get ready for your class. And put on the good clothes I left on your bed. Don't be going into the church looking ridiculous.

Normally I would protest her choice of clothes. The collars were too big, the pant legs too straight. But I had done all the disobeying I would be allowed for the day. I slunk past her and went into the shower, and when I got to my bed, I eyed the clothes she wanted me to wear as a man eyes shit stuck to the sole of his shoes. The massive collars. The faded straight-leg high-water slacks that fit nicely a year ago. They were all hand-me-downs my cousins wore in decades past, donated by my aunt when we were poor. To wear this outfit was to not accept our victory over poverty.

I began to squabble with her when I got out the shower, a damp towel wrapped around my waist and my bird chest sticking out.

Mom, you got me looking lame.

You are lame, she replied. Now put on the clothes. This lasted several minutes until my father came up the stairs. He squinted and flattened his mouth into a line, his mask of irritation.

Boy, get ready so I can drive you over there and get back in time to watch *60 Minutes*, he said. I slunk away and changed into my ridiculous outfit.

My father, despite hustling me, knocked about, collecting his things while I waited for him by the door, and ended up dropping me off after class began. I shuffled into a tiny room with tiny chairs and five faces I had never seen before. The rector barely seemed fazed; he didn't at all pause or stammer at my interruption. The students—all slumped left and right in uncomfortable poses—sat around a circular table while the rector paced. He wore a black turtleneck and jeans. His bald head appeared freshly moisturized and nearly sparkled, depending on where he stood.

I sat on the periphery of things, behind the circle. In front of me was a girl with long, straight black hair that shone like the rector's pale bald head. The rector stuttered a bit when I snatched a seat outside the group, but he carried on with whatever he had been talking about. He spoke in his normal mumble, and without a church podium, he paced. After he finished a point, he asked the group to make a space for me. The girl with shiny black hair and the skinny boy next to her parted and I pulled up my chair.

There's room for all of us at God's table, the rector said.

This God's table? I asked. So it doesn't belong to the church? I glanced quickly at the girl to my left—I assumed somehow, because she was the prettiest, that she was Alana—to see how she responded to my joke. She, like the rector and everyone else, pretended it never happened.

The rector asked me to introduce myself, and I told them my name and that I had spent most of my years on the Southside (this I said with tough, staccato inflections) before moving north. The girl with straight black hair was indeed Alana. There were two other girls. A short girl with a tough creasy face, whom I privately nicknamed the Raisin, and a girl with a soft pretty face and unnaturally meaty arms who, no matter what her name was, became Popeye. Then there were two guys. They looked Italian or something; I couldn't place it at the time, but somehow different than the few white people I encountered in those days. The smaller one announced proudly that he was the older fraternal twin, Mauricio he said his name was, but we could call him Maurice. The younger twin, taller, handsomer, and more confident, informed us all that he and his brother were Alana's cousins on her mother's side.

While the rector droned, I ignored him and looked around the room. Here is where they held Sunday school and the parallel children's service. Pictures of smiling white biblical cartoon children adorned the walls. Some were shepherds. Some knelt and prayed. Jesus hung on a wooden cross.

Tomás, the tall twin, raised his hand. My uncle says Jesus was black, he said, and then paused almost as a challenge to the rector.

He was God, what does it matter? Alana said.

No, Tomás replied. He was a man. Tomás turned to the rector. Wasn't he a man, Rector Byron?

Yes, the rector replied softly. But he was a special man. The only begot—

See, so it does matter what Uncle Jonah says. My dad gets mad when he hears Uncle Jonah say that. Says there is no way Jesus was a nigger—

Tomás, will you be quiet! Alana said.

Tomás, the rector said, we won't have that kind of lang—

What? I was only repeating what my dad says. I like Uncle Jonah. He's one of those *strong black men*. My dad says he likes him too. But I got my doubts about that. He don't like that his sister married him; I can tell. But I don't see nothing wrong with it. I like Jesus, and if Jesus was black, then there can't be anything wrong associating with black people and marrying them and stuff. I might marry a black woman, seeing as how Jesus was black. He was black, right?

We all gazed at the rector's shiny white head, waiting for a reply to what now seemed like the question of the ages. Even White Jesus, hanging from a cross on the wall, seemed to lean in to hear the answer. I had never given the issue of Jesus's race much thought, but now it was something burning. The rector made several false starts before speaking.

Perhaps we should take a bathroom break, he said finally, standing from the table. Before anyone could respond, he was through the door.

Of all the things I remember from that night—Alana's neck, the rector returning and pretending the previous minutes never happened, small talk with the Raisin and Popeye, the rector's admission that Noah was a drunk (which made me think of my father's old ways), Tomás grilling me for whatever reason—what I recall most brightly is Tomás standing in the hall looking sheepishly to the floor apologizing while his cousin chattered at him. Man, those wild dancing arms of hers.

That night I ate dinner after everyone else. My sister, I learned, had come for a quick bite and gone back to her dorm room. I picked at my rice, thinking about Alana Spencer, so forceful and powerful, backing down her blowhard cousin. And I thought about White Jesus, and I tried to picture Black Jesus but couldn't. My father sat under a dim lamp reading the newspaper. My mother sat by me, drinking a cup of grape juice.

What did you learn tonight? she asked.

That Jesus was black, I replied.

What? The rector told you that?

No, a kid in class.

Jesus was the son of God. God's representative. He was Jewish. And it doesn't matter. Damn negroes want to make everybody black.

It wasn't a black kid. He was a white boy. I think he's from Port Yooga.

I never seen white people in our church. Besides Rector Byron, of course.

Maybe they go to the eight-o'clock service.

Look, don't you pay attention to foolishness. Learn about the church and God and don't listen to people talking nonsense. White boy or negro.

I looked over at my father and noticed the slim smile on his lips. He didn't raise his eyes from the newspaper, so it was hard to tell whether he was grinning at us or the funny pages.

I was just teasing my mother. Wanted to see what she had to say. But watching her reaction, I figured anything that annoyed her so much was worth believing in.

Alana Spencer. The name bounced around my skull after that first class and much of the next week. Imagining her became a nice mechanism of escape, especially in church. My mother often caught me staring into space when I was supposed to be singing or praying. You are the one who has to account for your soul, not me, she often whispered in between songs, and it was always loud enough for people around us to hear and give us strange looks. I wondered why Jesus would care if we sang songs in his honor. Why it mattered that we dropped to our knees like the naked women in the Cinemax movies I stayed up on weekends to watch. The need for praise seemed like a black trait. But then I figured that was a ridiculous thought.

I found myself again along this path of thought in confirmation class as the rector spoke. I looked at Alana. She glanced over at me.

You okay? Tomás asked.

What?

Like you want something, but you're afraid to ask. His brother laughed the laugh of a sidekick. Tomás continued: You keep staring over at my cousin.

Tomás! Alana called. Her brown turned a reddish color. I felt a shudder or something in my core. I didn't speak. I wanted to punch Tomás in his gut.

Are you all paying attention? the rector asked. My life had made me a master in the art of misdirection, and there was the rector making himself a target.

Yes. Yes, we are, Your Supreme Highness, I said, giving him a salute and a slight bow. Not a single classmate offered even a chuckle.

If you're done, Robert, we can go on, the rector said.

Wait, I replied. I have a question. A serious question. You said when we reach the altar, you'll ask us a series of questions to answer in front of the congregation, right?

Yes. *Do you accept Christ? Do you believe in His Father?* That sort of thing.

What if I say *no*?

Well. The rector paused. Well. Um. You. Ahh. I mean, it's . . . Robert, do you plan to say no?

No, I said. I'm just curious.

Because if you plan to say no, we can talk after—

Your Highness. Rector. I'm just wondering—

At that moment the rector called for a bathroom break and we all shuffled outside.

It would be my moment, I figured. If I could just get Alana alone. She stood in the hallway underneath White Jesus with her cousins on either side of her like holy bodyguards. I felt like cracking Tomás in the face and whisking off with his cousin. That's how my father said his father met my grandmother. Granny said that was untrue, an exaggeration, but her smile told all. My grandfather was some kind of gangster, and his son hated gangsters. Gangsters leave nothing for their families but hurt and bullshit, my father once told me. I didn't know if that was true, but goddamn they get the girls. There was none of my grandfather in me—I had never met him—and too much of my father. I wondered what he would do to pull a girl like Alana. Probably sink into himself and hope she noticed the quiet dignity of his hard work. Sink too deep and you find the path of destructiveness my father walked and then wrenched himself from with nothing but the force of his own will and Jesus's hand.

I was paralyzed. Had no clue how to proceed. What would Jesus do? Earlier we had gotten the rector to admit that Jesus ran with whores. Jesus got bitches! Tomás said, and then grew quiet and embarrassed when his cousin frowned at him. Standing there watching Alana from the corner of my eye, I tried to imagine what Jesus had said to woo that young slut, the first nun. Which witty parable he spouted. I had no parables.

When the rector called us back in, he reopened the session with a prayer. Everybody bowed their heads. I kept mine raised and focused on Alana.

The wispy hairs that curled on the back of her neck. That was the first image I recalled when I was in bed that Sunday after my parents turned off the hallway light. I always waited for darkness beneath my door before I eased down my pajama pants and pulled up the image of Alana's hair and some from Cinemax and an imaginary one of Alana straddling me and a hug I experienced in the school hallway and the feeling of a butt I grabbed at school that last week, the girl, my friend, yelping in shock and then chasing me through the halls, squealing in a laughter that was more embarrassment than pleasure, but at the time I had the formula flipped and I laughed and ran with joy, looking back to see the movements of her breasts beneath her T-shirt and the girl became Alana and Alana became as naked as a woman on Cinemax and all became as white as Jesus up there on his high cross looking down at me in pure disgust and judgment and I closed my eyes; I was drowsy and disoriented as if his blood had mixed with mine, and soon all became black, Jesus black.

Teachers called during dinnertime. Or just before it. Or just after it. There was a time I didn't think I'd make it three consecutive dinners without the sharp trill of the phone stopping time. Ms. Baker had a way of fooling me. She used a sweet voice for the phone, not that buzzard voice she spoke with in class. And she would call my parents by their first names, no Mr. or Mrs. *Is Robert there?* she'd say. So I would then happily hand the phone over to my father not knowing it was all a setup. And there would be laughter causing me to ease back into a state of relaxation and calm. In the old days, as soon as the phone returned to the cradle, the smile on my father's face would fall away, replaced with a sneer, and he'd speak in his deep rageful monotone: Go to your room and take off your pants. And I'd sit in my room shaking and sweating, waiting for my father to turn up with an old, ratty belt in hand.

When the phone rang the Monday night before confirmation, I was on guard. It was sometime after dinner. I snatched the phone from the cradle and played with the tangled cord. I breathed deeply and took on the heaviest voice I could manage.

Brooks residence.

Who do you think you're fooling, big head? It was my sister.

Ms. Baker be calling here like she got nothing better to do with her time. She don't like me. I got to protect myself.

How about protecting yourself by doing your work and not causing any trouble? That too hard?

Shut up.

I'm tired of you already. Put Daddy or Mommy on the phone.

What if they don't want to talk to you?

Boy!

Hold on.

I took the phone from my ear and made to find one of my parents, but

Alana flashed before me, a bright blinding vision. I had just been read-ing about angels appearing before Jesus, Mary, the disciples. Illuminated messengers spurring the ordinary to take their place among a heavenly pantheon. They came with solutions to impossible problems. I put the phone to my ear. Hey, Big Sis—

You again? I thought you were getting Mommy or Daddy.

Let me ask you something. There's this girl named Alana in confir-mation class—

Aww, little Bobby's getting into girls. Proud of you, man.

Stop playing. Tell me what I need to say to her.

Little brother, I taught you nothing before I left. I'm a bad big sister. Now puberty is upon you.

Never mind. I see you won't be serious.

All right, all right, I'll be serious. Bobby, there aren't any magical words. Guys who think they need to sound all Billy Dee smooth annoy me. Just make conversation with her like she's a human being. Any ol' human being. That's all she is anyway. She's not Jesus. She can't raise the dead. No need to get all tongue-tied. If you talk to her and she still seems like she's worth talking to, ask for her phone number or ask to meet up somewhere. It's not a big deal, Bobby. Now put Mommy or Daddy on the phone.

That night I sat in my room doing my homework, but really listening to my parents' end of the conversation with my sister, when it dawned on me: In just six days I would be a man.

I stopped doing my work and rested in my uncomfortable bed that featured wooden slats in lieu of springs. I had it since I was three. Some outdated theory once said this system was good for a child's spinal devel-opment, but in practice it turned me into an insomniac with stray back pains. I imagined my parents would rush to replace the bed once I became a man instead of ignoring my complaints.

I fell asleep with that thought and woke the next morning still in my clothes; my bedroom lights shined in my face and my mouth had a raw, unbrushed taste. For a moment I thought it was Saturday and lay there in a dazed state. My eyes felt scratchy and unrested. I turned to enjoy several more hours of sleep when I realized it was Tuesday. How was it that no one yelled at me to change my clothes and brush my teeth? At least someone usually slipped in while I slept and turned off the lights. Was this a taste of manhood? How everything would be after Sunday? All responsibilities now resting on my shoulders. No one to chase me out the door.

I found it hard to focus that week. I was at school, but I was also elsewhere, mostly with Alana. Teachers, particularly Ms. Baker, would call on me and I would flub my responses to wild laughter from classmates. No matter. I couldn't help imagining different combinations of words to win Alana's attention. It was like cracking a locker combination, seemingly impossible. I threw together random words like the random numbers I pulled together that one time I guessed Edward Covington's combination after three days and hundreds of tries. Seemingly impossible, but I did it.

Wednesday afternoon I arrived home just after the mailman's visit and noticed that my mother held the day's envelopes, postcards, and circulars in her hand. Later, while she cooked dinner, I spotted two notices from the school on my father's dresser. The famed yellow envelopes of interim deficiency reports. My mother had slit them open and read that I was failing math and science, but said nothing. She just prepared the spaghetti like it was a normal day. If I hadn't dawdled by the bus stop, I could have snatched them and discarded them. Though after the rare beating my sister once received for that crime, I was always reluctant to toss them. My only option now was to read the half-truths and attempt to devise broad strokes to fill in the incomplete picture painted by my teachers' reports.

Sitting through dinner, my left elbow nearly touching my father's, I said nothing of the interim reports and neither did he. My gut quivered during the silences, waiting for the lecture on taking my work seriously. The exasperated screams. Accusations of wanting to be a ne'er-do-well. But none of that happened. I wondered if I should preempt my father, apologize for the poor showing and promise to do better, but I shot that down. I knew my father well enough to know it would be taken as a sign of weakness.

After dinner I retired to my room, nominally to do my homework, but really I sat at my desk, threw my head back, and imagined what I'd say to Alana come Sunday. Perhaps there was a song that encapsulated everything I felt and I could quote it to her. After all, hadn't everything that ever needed to be said about love been said in an R&B song? *From the first time, Alana, that I saw your brown eyes . . .*

Three hard knocks on my door startled me. No one ever knocked. Knocking is nonsense when you own the house, my father said once.

Come in, I called.

There stood my father in the doorway. I breathed deeply. I had practiced what I'd say about the interims all day since I had seen them waiting for my father on his dresser. The mental rehearsal was limited, though, interspersed with thoughts of Sunday's wooing of Alana. I fumbled with my words in my mind.

Bobby, he said. I opened my mouth to offer a blubbery explanation, but he cut me off. Tomorrow, I'm gonna come home early so we can go down to the mall and get you a suit for Sunday. You can't be looking like just anybody during your confirmation.

I thought of Alana so much on Thursday that my head pounded by the time school let out. When my father came home to take me suit shopping, I was lying on the living room couch, hoping my closed eyelids would make the throbbing in my head dissipate.

Boy, you not ready? my father called. Didn't I tell you to be ready when I got home?

The boom of his voice vibrated against the ache on the right side of my head. I moved slowly through the motions of changing into my going-out clothes, fearing that sharp, quick movements would rupture my brain or, at least, cause a sudden pulsing.

My father stood by my door grumbling and complaining as I changed. But when we finally went out to the car and the radio got to cranking, he put on a big grin, singing along with Teddy Pendergrass. The key to everything, son, is to calm down, he said. Don't let too much move you. So much depends on a million things that are out of your control. Took me a long time, too long, to figure that out.

I said nothing, distracted by the streaks of sun that beamed down from space to stab themselves into my eyes and stir my headache. I screwed up my brow and must have looked angry or confused. To tell the truth, I was a bit confused, as my father, quick to anger and judgment for most of my life, was always being moved by petty annoyances. I often wondered if and when the old monster I loved and feared would return.

Why you frowning? he said. You still upset that your old dad wanted you to move with purpose?

Naw, Dad. I'm fine.

The sun now caused the pain in my head to slowly throb.

Something's wrong, my father said. People don't just frown for no reason at all.

Dad, could you let it drop?

We exchanged not two more words all the way to the store. My father didn't even bother to sing when Al Green came across the radio, and I felt I had ruined his good mood. But once we got into the store, it only took the sight of a few fine suits to rekindle it. He pulled a gray one with thin brown lines from the rack and danced like James Brown with it against his chest.

I'm gonna have you looking sharp, he said. I don't care how much it costs me. A man got to have one of these. Two when you really become a man. But one is good now. You like this?

I shrugged, not from indifference, but rather from the fact that the suits all had a sameness to me. I was becoming a man, but my sense of fashion was far from refined. Sure, I could tell that the three-piece number in yellow and black plaid was a clown suit, and I could also marvel at the $500 Italians, but everything else had a uniform quality. I lacked the visual vocabulary, the key to the code that all men were reliably expected to crack.

My father pulled suit after suit from the rack. Try this one!

I gazed at myself in the mirror wearing a black striped suit that came with a vest. It made me look like a banker or a gangster from the 1920s. I stood on a raised part of the floor and for once I was higher than my father and everyone around me. I looked sharp. There's no way I could deny that. Or at least I would look sharp once the tailor went to work.

Two figures passed behind me; I could see them clearly in the mirror. The twins from confirmation class. They were with a tall oaken-skinned man. He had Alana's cheeks and nose, so I assumed he was her father and that she must also be around. Here I was standing in a baggy whale of a suit that swallowed me whole, accentuating every outward thing that was still childlike in my appearance. I wanted to become small. Not small in the way that I was, but a tiny thing so I could spy on Alana when she happened by.

Maurice spotted me and chuckled, pointing. Tomás grunted but otherwise ignored me, even when I waved. Maurice turned from me and glanced through the suits. When Alana walked up behind her cousins, my hand was still in the air. I shouted a *Hey!* that sounded to me like the flat bark of a seal. She responded with a pursed-lipped smile before turning to help Maurice choose a suit. The tailor returned to tug at the ends of my pants. My hand hung in the air, a frozen wave. I realized I had been holding it above my head as if I were now some kind of black Statue of Liberty. My father arrived with two more suits. Son, he said, the one you got on looks good, but you'll look like my little superstar in one of these. Maurice and Tomás pointed and snorted once more. I thought I saw Alana smirk, but whatever passed across her lips was too brief for me to place. I pretended not to see Alana and her cousins walking about below me as I glanced at them out of the corners of my eyes. Soon they disappeared into a dark-hued maze of haberdashery. I took solace, standing there in the mirror, in the fact that my voice hadn't cracked, but on my way home I realized that what actually did transpire was no better or worse than my voice momentarily dancing off into a higher register. In fact, that could be explained away as the uncontrollable whims of my malfunctioning hormones. What excuse could I ever make for such a bizarre display?

The Friday before confirmation Sunday I spent much of the day wondering about the strange mechanism of the mind that made seconds slow in anticipation of major events. It's still a mysterious thing to me, especially since it no longer happens much now that I'm older. Nowadays a minute is a minute and a day is a day and the ones leading up to something exciting feel no longer than any other minute or day. Perhaps I had experienced so few days and minutes as a young man that my sense of wonder could stretch time until it felt misshapen. Perhaps when I'm old, all of life will feel like little more than an instant, and maybe that's why God's day is a thousand years. What's a minute to the man who has all the time?

At home, I did no homework but instead slept, watched music videos, and masturbated to make time move faster. In class I slept, and it was perhaps to Ms. Baker's delight, because it gave her another opportunity to call my parents, which she took advantage of Friday night.

My mind was so cloudy and loopy, floating through a haze somewhere far from earth, that I neglected to properly monitor the early evening phone calls. What kind of person has nothing better to do on a

Friday night than call parents, anyway? I picked up and didn't recognize Ms. Baker's voice until after I had screamed through the house, alerting my mother that she had a phone call.

I paced about while she was on the phone. I heard my mother giggling as if she were talking to one of her girlfriends. If my sister were here, we could huddle and develop a strategy. At the very least she would make me smile through my anxiety. I felt sweat pooling at the seat of my pants. My testicles shriveled. I wondered about the evolutionary function of testicle shriveling. Ms. Baker had said every action of our bodies evolved to ensure survival in a brutal and dangerous world. Perhaps a man can flee predators faster once his testicles have shriveled up into his body. I don't know. Funny time to recall Ms. Baker's lessons. Though I never listened and I failed the tests, some of what she said had gotten through. But the Jesus I was about to confirm my dedication to never mentioned evolutionary functions.

I took a deep breath and closed my eyes, and then I retired to bed. It was early, but I figured my parents wouldn't bother me in my sleep.

Baby, my mother said as the door creaked open. Baby, wake up. Ms. Baker just called. I saw you open your eyes. Don't shut those things again. I know you're awake.

I turned a little bit and wiped my eyes.

Sleeping in class? All you do is sleep here.

Ms. Baker's class is boring.

Don't you want to be a doctor?

I nodded despite the fact that I hadn't wanted to be a doctor since the fourth grade when I realized that it would require more math than my fragile intellect could stand.

Well, how's that going to happen with you sleeping in science class? I wouldn't want you to be my doctor. I need greater effort and focus from you. This disappoints me, because I know how smart you are. I see it every day. I know you got more brains than the average person in that big head of yours. I'm going to talk to your fath—

Wait, Mom, I cried out. This is a small thing. You don't need to—

Let me finish, Bobby. He's good at setting goals and coming up with plans. That's why we live here now and not back on the Southside. That's how we got your sister off to college. We never set too many goals with you. Not as often as we could. Maybe he'll be mad and he'll fret and stuff.

Maybe he'll yell, but you got me in your corner, Bobby. Your father too, but I'm in your corner in that mother way. In the end, talking to Daddy'll be for the best. Ms. Baker told me about the insect collection project. I haven't seen you pick up so much as an ant. Instead of sleeping, go hunt some of the roaches around here.

We don't have roaches, Mom.

I'm so used to living with those damn things back in the old apartment. Your sister had no problem with this project. This is the one time being over in that neighborhood would have helped you with your lessons. Go back to the Southside and get some roaches.

My mother started to walk from my room. At the doorway she turned and said words that hit me like a switchblade to my gut: Don't continue to disappoint me, Bobby.

When my father got home that night, he grunted toward me and disappeared into his bedroom to change from his work clothes and to chat with my mother. If she discussed Ms. Baker's call that night, I never heard anything about it. He said nothing much at the dinner table, staring off into his soup. After dinner he retired to the couch and fell asleep as if he too were trying to pass the time with slumber.

Late night Friday and Saturday blend together for me. I spent those hours in the basement watching *Desert Passion*, *The Bikini Car Wash Company*, and *Private Obsession* on cable. None of us could have possibly imagined the wonders of cable back when we lived on the Southside, and now I couldn't conceive of becoming a man without it. I remember each particular movie that played that weekend (though not which night each was on), as they were my favorites and I would check the cable guide weekly in an effort to never miss a late-night viewing when I could help it. These three movies were such dazzling cinema. The dizzying flashes of flesh. Somehow these pictures assured me that the future, Alana or no Alana, would be fine. Who would need Alana with the coming cavalcade of bodies like the ones on-screen?

Above in the kitchen, whenever I heard my mother or father rustling around, I lowered the volume, particularly if there was moaning and panting on-screen. But this weekend it felt as if the clouds had parted. No one came into the kitchen or shouted from the stairs ordering me to come up to bed or otherwise interrupted my cinematic education. Watching some nude woman or the other, I began to think of it all as strange. My favorite three naked movies, as I called them, airing with no interruptions in the days before Jesus would declare me a man? At first I regarded it as a gift, a last chance at guilt-free sinfulness before I was required to take responsibility for my own sins. A kind of bachelor party. I began counting tits, and at about the seventeenth pair, I realized my gift theory was full of holes. Jesus and his obsession with chastity wouldn't even allow himself the carnal pleasures I allowed myself on that couch.

This was the temptation the devil paraded before Jesus those forty days and nights in the desert. Come to think of it, that Saturday night it was *Desert Passion* that played, and I regarded it as a joke between me and the Almighty, and also as a clear sign alerting me to what the trickster Jesus was up to. And as much as it was a joke and a sign, it was also a dare to resist lasciviousness. I imagined Black Jesus up in Heaven laughing like hell at his twisted sense of humor.

I watched the movie until the end when the half-naked women disappear into the hot, unforgiving desert, and I went upstairs to bed. I lay there staring at the dark, thinking of the trial given to me from on high. I closed my eyes and tried to fall asleep, but images of the women from the movies and thoughts of Alana passed through my head. What a cruel test, I thought as I wrenched down my pajama pants and gripped my erection. Fuck it, I whispered. I'll fail.

What stopped me was the sounds of voices through the wall that separated my parents' room from mine. They were awake. Briefly I imagined they had heard the creaking of my old bed—as I sometimes heard the creaking of theirs—and were debating whether to bust down my door and confront me, but even I could recognize the ridiculousness in that.

Their voices became heated and loud. Mostly it sounded like muffled tuba playing, but I understood snatches.

I heard the word *stress*. I thought my father said my name and then my sister's name. The name of her school. I stopped breathing to concentrate. I felt the warmth of my shaft in my hand, but I didn't let go. If anything, I held it tighter.

My father cursed. I sat up to hear more clearly.

Look, Robert, I can take Bobby and move back to the Southside if I need to. I don't care. I've only been not-poor for a little while.

Like you can handle a boy like Bobby all on your own. Every minute a phone call from the teachers. Like you're doing a good job getting him to do his schoolwork now.

That's not fair, and this is not about Bobby—

He shouted over her, repeating the same thing he had just said. My mother too repeated her words.

Will you shut up, Robert? This is not about Bobby. You're just trying to change the subject. Bobby's not the reason—

You're right, he's not. You are.

You're a drunk.

I haven't been drunk in years. I don't plan to ever be drunk again. I drank half a beer because the shop is stressing me and you're stressing me and Bobby's stressing me. And then I told you about it. I didn't try to hide. I confessed like Rector Byron told me to. Didn't he say I'd backslide, but that when I did, I had to tell you and tell Jesus? Well, here I am and this is what I get?

Let's pray, Robert.

After that, I heard grumbling and then silence. I rested my head back on my pillow. I wanted to rush out and ask all that was swirling my head: Is it true? Was it just half a beer? Did you tell my mother and Jesus everything? Am I really to blame? Are you praying to White Jesus or Black Jesus and do you really think he's up there making it all better?

That Sunday morning—the day of my confirmation—my mother and I went off to church and my sister met us there. My father stayed home, saying he wanted to spend the morning finishing the table and getting the house ready for the party that would follow the evening's service.

God'll understand, he said as my mother hurried me out the door.

It was the usual service. The rector told corny jokes during a generic sermon. I refused to raise my croaky voice in song, even as my mother glared. Having stayed up most of the night before, I dozed during the prayers and all the various still moments. When I dipped off, my sister kicked my ankle and my mother popped my cheek.

During the announcements, the rector asked all the confirmation candidates to assemble in the narthex at 6 p.m., no later. I was awake and alert. I even looked over at Alana and imagined we shared a moment. I'll never forget the word *narthex* or sitting there paying close attention to the announcements, thinking I was having a mundane, forgettable time. One that wouldn't define me and one I'd never think back to as I went on to live my life. The word *narthex* was just a strange word I somehow dimly knew the meaning of. How could I ever imagine that my future would turn on the precision in defining such an odd and beautiful and gothic little word?

My mother slammed the door of the gray Oldsmobile. I sat in the back and stared out the window for the short drive home, and my sister sat up front.

First my mother started in, Couldn't you act like you care one Sunday in your life? It's your confirmation Sunday.

I know, I replied.

And got the nerve to talk back, my mother said.

Bobby, why don't you shut up and listen for once? my sister said. I was shocked by her rebuke.

You slept for the whole service, didn't pay one bit of attention, my mother said. You are the one who has to account for your soul, not me.

My mother and sister took turns going back and forth. We stopped at a red light and I thought the car would never move. The sound of my mother and sister chattering against me became an impenetrable wall. They no longer used words; it sounded to me like the muffled noises I heard between the walls when my parents prayed. I said not another word, because I could barely understand what was happening.

He's not paying you any attention, Mom, my sister said. I don't even see the point of talking to him. He's going to learn the hard way.

I don't want your brother to learn like that, so I'm going to make him damn well straighten up. Bobby, listen. You awake?

My mother pulled into the carport at the side of our house. We all exited the Oldsmobile and approached the door. I felt worn and beaten.

I bet you don't even know where you're supposed to meet tonight, my sister said.

Of course I do.

I waited for my mother to put the key into the lock, but the three of us just stood at the door.

Where? my sister asked.

I paused. I felt no need to explain anything to anyone. After all, in a few hours I would officially be declared a man.

Where, Bobby? my sister asked again. Where are you and your girl-friend and everyone supposed to meet, Bobby?

I looked at the keys jangling in my mother's hand. She stood, refusing to put them into the lock. I grasped for the word, but it perched itself far outside of my mouth, not even anywhere near the tip of my tongue. Since my mother and my sister waited, I hoped to satisfy them with an approximate answer.

In the place where we meet, I said.

My mother reared her free hand back and slapped it against my cheek. I stumbled and looked over at my sister, her eyes and lipstick-red mouth open in shock.

A man wouldn't cry, but I was still a boy and the smack shook loose teardrops big as blowflies.

Don't even have any clue where you're supposed to assemble, she said. It's the narthex, Bobby. The narthex. Not *the place where we meet*. The narthex. Now, shut up with all that damn crying.

I couldn't shut up, though. My sister watched me with a sort of prideful smirk I had never seen on her. She also told me to shut up as my mother pushed the key in the lock and shoved open the door.

My father, standing in the living room holding a rag to his beloved table, saw the tears streaming from my eyes. He watched them, and his face fell and creased, turning into the thick twisted visage of a bull.

What did he do? he said softly, and before anyone could answer, he snatched me by the collar of my shirt. What the hell did he do? my father shouted.

I—

He flung me across the living room as if I were made of cloth and stuffing. I stumbled and slammed into his table, cracking the wood and knocking loose the leg my father had spent the last couple weeks fixing.

Dazed, I struggled up. My father shoved me back down and I heard the wood again crack beneath me. He balled his fists and punched me in the chest. I doubled over and he slammed a fist down on my back.

What the hell did you do? my father screamed. He opened his hand and slapped at my face. I tried explaining through the tears. I gave each blow an amplified howl in an attempt to appeal to my father's humanity or my sister's love or my mother's pity. My mother shut the door, as if to keep the whole neighborhood from hearing our drama.

Sick of you, man, my father muttered.

I could see my mother and sister hanging back, expressionless, as my father punched me and slapped me and swung me around, flinging me back and forth across the living room.

When the beating was done, he stormed off to his room and slammed the door. My mother followed without even looking back at me quivering and crying and curled into a question mark on the floor.

I looked to my sister and saw a wisp of her heading for the basement.

I lay there by myself sobbing and dazed for what seemed like an hour, but time no longer had any meaning to me; it could have been a minute, it could have been a day. The house had a stillness that I equated with late at night after I finished my movies and dragged myself to bed. Through the quiet I heard my father's voice speaking softly to my mother: What did he do?

I said nothing at all to my sister for the rest of the day. When my father and I passed each other, we looked off into the distance or at some spot on the floor. My mother, toward late afternoon, pretended as if we had just experienced an ordinary morning. She told me jokes and chatted about the comics page. I responded with low grunts and nods and eventually walked away from her.

I put on my new suit. I admired myself in the mirror. I rolled my tongue over the swelling at my lip, the blemish that ruined it all, the stark reminder of my status as a member of the childhood underclass. My mother pushed open the door to my bedroom.

Bobby, you look so handsome, she said.

Thank you.

I'm going to call your sister in here so she can see how handsome you look.

Why don't you call Dad too so you can all take turns beating me?

You stop it, Bobby. Tonight's a special service. Don't turn it into something else.

I got beat for no reason and you know it.

Sometimes these things build up, Bobby. Now straighten your tie and stop frowning; it makes you less handsome.

I carried the icy silence of the car ride into the narthex, thinking mostly of the slap that preceded the beating. I wondered if the swelling at my lip came from that blow or from the later assault. When I saw Alana, I realized I hadn't thought about her for hours, and I couldn't bring myself to talk to her or even to make eye contact. I hung back while the confirmation group chatted with a newfound collegiality. When they spoke to me, I responded with just a word or a shrug. Mostly I looked off, dazed. Who was I to try to talk to Alana? I couldn't even defend myself from the beatings children get. In less than a half hour she'd be a woman and I'd be what?

While the rector gave us instructions in his soft-dull voice, I barely listened and figured I'd just follow the lead of all the other kids. When the music started, I fell in line behind the Raisin and we did our procession into the nave. I looked left and there stood my family. My sister took pictures, my mother waved. My father seemed to be smiling a bit. Assorted aunts, uncles, godparents, cousins, and family friends had sprinkled themselves throughout the congregation.

Through the songs and speeches and other garnishes thrown in to extend a service that could have been five minutes, I tongued the swelling at my mouth. It had a hot, blood-tart taste. I hated my father, my mother, and the sister who betrayed me. I hated them all.

Alana went first, then Maurice, then Tomás. I watched as the rector asked them about receiving the Lord and they nodded and voiced their agreement to receive Him. Then Popeye accepted the Lord and then the Raisin accepted the Lord.

The rector finally called my name. I again tongued the swelling on the inside of my lip. I eyed the floor beneath my feet and didn't move. My legs felt leaden. So did my arms. My head became a bowling ball. The rector called me again, and a murmuring rippled through the church. I rose from my seat and did a Frankenstein walk with my dead limbs. I reached the altar and knelt before the man and looked up to a shower of multihued light cast down from the stained glass windows. The rector spoke, and I flinched from the lightburst. I could see White Jesus, but not much else. The rector's head shone golden. Do you accept Jesus? he asked. I squinted, trying to see his face. Above me, White Jesus leaned in to hear my answer. When I didn't immediately respond, the rector leaned too. He didn't look like a being of gold anymore. He looked tarnished and cracked. He leaned further and became a shadow.

There was more murmuring from the audience. I never knew that a few seconds could feel like eternity; a long time and no time at all. This is what White Jesus's heaven must feel like. A day to God is a thousand years. I nodded. The rector's expression was of puzzlement and annoyance. He required a verbal answer. The one that sat lodged in my throat. I looked out onto the crowd. I saw my sister clear as I'd ever seen anything. My mother was hazy and my father was just light. I looked up. White Jesus's arms were long, his muscles defined. He looked sad, though. He had never had sex, like me. Never masturbated to relieve the tension, because that was a sin and he was sinless. Never watched naked women writhe about on Cinemax or whatever the ancient equivalent of that was. Just what did he discuss with those whores? With the one he loved but never fucked? What did he do with all that yearning? I closed my eyes and the rector asked again. I thought about White Jesus feeling the lash of his father's hand striking him, choking him, whipping him, opening wounds all over his body. What else was the Passion but a cosmic spanking? White Jesus and I shared that in common. Just like White Jesus, I was confused by the bruising, and after my lashing, alone in my room I called out *Why?* but received no answer. And when the rector asked a third time, I mumbled, Why? And perhaps God magically turned it into a Yes for everyone's ears, because the rector blessed me and carried on. The church people promised to support me just as they did with everyone else and they slipped into song and I returned to my seat feeling wrung out and exhausted and no one ever asked me about my response. Did they not hear? Did none of it matter? Did they not know?

Well, in any case, I knew and I know and I've always known what really happened the day I received my confirmation.

Party Animal

The Strange and Savage Case of a Once Erudite and Eloquent Young Man

Of all the cases of Reverse Animalism[1] that we have either read about or observed firsthand, the case of Louis Smith[2] is the most puzzling, if in many ways the clearest. And if we may make so bold a statement, it is a case that is often misunderstood owing to its mishandling. Smith's backwards evolution and descent into what can only be described as simian behavior could well have been avoided if responsible parties—i.e., school officials, parents, the courts, and so on—had been more attentive and

---

1. The disorder is most often called Reverse Evolution. The authors of this study find that term problematic, as it is imprecise and, frankly, politically fraught. We propose the less controversial Reverse Animalism, as evolution, like climate change, is simply a theory and not a unified and complete one. We find it awkward to compare a real condition, albeit one many researchers and psychologists have trouble acknowledging as genuine, to a theory that has hardly been proven. The authors of the study will continue to use the phrase "backwardly evolved person" or BEP when referring to one who is suffering from the disorder, for want of a better term. We find the phrase "reverse animal" condescending and disrespectful, as sufferers of Reverse Animalism are, after all, still human.

One of the frustrating things about researching this disorder is that the scientific community currently lacks an accurate vocabulary to properly discuss Reverse Animalism. Because of a certain dogmatism and mental ossification among researchers, developing politically neutral and accurate terminology has been difficult. We believe that adopting the term Reverse Animalism is a small

aware of the symptoms[3] of Reverse Animalism. Then perhaps Louis Smith's mental state could have been salvaged and he might have been rehabilitated and released back into society. As it stands now, the man who as a child was once referred to as "the erudite young Louis Smith"[4] is beyond reclamation. Despite advances in treatment of the disorder, the scientific community has dragged its knuckles for too long, and as a result the subject of this report is destined to live out his life as more animal than man.

We intend in this study to present the facts of Louis Smith's descent into bestial behavior in order to afford what we believe to be the first clear, published look at Reverse Animalism. In examining this specific case, we hope to challenge the public's preconceived notions about the

---

but crucial positive step toward creating a precise language around the disorder. Readers more familiar with the term Reverse Evolution are reminded that Reverse Animalism and Reverse Evolution are synonymous. Also, it is good to keep in mind that we are discussing a psychological disorder and not the proposed scientific phenomenon that posits a reversal of the so-called evolutionary timeline or a literal reversal of evolutionary biology.

2. The subject's real name and some identifying details have been changed to protect his identity. He is an African American male who resided on the Northside of Cross River, Maryland (with the exception of his brief time at River Run Mental Health Facility and his days in the Wildlands of Cross River), in the years covered by this study, which runs roughly from his tenth to his nineteenth year. All other names have been either omitted or changed.

3. The symptoms of Reverse Animalism can vary but often include taking excessive pleasure in excretory functions; a lack of interest in traditional basic hygiene, including bathing, shaving, and combing of the hair; an abnormal, sometime prurient, interest in domesticated and, later, wild animals, particularly mammals, including but not limited to dogs, wolves, bears, horses, monkeys, and apes; and a gradual loss of language functions, beginning with a slow shedding of vocabulary and ending with grunts, howls, and gestures substituted for speech.

4. Louis Smith earned the sobriquet "erudite" as a child. He had a stellar academic career up until high school, where he experienced a sudden and shocking decline. We now know that this decline can be attributed to his condition, but at the time, to his family, it was quite puzzling. Louis had once won awards for public speaking and for a time studied French and Spanish alongside his native language. Here was a boy who received all As and positive reports throughout his elementary school career, a boy who once placed first in the school's spelling bee and did well in the regional competitions. Suddenly he began failing classes and incurring suspensions for fights. These fights, placed in their proper context, were really, to Louis at least, challenges for male dominance over his peers, who to his devolving mind were really a herd or a pack.

condition and to stimulate badly needed discussion. Also, we aim to spark a greater awareness of the disorder and would like to foster a great leap forward, both in understanding and in treating Reverse Animalism, for the sake of our society and of the increasing number of people afflicted with this troubling disorder.[5]

It is a popular misconception that Louis Smith at age nineteen simply and inexplicably stopped shaving, then bathing, and within six to eight months ceased speaking, to communicate instead in hisses, grunts, and growls until he became a nuisance to society, an irritating vagrant who wandered from nightclub to nightclub, somehow crossing velvet ropes in order to fondle and "freak dance" (i.e., rhythmically gyrate the male genital region against the buttocks or genital area of a partner in an erotically stimulatory manner) with the opposite sex in ever more primal and base fashions. This view has, unfortunately, been put forth in report after report, most notably the Meratti Pharmaceuticals report.[6] This version of events, however, does not take into account that Reverse Animalism never simply arrives like an unwanted visitor. Instead it has a gradual onset. Many small symptoms, such as an impulsive surrendering to one's base desires, appear before the larger symptom of losing the ability to communicate through or fully comprehend human language.

---

5. Approximately 1 million people in the United States alone suffer from some form of Reverse Animalism. Most cases are very mild. The vast majority of BEPs are never diagnosed and never know that they are living with Reverse Animalism. In this report we discuss, for the most part, the symptoms and stages of the harsher manifestations of the disorder.

By some estimates, there has been an almost 1,000% increase in the number of diagnosed cases in the past ten years. This shocking increase has inspired many theories, but no definitive one as yet. Extreme cases, such as the one discussed in this study, are, for reasons not yet fully understood, becoming more common.

6. R. Burns et al., "Undoing the Descent of Man: New Effective Approaches in Treating Reverse Evolution," *American Pharmacological Concerns Quarterly*, Fall 2014, 1–14. We find the Meratti report to be a self-serving piece of corporate propaganda that only aims to absolve Meratti of any responsibility toward Smith. After his capture, he was treated with a cocktail of medications and briefly became part of an ill-conceived study of Panofil, an untested Meratti Pharmaceuticals product. This medication, we believe, likely accelerated the progress of the disorder and should not be administered to anyone who suffers from Reverse Animalism without further study. Meratti, Inc., predictably disagrees.

Louis's intellectual peak seemed to be in the sixth grade, when he was named cocaptain of the Walter J. Clash Elementary School debate team. An English teacher handpicked him to join the team after witnessing his eloquence in discussing *The Diary of Anne Frank* in class. The teacher recalls that Louis was often very aggressive toward male opponents and teammates. A victory would find Louis laughing at his opponent, somewhat obnoxiously, and shouting him down. The occasional loss often caused him to retire to a corner, not speaking for some time. Ironically, these were the traits that convinced teachers that Louis would make a good debate team captain. And by all accounts, he was. The team often found itself victorious, and his English teacher credits Louis. The teacher and debate team coach had this recollection:

> I had to lecture Louis on sportsmanship more than once. He didn't take losing, or winning for that matter, very well. But he was a good leader, everybody followed him. Once, during a real crucial debate—we're at a school in the next town [Port Yooga, Virginia], an all-white team—Louis's cocaptain C—— just blanks. In front of the whole school, a packed auditorium, all the parents and teachers, this fifth-grader, a real eloquent and bright kid, is just frozen there. Costs us the whole tournament. Well, Louis is not saying much about the whole thing for most of the bus ride back. Everyone's quiet, just contemplating the match. I stand to give the guys a standard pep talk. I tell them that it wasn't C——'s fault. Louis cuts me off and starts yelling. *No Mr. G——*, he says to me. *It's not all right.* Then he stands up and turns to C——. *We trained for months for this tournament and you blew it for us. Now we have to go home to nothing. Nothing. Thanks a lot.*
>
> I'm speechless. C—— starts crying, and all I can do is ask Louis to sit down. He glares at me for a few moments before taking his seat and staring out the bus window all calm and docile, but obviously he's pissed. It wasn't my finest moment. It's probably when I lost control of the team. But Louis was only saying what everybody, including me, was thinking.

Louis Smith's earliest recorded clear symptom of Reverse Animalism, though almost certainly not the first, was an incident in the eleventh grade in which he, out of boredom one day in gym class, fondled the fleshy portion of a young girl's posterior.[7]

Horrified, the young woman screamed and fled the gymnasium. The young man, who had fallen to the ground, feigning a loss of balance, sat on the hardwood floor with what many say was a hurt, almost childlike expression on his face, as if he had just courted this woman and experienced the deepest rejection.

Louis Smith attended District Central Senior High School at the time. The school began drawing up plans to expel him, the default punishment for sexual assault, but Louis and his mother were two steps ahead of District Central and the Cross River Public School System. Instead of fighting his suspension and impending expulsion, Louis's mother simply withdrew him and enrolled him in another school in Port Yooga, where it appears that he kept his Reverse Animalism in check. He returned to District Central the next year as if the incident had never occurred, thus neatly circumventing the school's disciplinary procedures

Upon his return, Louis Smith found District Central a cold and unforgiving place. Said one school official: "He really became an outcast at District Central, like he was marked, with a scarlet A on his forehead if you will. Or, more accurately, a scarlet F, for Fondler."[8]

---

7. The subject admitted to grabbing the young woman's backside but claimed it was an unfortunate accident. Never having much coordination, he told school officials at the time of the incident, he lost balance during a game of basketball and fell. His arms went flailing about and landed on the young woman's "butt cheeks." Later he changed his story, claiming that his fall was the result of "horsing around" with other males in the class. In other words, he was pushed. His alternative explanation was that there was a second groper, who took advantage of his fall to stealthily fondle the woman and place the blame on him. These interpretations of the day in question are much disputed by the young woman and eyewitnesses. Several close acquaintances have said that Louis, before he stopped speaking, claimed that he accosted the young woman out of boredom. After a lengthy investigation, a second malefactor was never discovered, and school officials determined that no one else was involved in his fall. Having examined the record and interviewed hundreds of people, both intimately and tangentially connected to young Louis Smith, the authors of this study have concluded that the boredom motive is the most persuasive.
8. The speaker, who served as a gym teacher while the subject attended District Central Senior High School, is the only DCSHS official who admitted to knowing Louis well, and even he said that their interactions became rare once Louis began to withdraw.
"He seemed like he wanted to be left alone," the gym teacher recalled. "So I left him alone."

Where there had been friendship, or easy acquaintanceship, according to interviews, Louis now found scorn and cold shoulders. It is reported that he often went entire days without speaking to another person.

Frank, a schoolmate of the same age and racial background, relates an incident that is likely typical of Louis's high school experience as the cloud of Reverse Animalism slowly descended upon him:[9]

So we're all sitting around the lunch table, me, A——, S——, B——, R——, and Carson. We're all talking shit, clapping on one another, and here come Louis, lumbering over, swaying back and forth. He was a big dude. Imposing, but he was a pussy. He snatched a seat— and up to this point in the school year I ain't say shit to him. I know most of the dudes at the table ain't talk to him neither. It's not like we was offended by what he did. I know I wasn't. I guess I should have been, but you know, I was a kid. Shit, I wanted to fondle D—— too; she looked good. Everybody wanted to fondle her. But we didn't, though. That's the difference between me and him. I guess me and Louis used to be cool. Not really. It's like we grew apart. But anyway, he sits down and everybody gets quiet, starts looking around to one another. Carson is on the other side of the table. Out of nowhere he's like: *So, grab any girls' butts lately?*

According to Frank and others, there was laughter all around the table, except from Louis, who just sat there humiliated.[10]

One of the most frustrating aspects of this case is how little we know about the subject's progression from man to beast. His family, of course, did not maintain careful records, so we are uncertain, for instance, when

---

9. After some debate, the authors have decided to leave Frank's vulgarities uncensored. We believe that, while potentially offensive, they serve to evoke the world that was slipping from young Smith's comprehension.
10. Carson has a different memory of the occasion and insists, rather angrily, that it was actually Frank who made the "fondle any girls' butts lately" quip. The authors are not interested in determining who said what on that day. Based on interviews we have conducted, we are satisfied that it occurred in some form and feel that it is a good example of the isolation that Louis Smith felt at District Central after his return. We use Frank's description of this particular incident because it is the most evocative, not because we feel it is more true than Carson's or, for that matter, anyone else's description.

he began defecating and urinating in the cat's litter box. We speculate that he may have done this for years and simply hidden the results. A lack of control of excretory and masturbatory impulses are common signs of Reverse Animalism, and in fact the condition is usually discovered because of an inappropriate public display of such impulses. Many interviewed said that, though they thought little of it at the time, Louis's enjoyment of public urination should have alerted them to the problem. He often bellowed or howled while the yellow stream trickled through the open air.[11] Evidence of public masturbatory phenomena in this case is slim, though it undoubtedly occurred.

Upon graduating from high school, Louis enrolled briefly in Cross River Community College, dropping out in the middle of his first semester after complaining about the assigned readings, which he described as becoming increasingly difficult for him. Books, he often told Frank and others, were best for keeping his tables leveled. As an elementary school student, Louis had loved reading.

As time passed, his posture became more and more hunched and apelike.

Louis's postcollegiate life consisted mainly of watching television and playing video games, or picking up odd jobs here and there. Later, when his mother no longer allowed him to stay at home during the day, he wandered aimlessly around Cross River. His main focus became club-hopping; he was fast turning into, quite literally, a Party Animal. The club-hopping was an activity he often pursued alone, arriving and leaving unaccompanied. At times he would run into acquaintances from District Central, who would make awkward small talk, mostly about high school.

It has been posited that perhaps the often primal rhythms of the music in the nightclubs awoke something in him. This is an attractive theory oft proposed in cases of Reverse Animalism. People tend to look to outside factors as triggers for the bizarre behavior of BEPs, although external factors ultimately offer unsatisfying explanations. Frank recalled Louis's nightclub behavior in an interview: "Man, you should have seen him dancing, just thrashing all around. He used to get real lost in the music and then he'd start to feel up on some ass, any female ass around

---

11. This description is not ours. Like everything else in this study, it is derived from interviews and a careful perusal of available public records.

him. He'd be all nonchalant about it and then act surprised that anyone thought he was strange. As if everyone else was off. Sometimes I really do wonder if he knew any better at all. My man A—— says dude knew exactly what he was doing, but I'm not sure."

Louis was banned from The Garden, a nightclub on Cross River's Southside, after an incident in which he repeatedly inched down his pants while dancing with women.

One wonders if he could control himself at all anymore or if the disorder had completely deranged him. Carson describes Louis speaking in a strange and stripped-down language on the night of his expulsion from The Garden, a language that was choppy and difficult to understand. He spoke in grunts and facial gestures more than words. Just how far along was he?

For those with Reverse Animalism, there is only the present.[12] There is no free will, just instinct.

Frank recalls a moment outside Club Illusion in which a shaggy Louis Smith growled like an angry gorilla in recognition of him, as if instinct told him to be wary of Frank.[13] In the period after that, Louis most often

-----

12. One of the key differences between animals and humans is that animals seem to lack declarative memory, the memory of facts. There are two types of declarative memory: semantic and episodic. Semantic memory comprises facts that exist independent of time and place—when a person recalls that the Earth is round, she is using this type of memory—while episodic memory comprises facts dependent on time and place; when a person recalls the *moment* he learned that the Earth is round, he is using this type of memory.

Declarative memory is distinct from procedural memory, the memory required to do things that feel relatively automatic, such as walking, sitting, or riding a bicycle. This is the way an animal learns to stay away from a hot stove after a burn, even if that animal lacks the language to describe pain or the understanding of time and space that would allow it to create a narrative out of being burnt.

These separate types of memory reside in different parts of the brain. BEPs appear to completely lose their declarative memory, and their procedural memory also appears to devolve. How or why this happens is not fully understood.

Animals call on procedural memory when performing simple tricks. In fact, we managed to teach Louis, while he was in captivity, to knock twice on the floor to signal his pleasure with a meal and three times to signal his displeasure. Attempts to teach Louis simple sign language, however, failed, as did attempts to have him relearn basic words such as *da-da*.

13. This is no doubt an example of Louis's procedural memory warning him of danger, as his instincts *remembered* the pain of being shunned by high school peers.

roamed the streets, soon building a nest for himself in an alley in Downtown Cross River, near the nightclubs.

His mother said she did not know what to make of his sudden absence or his strange silence whenever he was around; this was as he was becoming a rarity in her home.

The night of August 16, 2004, Louis awakened from a long nap in his alley home, stretched his arms, and growled when the dyed golden hair of a passing woman caught his eye. He drew close behind her, though she did not realize he was there, according to a statement she gave to police. Louis reached out and grabbed some strands at the back of her head. The woman panicked, yanking free from his grip, leaving Louis holding a clump of hair. She screamed and ran. A confused Louis bawled after her, a gut-wrenching primal wail the woman said she associated with the fictional hero Tarzan. He lumbered behind her, still howling. But he soon lost interest in the pursuit and settled onto the sidewalk, where he proceeded to loosen his pants. When the police arrived, Louis was still crouched on the sidewalk, defecating.[14]

Police circled[15] him as he squatted on the ground soiling his torn blue jeans. According to onlookers, it seemed he had long forgotten about the

---

14. Regrettably, the woman in question declined to be interviewed for this report. We had hoped to discuss the incident with her and achieve a fuller understanding of what actually transpired, but we are able to infer certain things from the police report and interviews with homeless people who witnessed the incident from the moment Louis woke until his arrest. Louis at the time was not completely lost in his bestial personality, as he still wore clothes. According to the description provided by the police, he wore a brown sports coat over a navy blue T-shirt. He also wore tattered blue jeans and nothing on his feet. We assume his clubbing days were behind him.

We cannot be certain, but we believe he did not mean to attack the woman. Primitive humans, like their simian counterparts, often showed affection by grooming one another. This consists in part of picking insects out of each other's hair. It is not inconceivable that upon seeing a pretty woman, Louis rushed to show affection by grooming her. Being a modern woman, she naturally became frightened by such attention.

15. Circling Louis was a risky move and could have ended disastrously. This is where a better understanding of the disorder is imperative, for it will lead to sounder methods of capture that will be safer for BEPs, rescue workers, and the community. It is not an exaggeration to state that the Cross River police, like many police departments across the country, approach most situations with their

woman with the dyed golden hair. At that moment, defecation was his whole world.

Cornered by police who looked at him with disgust while speaking a language he could no longer understand, Louis decided, like any trapped animal, to go on the offensive. As they approached, he flung his warm new feces in their direction. Excrement splattered against the officers as they rushed to subdue the bawling Louis Smith. They wrestled him to the ground, cracking his skull and three of his ribs in the scuffle. Louis Smith, that poor confused creature, must have had no understanding of what was going on.

Having gone through this experience, Louis in captivity rapidly sped through the stages of Reverse Animalism,[16] often hooting like the pri-

---

guns drawn and their fingers poised on the trigger, particularly if the suspect is, like Louis, African American. If police understand that a suspect is suffering from Reverse Animalism, they can use techniques of capture that do not involve killing or maiming. The authors believe police departments across the country should be trained to recognize the disorder and safely subdue suspects who may be suffering from it.

A 2012 study of the CRPD conducted jointly by researchers at Harvard University and Freedman's University in Cross River (H. A. Colmes and Marjorie Ray, "Trouble in 'Black Paradise': Examining Race and Violence in the Cross River Police Department," *CrimCon* 26, no. 3 [2012], 42–59) found that officers in Cross River, regardless of race, were more likely to use excessive and deadly force against African American and Latino suspects. It was determined that the CRPD, a largely African American force, was seventeen times more likely to use deadly force against minority suspects than similarly sized police departments. We do not intend to turn this study into an indictment of the CRPD. It is to their credit that Louis was not shot and killed during his capture.

Accepted techniques for subduing a Backwardly Evolved Person are not unlike techniques police already employ to capture wild animals. The use of stun guns, nets, and even tranquilizer darts can be very effective.

16. The stages of the disorder are the subject of ongoing debate. We have outlined them as we understand them:

- Stage I: BEPs withdraw from social activities. A preference for animal company over humans emerges, as well as an exaggerated empathy for animal suffering coupled with coldness toward human suffering. BEPs start showing a lack of control over base desires. Memory starts to fail.
- Stage II: BEPs may begin to mimic the behavior of domesticated animals. Activities such as eating pet food and forgoing the toilet bowl for the litter box are not uncommon. BEPs often develop a pattern of urinating, defecat-

mate he had become. The River Run Mental Health Facility on the Southside of Cross River had—and sadly still has—no procedure for controlling a person who insists on grooming peers who are, no doubt, struggling with mental disorders as serious as his own. Louis often violently attacked other males for supremacy, sexually accosted female patients, and swung through the facility, hopping from wall to wall as if they were jungle trees. Before long he resisted even wearing clothes.

It was a controversial decision to turn Louis Smith loose into the wild to live out his life as a simple primate. Some found this course of action an unnecessarily cruel choice. Many mental health advocates, those with little understanding of the stages of Reverse Animalism, who have often never encountered a BEP, said a round of treatment aimed at bringing Louis back into society or, at the very least, easing some of the symptoms, would have been best. But the decision to turn Louis loose is one we stand by. There is no coming back from this particular descent. Much might have been gained from studying him up close, but was his life created especially for curious researchers? If we were to keep him unhappy and in captivity, how would we be any different from common slaveholders? In addition, we had to think of the safety of the other patients at River Run. Proposals to hold him in captivity at the Cross River Zoo, the Alfred McCoy Museum of Science, or B. J. Arcom's Traveling Parade of Oddities were quickly rejected. Louis Smith is not the Hottentot Venus,[17]

---

ing, and masturbating in public. BEPs become lax in their hygiene, and their vocabulary begins to slip.
• Stage III: BEPs cease wearing clothing and speaking. They appear unable to comprehend human language. At this point, many researchers agree, forward evolution is unlikely, though there has been some progress with Stage III BEPs in recent years.
17. The Hottentot Venus was the epithet for at least two African women who were paraded around Europe as part of a traveling sideshow during the nineteenth century. Men were allowed to gawk at and touch their large buttocks, a feature that was a rarity in Europe. The most famous Hottentot was born Saartjie (pronounced SAR-key) Baartman in what is now South Africa. After her death the woman's skeleton, genitals (which Baartman never allowed to be displayed while she was living), and brain were exhibited in a museum in France until 1974. Her remains were returned to her homeland only in 2002, seven years after South African president Nelson Mandela requested their return. It is this type of spectacle that the authors of this study have sought to avoid.
The Hottentot Venus was well known in her time and even after. In the 1939

and we, it is to be hoped, have moved forward as a society from such gross and primitive displays. If we were to return to such a disgusting spectacle, how could we even call ourselves modern men and women? The authors could not answer that question in a way that we were comfortable with. We took what we believe was the most honorable route and released him into the wild where his current mental state tells him he needs to be.[18] Louis Smith, or the man who was once Louis Smith, lives in the Wildlands[19] on the edge of Cross River, which is home to all types of creatures, according to myth and urban legend.[20] The once erudite young Louis Smith now roams naked, but happy and free.[21]

----

cinematic version of *The Wizard of Oz,* Bert Lahr as the Cowardly Lion asks in song, "What makes the Hottentot so hot?" He answers his own question with the word *courage.* The correct answer, though it is not said in the film, would most logically be: her derrière. Or perhaps *Wizard of Oz* songwriters Yip Harburg and Harold Arlen meant that it took a certain measure of courage to live through such degradation.

The authors of this study do not adduce Lahr to be flip. Louis Smth, we believe, bears an uncanny resemblance to Lahr as the Cowardly Lion in both stature and complexion, particularly after his backwards evolution.

Ironically, though we sought to protect Smith from such an undignified exhibition, he would likely have been a big fan of the Hottentot Venus and, had he been living in Europe in the nineteenth century, would have gladly paid to gaze upon and fondle her backside without giving two thoughts to the racist and misogynist nature of such a display.

18. To be sure, there was much debate amongst the authors of this study about the proper course of action. We turned down a great deal of money to protect our integrity. B. J. Arcom of B. J. Arcom's Traveling Parade of Oddities was particularly aggressive, offering hundreds of thousands of dollars, though he never breached the $1 million mark. We are all proud of our decision.

19. The Wildlands, as it is commonly known, is a largely undeveloped portion of town that borders several parts of Cross River. Hunting, fishing, building, and other activities are severely limited within its borders; however, there are corporate interests and politicians diligently working to change that. The Wildlands is a fascinating place to study, as much of it remains virtually unspoiled by human hands.

20. There is some evidence that Louis has even found a mate in Lily of the Valley, a female gorilla who escaped from the Cross River Zoo. She has thus far avoided capture, and one theory is that Lily has a more intelligent accomplice helping her flee.

21. The authors do not want to give the impression that we have turned a dangerous psychotic out into the Wildlands to terrorize an unsuspecting populace.

We keep track of Louis's progress by the use of an electronic tag implanted underneath the skin at the base of his neck. Often researchers travel to the Wildlands in order to observe his progress. One researcher, the late Dr. Adam Connor, who before his untimely passing left this project to serve in consultant roles at the Cross River Zoo and the Alfred McCoy Museum of Science, wrote an interesting journal entry about his first experience seeing Louis in the wild, from which we would like to quote:

On Seeing Louis Smith: My Encounter with Reverse Animalism

He's a shaggy creature, like a Sasquatch, but not as tall as you'd expect one to be. I first saw him about an hour into my observation.

With his gritty hands, he clung to the mossy green branches of a tree as if it were a natural thing for a human to do, but he isn't a human, not anymore. . . . Upon seeing me he howled. Perhaps in terror. I've been told that he's come to distrust humans based on his past treatment.

I was amused by the howl. It rang loud and sounded as if it came from the center of his gut. My mouth hung open upon seeing him leap to another tree like he had been born to perform this feat. I watched the creased bottom of his feet, his dirt-and-hair-covered legs, the scraggly whiskers around his flaccid uncircumcised penis and testicles, the decaying leaves in his nest of a beard. His head had become a forest. Scars and bleeding open wounds covered his body, as if he had just battled a bear and narrowly defeated it, but he did not appear to be in pain. The former Louis Smith was truly a sight. . . .

Before this point I had never seen him, this man who believes himself an animal. He was like a character out of childhood myth. I had nearly forgotten that I was observing him as part of my job. I reached for my camera, slowly putting it together so as not to scare him. He watched what I did curiously. I wondered if there could be any understanding in him at all now; if he remembered what a camera was; if after his treatment by police, every black object in the hand of a human evoked the baton that broke his ribs and bruised his face. Did he have any memories at all, or did he just have instincts?

I snapped a picture and Louis screamed. It was a deep and painful scream, emotive and reedy. Even the trees must have shivered. It echoed throughout the Wildlands. . . . I kept taking shots, gripping the camera tightly as much out of fear as out of fascination. It was like a talisman, the only bit of protection I had. Louis was much taller than me. His muscles were defined, almost as if he worked out at a gym. This is a funny thought, because Louis knows nothing of gyms anymore. He'd be scared inside of one, running about untamed, horrifying normal men and women, a naked animal on the loose in the middle of civilization.

He leapt down and charged me, using his arms to propel himself forward. It was as graceful as it was odd. Before I knew it, he was upon me. . . . I could smell his rank scent, it filled my sinuses and inhabited the back of my throat. I swallowed it, taking it inside of me. It rested in my gut. He slapped the camera from my hands and it fell to the earth and broke apart.

Just by instinct, I reached to pick it up. Louis bellowed and threw me like I was a sack of clothing. I landed on my back, my heart pounding like the primal drums many native tribes used to communicate. I was motionless. He pounced and stood over me. His face

---

was twisted into an angry scowl. There on the ground, I eased backward. What is the old cliché, I wondered, is it that animals can smell fear? I must have been rank with it. . . . Seeing my expression—I can only assume it was my expression—his face eased and I watched the anger fade. His features became confused and slightly more human. Some spark seemed to fly through his brain, like he had suddenly remembered his humanity. All the science I studied told me that was now impossible, but I saw it on his face through the mess of unkempt hair on his cheeks. He breathed in deeply, as if sighing, and moved his jaw up and down. Was he attempting speech? . . . There I was, a distant reflection in his moist eyes . . .

Klan

There was then the time the Klan galloped through the main yard of Freedman's University late in the evening. The perils of an open campus.

Four white-sheeted ghosts on white horseback riding in procession. The Klan member in front and the one in back held tight to flaming torches. The other two, on and off, waved the glowing white screens of their cell phones in their white-gloved hands. I remember the procession as a blur of white and fiery orange and gray from the smoke.

They trotted circles around the statue of our founder as if to menace the dead white man. The ghosts followed that by circling the flagpole, which held a fluttering Old Glory along with the town flag—the book and the sword that make up the Cross River crest in a square of white set against a field of red at the top half and a field of blue at the bottom.

It surprised me how frozen the ghosts made us; I include myself in this. If they tore down our town pride—the banner our ancestors held as they hacked limbs to wrench themselves free—perhaps we'd dash into confrontation, but absent that we became cowards. The Klan members pulled at their reins and some of the horses stood on their hind legs and whinnied and they all then galloped off. For the first time in ten minutes, I released the air I held deep within my chest.

When I started at Freedman's, during orientation, a speaker who was an alumna and board member talked of sitting in economics class next to a shy young man with a thick West African accent. They struck up a friendship, she said, pausing to wink and nod, which I took as an insinuation of a more intimate relationship. The woman ended the story with his name, and I recognized it as the name of the warlord-turned-dictator-for-life of a small African republic. We were supposed to be impressed by the prominence of our alums, and at the same time we were encouraged to wonder what sort of world-shaker sat beside us.

One day the dictator will be overthrown and executed or tried in The Hague for crimes against humanity.

I thought of all this today because Malcolm Bailey began our job interview by reminiscing about the Klan ride. He remembered seeing me bloodless and terrified, and at this he chuckled. All I recall of him is the humanities class where we met and how he wept over Okonkwo when things finally did fall apart.

I didn't mention that, of course, even when he told me of the deal he made with the warlord to acquire cheap gold for the electronics we manufacture. I say *we* because it was clear then that I had the job if I wanted it.

The last thing he said to me—leaning in real close and whispering— was, They never caught those Klan members, huh?

I don't believe so, I replied.

Psychology class, brah, he said. *Psychology 302: Special Topics in Race and Something or Other.* Don't tell nobody, but that got me an A. Changed my life, too. He tapped the desk three times, and it sounded to me like the clopping of white horses across the Yard. Changed my life.

Razor Bumps

If I be shaven, then my strength will go from me, and I shall become weak, and be like any other man.

—Judges 16:17

My head—the briar patch it had become—was like the Wildlands, host to all sorts of mythical beasts, for instance Br'er Rabbit, who each night for a month or so untangled himself from my locks and leapt across the living room, leaving to enjoy an adventure or two before returning to the thicket of my dome. That's according to my wife, who during the Great Hair Crisis of '05 took it upon herself to become, at my expense and before no audience, the stand-up comedienne she had always dreamt of being.

Her routine irritated me because of the truth in it. I did look ridiculous with my misshapen Afro. Powdery white dandruff dusted from it whenever I turned my head, and knots like asparagus spears burst in all directions. The Barber—everyone referred to him as The Barber except for those that hadn't had a cut from him—once a great artist, was no more. Sure, he existed. Breathed. Bled. Farted. But he no longer lived. It must be torment for a god to wake up mortal. Not even an exceptional mortal, but a barely competent one.

But then I'd see a head cut with The Barber's exquisite touch. The sharpness of the hairs. The crispness of the lines. Those sorts of haircuts reminded me that no one else was capable of a perfect cut, and once you've had perfection, who could settle for mediocrity? Even excellence? When I saw he was still capable of such heights, I imagined the crisis had ended and everyone would return to The Barber to get cut like we did in the glory days.

I sat in his chair that night knowing this wasn't one of those times. I was under no illusions that I'd get a good or even a mediocre cut. But I could no longer stand the mockery. Not just from my wife but from strangers. Children on the street. Whispers at work. Mocking eyes. Mocking laughter. Though it was the woman I married who mocked most maliciously.

I was taught to laugh with a bully. That way the harassment loses its appeal. An overrated strategy, especially when a bully is as determined as my wife.

Buckwheat, she would cry. Get a haircut!

O'tay, I replied.

The Barber frowned when I walked in that night, but quickly he corrected his face and greeted me with a head nod. He could be a grumpy son-of-a-bitch sometimes. After the door shut behind me he flipped a switch to his right, shutting off the glowing blue *Open* sign in the window; he walked to the door and locked it, leaving a cascade of keys dangling at the entrance.

A customer sat in The Barber's chair and three people waited ahead of me. Uncomfortable black seats sat pressed up against the wall, and on either side of the chairs messy stacks of magazines overflowed on small tables. Digging in for a long wait, I snatched a wrinkled copy of my favorite music magazine, *Riverbeat Currents*, from the top of the pile and leafed through it. After some time I realized that it was the same issue I always seemed to pick up during these excruciating waits, giving every visit a distinct sense of déjà vu. I tossed it aside and picked another.

The exchange between The Barber and his customers shifted from football, which I cared nothing about, to the coming weekend's fight—which again, like all sporting events, mattered little to me—and I sank lower in my seat, hoping no one asked my opinion. The week before a haircut I always did enough research to fake my way through a sports conversation. I cursed myself for forgetting to research the coming weekend's fight.

The Barber removed the black cape from his customer and shook the excess hair from it while arguing that the champ's time was done.

The customer stood, his head a mismatch of two different hairstyles. He peered into the long rectangular mirror on the wall behind the barber chairs. It hung above several tables that all stayed cluttered with bottles of baby powder, shampoo, rubbing alcohol, and a motley assortment of aerosol cans. The man sighed, handing over his money. I wanted to drop the magazine and dart from the shop. The other customers looked on, solemn and wide-eyed. The nearly bald man who had been sitting to my right shuffled slowly to the hotseat as if walking to the electric chair. He had little to lose. The other customers and I would have to wait two embarrassing weeks for our heads to fully recover.

A silence descended upon the barbershop. A man at the far end wept a bit. Nobody noticed but me. The guy sitting nearest the door announced that he had forgotten his wife's birthday and slipped out, promising to return the next day.

The Barber changed the channel from ESPN to the nightly news. It was nothing but heartbreak. A terrorist had made another bold audio-taped announcement full of mockery and threats; a woman's life had become a smoldering wreck, a public tragedy only because she had once been a pop star; a war dragged on, taking the lives of four more soldiers; and right here in Cross River a mysterious case was still unsolved: the death of an undercover cop from a neighboring town, killed several weeks ago on the bad side of our city, a few blocks from where I now sat. The killer had fled into the night and was no longer a man but an idea to puzzle over.

The Barber changed the channel again and the suspect, or rather a rough sketch of what he might look like, peered from the television. He appeared barely human; instead he was vaguely ectoplasmic, or gelatinous, what with the use of light charcoal grays to provide texture and the simple ovals for eyes, curved lines to represent a nose, another wider oval for a mouth, knurled protuberances for ears, and a mess of lines for hair. Apparently this cop was killed by a collection of shapes. And then there was the photograph of the officer, a yellow-skinned man with smooth slicked-back hair and a long jaw. The Barber stopped his cutting and stepped back from the chair, his lips parted. He appeared shaken, and his hand trembled as he returned to cutting the balding man's head.

You all right? the patron to my right, the next customer in line, asked.

Yeah, I'm okay, The Barber said, but after a moment he wiped tears from his cheeks. Man, he said, I knew that dude. The cop, Carlton, he was just up in here right before he got killed. The day before. I used to cut his hair, and then he decided to get that perm. I was always telling that man to let me cut the perm from his head.

Damn, I said, attempting to join the conversation, hoping some camaraderie would garner me a better haircut. That's some fucked-up shit.

News of this case had played on day after day, though I hadn't paid much attention. The newscasters presented little new—in fact there was nothing new despite its prominence on the broadcasts. Somehow, and I'm not certain how, according to the newscast, an obscure local rapper who had released an album menacing the police was at fault. The rapper had named himself L'Ouverture and he called his album *Problem With Authority.* He appeared on the television screen attempting to defend himself, standing in front of a bank of microphones with four angry-looking men behind him.

This is art, he said, not self-help. I never told nobody to kill nobody.

See, that's why my kids don't listen to that trash, said the balding man sitting in The Barber's chair. He ran his hand over the patchy flourishes hanging about his ears and his temple and said, I'll knock the shit out of one of them if I hear that shit coming from they rooms.

The Barber nodded and grunted in approval. So did the man next to me. The balding man stood from his seat, spun, and looked into the mirror. He inspected the raggedy lines that had been cut into the sprigs of hair on the curve of his head. Then he stared angrily at The Barber, but seeing his sad face, the man reached into his pocket and handed him a twenty. Refusing change, the balding man walked out.

The Barber smacked away excess hair from the seat with the black cape he covered his customers with and looked at his remaining two patrons as if to say, Who's next? The other man and I eyed each other without moving. I looked down at the magazine and slowly he rose and walked to the chair.

Damn, man, I'm sorry to hear about your friend, the man said. They got like ten cops for each block on the Southside now. More cops than ever. They multiplying like rabbits out here.

What you expect? The Barber said. They trying to find the dude that killed Carlton.

I ain't complaining, jack, the man in the chair said in a shaky voice.

Just trying to keep my head down. They need to ban that music, though. I ain't never in my life gonna listen to L'Ouverture again. Not like I listened to the nigga before, but I definitely ain't listening to him now. Don't take off too much from the top.

As if he hadn't heard him, The Barber cut deep into the man's hair. The talking heads on television screamed at one another, their voices shrill and grating.

It's no doubt that Officer Jones would still be alive if we didn't have miscreants making this sort of *music*, one commentator said. Another agreed, and then the opposition, a man who called himself Chairman R, said something predictable: I doubt it was a rapper who armed the killer.

Let me get this straight, demanded the host, a man with puffed-out cheeks that slowly turned pink and then red. You're defending a cop killer? I don't understand why you people al—

Who is this *you people* you're talking about? Chairman R barked back.

The commentators shouted over each other, their words becoming unintelligible. The noise was almost an entity.

The talk was interspersed with clips of L'Ouverture speaking to the cameras; of his recent interviews; of his latest music video.

As I flipped through the pages of the magazine, there he was scowling in an advertisement for his latest CD. I set that issue down on the table and grabbed another, and halfway through, as if he had followed me, there was a picture of him—this time smiling—spread over two pages and accompanied by an interview. And while I waited, I read. All I could think, though, was that he had a nice haircut. A very nice haircut.

Q. . . . .

A. *Yeah, well see, it's a name Black [Terror] gave me. This was way back before the Personality Kliq when I was running with his little brother [Shorty Cool]. I used to call myself Revolutionary Raymond the Versifier. Then I was Ignorance Killah. But I had to switch that up because niggas started calling me Ignorant Killer. I couldn't really rap back then, but I was passionate. I guess he saw something in me.*

Q. . . . .

A. *Naw, you couldn't tell me I wasn't the greatest rapper of all time. I thought I was Chuck D and a half. Every time I thought I had the most tripiotic rhyme, Black used to knock me down and send me home to write more shit. Ten*

157

years of just working on my flow, another five on lyrics. Niggas ain't got that type of patience these days. Shit, I ain't have that type of patience, but I trusted big brother. No matter what type of a dick I think he is now (and he is a dick). Black is gonna be big brother for life.

Q. . . . .

A. *Who, Black? Naw, he ain't know nothing about that revolutionary shit before he met me. You heard his early stuff back when he was Little Terror (stupid-ass name). That nigga was dancing around with a hightop fade like Kid 'n Play or some shit. I must have blown his mind, coming through talking about the Black Panthers and Mumia Abu-Jamal and Leonard Peltier, shit like that. I was giving him books to read like* Die Nigger Die! *and* The Spook Who Sat by the Door. *When he was starting the Personality Kliq he told me: Your name is L'Ouverture. This was after I gave him* The Black Jacobins *to read. It was as if I'd found my true name, like it wasn't Black that was renaming me, but God. Like God was working through him. I know that's bullshit, but whatever.*

Q. . . . .

A. *Now, D'Arby, why'd you have to go and ask that? You know that's a sore point. I'm not sure I want to address that. I'm not here to talk about no cop killers, and for that matter I'm not here to talk about Black and the Personality Kliq. We're supposed to be talking about my new group Problem With Authority . . .*

Q. . . . .

A. *D'Arby, D'Arby . . . You ain't even ask me no questions about that shit . . . Look, I'm in an awkward situation. People looking for me to defend rap music. I'm trying to promote this project . . . Problem With Authority ain't even rap music, the media's got it all wrong. It's Riverbeat. I thought Cross River would be happy that I was pumping our homegrown shit for the whole world to hear, but all I keep hearing is:* you killed a cop, you killed a cop. *I never killed a cop or told anyone to kill a cop. I just told a story about a nigga that couldn't take it no more. I got a band behind me. I'm singing and scatting like I'm Phoenix Starr. I got backup singers and a dude I'm training to be a great lyricist the way Black trained me—shoutout to my little sidekick, H. Rap Black (I gave him that name. It's a cool name, right?)—but don't no one talk about the music and my music's the most tripiotic shit out there. This album is just as good as any Kliq album. Fuck that, it's better. Much better.*

Q. . . . .

A. *Look, if the world were nice, I'd sing about flowers and trees, but this is*

*the world we got. The world where an unarmed black kid can get shot 37 times
on his way home by some trigger-happy pigs. Don't no one even speak about that
no more since that one cop got killed. Didn't Nietzsche say that he knew his name
would be associated with some great horror? Same way I feel, my nigga. I can't
control what people do with my music. Some people jam to it. Some people fuck to
it. People will even lead marches to it. And a very small portion will kill cops to
it. It's the soundtrack to the lives we livin' right here, right now.*

Q. . . . .

A. *Don't even call me L'Ouverture no more. My new name is the Black
Nietzsche.*

Q. . . . .

A. *I ain't answering that question until you call me by my real name.*

Q. . . . .

A. *Yeah, I'd call a cop if I had to. Call him a motherfucking pig.*

Sitting in The Barber's chair, my heart thumped like a mad drummer sat
in there thrashing about. My breathing turned shallow when I heard the
clippers buzz.

How you want it, chief?

He said this as if he didn't know who I was, as if he hadn't been cutting my hair for the past twelve years or so. A sure sign of barber slip-
page. It's not as if I ever once deviated from the usual: a close trim, even
all around, except for the back, which was always faded out.

Uh–uh–umm, I stammered, just a shape-up today.

You sure? You looking like Buckwheat. Nah, I'm just playing. You letting it grow out, huh?

I nodded. There was no way, I thought, he could botch a simple shape-
up. Even the most otherwise sublime and exquisite haircut is ruined if it's
not crisp around the edges. The shape-up is the most important part; nail
that and you can probably fake the rest.

Your brother was in here earlier, The Barber said.

Oh yeah?

We became silent, and the silence terrified me as I sat there perfectly
still, giving up my power to a man who had proved his ineptitude over
and over.

I heard a click and the buzzing of the clippers as he crouched before
me and stared at my hairline. His face was so close to my cheek I felt he

was about to kiss me. What really broke my heart was that he was not apathetic. He took just as much care as he did when he was the most excellent barber around. No, he wasn't apathetic, just pathetic.

I broke the silence to calm my nerves. Yeah, I said, my brother's about to have his first kid. I'm gonna be an uncle.

The Barber stepped back and snapped off the clippers. I turned my head slightly, looking up at him. His brow was bunched as if in a rage; his face moved in anguish.

Man, he was up in here today and didn't share that with me. He didn't share that with me at all.

Uh . . . I'm sure he meant to.

Yeah, probably, he said as he started cutting into my hairline once more. I'll just wait for him to bring it up.

He drifted into another silence, and I could hardly stand it. He looked, at moments, like his father, Sonny, Cross River's other legendary barber. By the time my own father herded my brother and me into that downtown barbershop, Sonny was already on his downslide. Still, my brother and I went to Sonny's—that was the name of the shop—well into our teens. It was a warm and inviting place with orange walls and mirrors all around. On the wall, the one across from the barbers' chairs, there was a row of seats where customers read magazines and waited. Above us hung a painting of dogs playing poker, the one with the sneaky dog holding some extra cards under the table in one of his back paws.

Sonny's chair was the one all the way in the rear of the shop next to a wall that he decorated with dirty postcards from places such as Mexico and Barbados and pictures ripped from nasty magazines: naked and smiling women in inviting poses. I wonder if my father ever thought twice about bringing me into Sonny's. I'd hate, for instance, if my brother brought my nephew into a place adorned with pornographic images, but it was a different time and no one ever talked about the pictures on Sonny's wall. I used to discreetly glance over at them every chance I could get away with, but my favorite part of the haircut was always when he spun the chair toward the wall to work on the back of my head and I could stare at the pictures without hiding, storing them in my mind so I could access them later.

Our father took us to Sonny's after our mother became tired of Dad cutting potholes in our heads. Maybe it wasn't so warm and inviting, as all my memories involve not wanting to be there. Such as the time, shortly after Marvin Gaye was killed, when I sat next to a fat man who overflowed from his chair. The fat man started speaking, unprompted, of discipline, which was a recurrent theme in the shop. My children, he said, ain't never gon' to be too old to get it.

It was a crowded shop that day, and everybody met his sentiment with nods of approval. I was seven, maybe eight.

My daughter's twenty, the fat man said, and she tried to talk back the other day, I knocked her ass down. Man, I tell you, if I can't get 'em, the nine millimeter's gonna get 'em. Like Marvin Gaye.

I flinched and eased from him, just slightly, involuntarily. This time the fat man was met with a silence that carried throughout his haircut.

Sonny gave the fat man the most exquisite cut, one that seemed far beyond his range at the time, one that allowed everyone to glimpse his greatness. And as the man left, Sonny wished him a good day. He pointed to me and I climbed into his barber's chair. Sonny leaned into my ear and in a voice just above a whisper he grumbled, That guy's a fool.

An eruption of conversation and mockery overflowed all around the shop.

Sure is a fool, ain't he?

When that dumb nigga get arrested for killing his kids, I'm testifying like shit.

I'll buck 'em down like Marvin Gaye's dad, 'cause I'm a tough guy.

I settled into the seat with the calming din of laughter and conversation all around and let Sonny cut my hair. If I remember correctly, it was a mediocre haircut. The fat man, I imagine, was the last time Sonny unleashed the full power of his artistry.

Sometime in my teenage years, Sonny brought his son into the shop to cut heads. I had seen him before, sweeping and taking out trash. This time, though, he was a barber, occupying the chair right next to his dad. Sonny had a look of pure satisfaction on his face watching his son cut. People tended to compliment Sonny on his son's work, saying things like, Man, you taught that boy well, and Sonny would nod and hide a smile, but even he was astonished at times by the things his son did with a pair of clippers. You could tell by the brief widening of his eyes.

All the young customers flocked to Sonny Jr., and as word of the young barber spread throughout Cross River, the wait became longer and longer. Once I remember a man with a West African accent sitting in the shop. He talked excitedly and smiled broadly. Said he came all the way from Nigeria to be cut by the finest barber in the world. I swore he was bullshitting, but the way this man cut . . .

His name was Sonny Beaumont Jr., though in those years we all started to refer to him as The Barber, and when you said it, everyone knew immediately who you were talking about. To call him anything else was absurd.

Sonny always looked on in pride until, one day in my late teens, his son left to open his own shop on the Southside. Cross River Cutz he called it, and Sonny would look grave and shake his head the few times I heard him mention it. Sonny didn't smile much or laugh after that, but truthfully I don't know that for sure, because it wasn't long before my brother and I left Sonny's for Cross River Cutz.

Sonny died during his son's golden period. This is the time people talk about when they speak of The Barber's genius. The son's response to his loss was to chase greatness in each cut so that his dead father could look on in pride. He'd stare at a head for several minutes before starting. Then he'd pace back and forth like a lion sizing up his prey. Soon he'd be moving his clippers over the contours of a head like God moving across the formless void to make a world. Around that time he brought in a guy to sharpen his clippers after every fifth cut. Those things hurt, but that was the price of a perfect haircut and I got a few of those before his decline. In the height of his artistry The Barber renamed his shop Sonny's II.

Young apprentices swept the floor for free. Several, it was said, even saved some of the fallen hair to study. His fellow barbers, those who rented neighboring chairs from him and competed for his meager over-flow, would watch and discuss The Barber's technique when they weren't cutting.

All those barbers eventually deserted him for other shops, or the most disillusioned left haircutting for good. The chairs next to him now sat empty.

While he shaped up my hairline that day, The Barber stopped to take a phone call and started back on a different side. I wondered if he'd lost his place.

Maybe it was our silence or the clipper's buzzing or the television's droning, but I spoke: Man, people are saying you lost your touch.

As soon as I said it, I heard the click of the clippers switching off. The television still droned, but The Barber said nothing. I remained frozen.

After a moment he switched the clippers back on and started cutting, and then he stopped again, spun the chair next to me, and with a sigh collapsed into the seat.

My man, he said, I'm tired as shit. If you wasn't a regular customer, I would have told you we was closed when you came in that door.

Sorry, man.

No need to apologize. I ain't just talking about today. I'm talking in general. I'm tired, jackson, tired as shit. I know what people be saying about me. You ain't the first dude that said it straight up. I am slipping. It happens to every barber. You start slipping, slipping, and then one day new kids come and take your place. I told myself it wouldn't happen to me, but I was fooling myself.

But you're so young. Your skills shouldn't be fading yet.

I don't feel young. I had like four, five, six careers, as many heads as I've cut. Made me a nice living. I was just too good. I ain't saying that to be arrogant. I should have raised my prices to protect my talent like folks told me to do. Them people kept coming like zombies or some shit. My man Phoenix Starr offered me nearly a hundred G's a year to go on tour and be the official barber for him and his crew. I turned that man down. I had to be amongst the people. I won the Golden Clippers award so many times they said I couldn't compete no more. I didn't care. All I wanted was a little shop of my own on the Southside.

You know, he continued, my dad had me practicing on my brother when I was just a little guy. I was cutting all the kids in my neighborhood after a while. For years I used to cut them neighborhood dudes for free, even after I got my own shop. Carlton, that cop that got murdered, he was the first dude besides my brother that let me cut his head. First to notice I was slipping too. He ain't say nothing. Just got himself a perm. All them dudes I used to cut found new barbers. Even my brother.

He chuckled bitterly and let his head drop.

I know better than anybody that I'm slipping. Shit. Ain't even as close to my customers as I used to be. People used to tell me they was having babies before they even told their parents. My cuts was the reason they even got to lay down with a woman in the first place.

What happened to you, man?

I'd been slipping for a while. I was so far ahead of everybody else that not too many people noticed. All the dudes I started out cutting, they knew, but I could hide it real well because all the barbers around here some trash. But the dude who used to sharpen my blades, he could tell, and he confronted me and I brushed him off like he was some stray hairs, man. He got mad and left me to go work with someone else. Still, it was going good enough until Carl got killed. Everything went crazy after that. Man, I had this notion—and my wife says it's bullshit—that I could have gotten on track if I just got a chance to cut Carlton's hair one last time.

Got this L'Ouverture fool, he continued, all over the television screen all day every day. Dude selling more records than he deserve off this shit. Ruin people's lives and then want to gloat about it. Talking all that political shit. It ain't politics, it's garbage. You know, Carl had a wife and two little boys. The oldest one's my godson. Young little handsome boy with yellow skin and a big nose. Got thick hair. Thick, thick hair. I used to cut it. His brother's hair too, and then Carlton stopped bringing them to the shop. Shit.

He sighed again. It was a deep sigh, and when he was done with it I felt he had emptied everything that was stagnant inside him. There was a certain point a barber went past that there was no returning from. Things were worse than I thought.

Let me finish your shape-up, he said, struggling from his seat. He flipped on the clippers and went back at it slowly and methodically.

When he finished, he handed me a mirror and I looked at my mangled hairline. He had pushed it back several inches and, of course, it was lopsided and jagged at points.

He carefully swept the stray hairs from the cape and sprinkled baby powder on the back of my neck. I offered him a twenty, but he waved away payment. I thanked him, put on my jacket, and walked from his shop. It was raining a bit when I stepped out onto the street. Several police cruisers zipped by, their sirens blazing. I heard the door lock behind me, and I looked back to see him through the window sweeping the floor. He held the broom close to him as if dancing with a woman.

L'Ouverture became like a ghost haunting my every waking thought. I took a nap upon coming home from the barbershop, and he even entered my dreams. In my nightmare he was a barber mangling my head.

I saw his angry frown, and then I saw his perfectly trimmed scalp and the perfect crisp straight line that sat perfectly above his forehead, ending on both sides in perfect right angles at his temples. His tight curls rolled into waves that bobbed up and down on the top of his head.

I wanted to stab his barber. Not just for me, but for a whole generation who were going through it. People I knew went from being beautifully trimmed to unkempt nearly overnight. Cross River hadn't seen so many Afros since 1972. A friend of mine described it as a crisis one day as he scratched at his bush. Flakes of dandruff fell onto his navy blue shirt like a light dusting of snow. My brother bought a pair of clippers and began cutting his own hair. It was a patchy affair, and his hairline was all out of whack, cutting diagonally across the front of his head. I had never seen him like this. If vanity were a religion, he'd be a fundamentalist. Each week my brother used to visit the barbershop. An aura of freshness always surrounded his head. My brother now appeared scarred.

At a family gathering, my little sister looked up at my brother's massacred curls and then at the ruins of my Afro and said, Y'all look like some fools.

She was right. We were loyalists, though. How could we see another barber? Such an act would feel like cheating on a sick lover. I wanted to hold L'Ouverture down and shave bald patches into his head. I wanted him to feel what we all felt. I wanted him to hear his wife howl, same as I heard mine when she came in the night of my shape-up and saw my jagged hairline.

Buckwheat, what did you do to your head? she asked.

The Barber did it, I replied.

The Barber?

She stood in the doorway, trying and failing to process what I said.

You paid for that?

I didn't respond. I walked to the next room and switched on the computer. My wife followed.

This is serious. God, you look crazy. Was he drunk or something? You should sue him for malpractice.

I don't look so bad; it's a new style.

New style? You look like some sort of pickaninny.

You don't love me anymore?

No, get a haircut.

I can't go back to him, baby. He's losing it.

Then find another barber.

You don't understand; he was the best. It's like saying find a new wife.

Buckwheat, if I died, I'd want you to find another wife.

But it wouldn't be the same. I paused. Wait, if I died, you'd find another husband?

We went back and forth for nearly an hour while I surfed the Internet, her insults becoming ever more ridiculous and cruel. At one point she hummed as I spoke, stopping only to tell me that she was humming the theme to *Little Rascals*. Somewhere along the line, I joked that I was planning to get dreadlocks.

Over my dead body, she said, waving her arms in the air. This made me more adamant.

Whatever. Next time you see me, I'll look just like Bob Marley.

She finally settled on this: You can go ahead and get dreadlocks, but they have to look nice, she said. Nothing too scruffy. I'll make an appointment for you at my salon.

Maybe I should get my toes done while I'm there, I said. I'm not going to a hair salon. That's girly. It's bad enough I have to sit around in a barbershop if I want to look normal, but now you want me to sit under a hairdryer discussing panties or whatever the hell it is y'all talk about. Uh-uh. I'll do it myself.

I'm going to see if Shane can see you tomorrow.

I heard her in the next room calling the beauty salon. She joked and gossiped with Shane before getting to the point. While she talked, my mind danced far away from her and from Shane and even from The Barber and what he had done to my hair. The bright flashing images of L'Ouverture on the computer screen pained my eyes, but I didn't look away. I read the bio on his website and muttered to myself, realizing every few moments that I was talking to no one.

Fucking piece of dog shit, I said. I played one of his songs, and it made me tap my foot, which made me even more angry. I searched for his address on the Northside and his phone number and every piece of useless information I could find. I stumbled upon yet another interview.

Above the din of my racing thoughts and the blaring music, my wife's screaming broke through. Do you ever hear anything I say to you?

When did you start listening to that garbage anyway? Damn. You got an appointment tomorrow after work.

Q. . . . .

A. *Yeah, from now on it's Black Nietzsche. L'Ouverture is more of an old-school name, something the Personality Kliq gave me.*

Q. . . . .

A. *It's no disrespect to Black [Terror] or the Personality Kliq at all. [Shorty] Cool, Ph. Dubois, P-Nut, Dark Kent, Octavio the Clown, all of them. I love them niggas. Poison Eros, the fifth Beatle, the tenth member of Wu-Tang, the female Phoenix Starr, she on my* Haitian Revolution *piece. She the first voice you hear, singing and shit. So, we ain't broken up. As soon as we get this financial shit straight and Black pay me the money he owe, we heading right back into the studio. And let's be straight up, Black is the greatest rapper and producer in Cross River history, one of the best in rap ever, even if the shit he's been putting out lately is a little weird. Why you laughing? Let's be honest, it's wack, right? Wouldn't nobody even care nothing about me if it wasn't for Black. His time is done, though. Black's an old man. He's out of touch. He need to move over and let us young dudes get some shine. I ain't the only one thinking like this. [Shorty] Cool got a solo piece. So do Octavio [The Clown]. P-Nut and [Dark Kent] working on something on they own. Even Poison Eros don't fuck with Black no more. I don't know what went down between them, but he messed up by screwing her over.*

Q. . . . .

A. *Let's face it, Black is gonna make more money off the Personality Kliq than anyone else.*

Q. . . . .

A. *Well, he owns the name. He produces most of the songs. I got to pay him to even use the logo; that's why you don't see the Kliq's logo on any* Problem With Authority *shit. I can't afford it. Slavery's done, or so I heard. I got a wife and kids to feed. Why should I be hoeing that nigga's field? L'Ouverture is done hoeing [laughs]. Let me not get too deep into that. I got into too much trouble last time some fool interviewed me . . .*

Q. . . . .

A. *He misquoted me, made up shit and took my words out of context—everything a real journalist is not supposed to do. That fool made me look crazy. Fuck D'Arby Reid and* Riverbeat Currents *magazine. It's another Cointelpro,*

they're trying to discredit me and shut down something progressive, and the peo-
ple ain't gonna let them do it. Tell your man D'Arby that when I see him, I'm
gonna punch him in his fucking face. I'm not Brad Pitt or someone like that. I'm
from the Southside of Cross River. We don't sue niggas. We punch them in their
fucking faces.

Q. . . . .

A. *That interview messed up a lot of shit. Got the Kliq mad at me. My record*
company mad at me. Problem With Authority mad at me. They not playing my
songs on the radio. They not playing my videos. Stores refusing to stock the CD.
People want to buy it, but they can't find it, so sales ain't where they should be. I
just wanted to be out on my own. I wanted to do what Black did. Wanted to show
the nigga that I'm a man too. That I ain't need him. I didn't expect this shit to be
so hard. I'm gonna be all right, but it's a trying time. A real trying time.

Q. . . . .

A. *Well, what people don't understand is that leading people is hard work. I*
feel like Huey P. Newton out this bitch. I got people's careers in my hands. I have
more respect for Black now. He still owe me money, but I got more respect for
him. [Ed. Note: THE ECLECTIC *contacted Black Terror for a response. He said:*
It hurts me when my brothers try to slander my name, but I still love that
dude and all my bills are paid.*] When you a leader, you got to think about all*
kinds of shit outside yourself. Like for instance, my drummer's kid got diabetes. If
I fuck around, he don't get insulin. I'm like Atlas, man. Call me the Black Atlas.
When that cop got killed, it really slowed down a lot of shit for me.

Q. . . . .

A. *No, I never think that. The music needed—fuck that—needs to be made.*
So I can't wonder what if, what if. My songs never ruined no one's life. The
dude that killed that cop ruined someone's life. I'm a musician, not a hypno-
tist. I couldn't make someone kill a cop if I wanted to. And let's not forget to
ask what the cop was doing. No one asks that. Look, man, that nigga Bigger
Thomas decapitated a woman. I blame Richard Wright for every decapitation
since Native Son *been published. Don't blame them A-rab niggas in Afghani-*
stan, blame Richard Wright.

Q. . . . .

A. *How am I being flip? Look, ask me something else, let's switch gears.*

Q. . . . .

A. *I'm glad you asked that, 'cause don't nobody ever ask me about that no*
more. The album's called The Haitian Revolution, *not* Problem with Author-

ity *as the media's been reporting. Problem With Authority is the band's name. Fuck Meratti Entertainment Group, by the way. They stopped supporting my shit as soon as the police complained. But anyway, it's a concept album about an immigrant, my character, Young L'Ouvertureman, who comes to America and gets picked on by his own folks, by the system, by everyone until he starts bucking back. It's some real deep shit. Designed to make my people stand up, fight back. Real soulful, real stirring.* My middle name's Unabomber, tell ya mama, *like I say on the record. The key thing about it is that it's a story, a very universal and human story. Plus it got some funky music—I got to give it up to the band—and some of the most tripiotic lyrics since Phoenix Starr left the earth.*

Q. . . . .

A. *Bad reviews don't bother me. Like I said, it's another Cointelpro. They scared of a nigga like me rising up and becoming the black messiah. From now on, call me the Black Messiah [laughs]. But all this bullshit goes with the territory. It's cool. I know I got a great album. If you don't like it, then you brainwashed. I'm light years ahead, man. You might not be able to figure it out for ten, twenty years.*

Q. . . . .

A. *Look, I make music for my people, point blank. People with feet on their backs.* The children of Reaganomics still choked by evil economics, *to quote a great man—myself. But truly, I don't give a fuck who else listens to it as long as their money is green. If crackers want to pay me to talk black liberation to them, man, it's all good.*

Q. . . . .

A. *I want freedom, justice, and equality for my people—the same shit everyone else wants.*

It was a Wednesday evening when I walked into Hair It Is and froze in the doorway as the eyes of the women in the shop fell upon me. They waited for me to speak and I tried, but nothing came out. A woman walked over and grabbed me by the hand.

You must be Buckwheat, she said. Your wife told us you were coming. We're not going to bite. Come on.

What the heck happened to your hairline? a hairdresser with short trimmed hair like a boy's called out, and a chorus of giggles followed her mockery.

Don't worry about her, the woman holding my hand said as she walked me over to a seat. You should have seen what her head looked like the first time she did it herself.

I tried to respond, telling her I didn't do it myself, but still I couldn't speak. She introduced herself as Shane. She had short elf-lock curls. They shone a lustrous white, and I couldn't stop looking at them. She led me to a spinning chair, almost like the ones in Sonny's II, but different, and immediately she set about washing my hair. Shane massaged my head, and her fingers were soft and smooth. A shiver passed over my scalp.

You want your nails done too? Of course you do, your wife said the works. She already paid for it, you know. You got a nice wife, Buckwheat. Just sit back and relax.

I felt a warm hand holding my left index finger and a file dragging across the nail. Someone removed my shoes and socks and began scrubbing away the dry, dead skin at my right heel, and before long the nails of my feet too were filed and treated with clear polish. I nodded in and out of sleep in their embrace. Finally I awoke to Shane gently shoving me. She held a mirror before my face. I was newly dreadlocked. Not a stray hair out of place, my locks swept back into neat rows. They had shaved my face so that it was as soft and smooth as a lady's thigh. The nails of my hands and feet shone. I was as pretty as a woman.

The beauticians applauded me on my way out, and this only angered me, though I didn't show it. Truthfully, I was enraged. Sitting in my car across the street from the salon, I slammed my fist into the steering wheel, dreaming all the while that it was L'Ouverture's face.

When my eyes caught themselves in the rearview mirror as I drove, I noticed that my eyelashes were long and pretty and when I blinked I looked like a cartoon version of myself. I had never noticed my lashes before. I wondered if the women had applied mascara while I slept as a joke. Perhaps it was my wife's idea. Yes. She told Shane to do it the previous night while I zoned out reading about L'Ouverture. It was retaliation for ignoring her. My eyes kept flitting back to my reflection. Even with the deep frowning crease that thickened my brow, my face still appeared soft and womanly.

Maybe it was my fault for keeping my eyes off the road, but this big black tank—it can only be described that way—veered in front of my Honda sedan, forcing me to jerk the steering wheel sharply to the left.

My tire bumped against the median and I swerved left and right across all three lanes before regaining control. A rapid pulse thumped in my throat. I slammed my foot on the gas pedal and cranked on my high beams, hoping to blind the driver in front of me. I became possessed by the spirit of a more aggressive man.

He moved to the right lane and I pulled alongside him, lowered my window, and waved my middle finger about. The man's windows were tinted and it was a dark night, making him somewhat unreal to me, like a ghost or a shadow. At that moment, as we pulled to a red light, I was content to leave it alone and make the left turn to head home. I raised my window and wondered what my wife would say about my hair. I imagined she'd be happy with my girlish appearance, and I shook my head side to side, feeling my hair gently bounce.

Just as the light turned, the man to my right cracked his window. I could see only the top of his head and a bit of his face. He stuck his hand out the window and gestured for me to lower my glass, and when I did he screamed, Bitch ass nigga! before speeding off.

With the shock of the moment, I didn't move for several seconds until the car behind me honked its horn. I sped off behind the black tank. It was several car lengths ahead, my stuttering Honda barely able to match the tank's speed, though I kept my eye on it.

So many thoughts tussled inside my skull. The man's face, what little of it I saw, was reminiscent of L'Ouverture's. It wasn't just the face but the waves in the piece of his hair that I saw. It was also the exquisitely crisp sideburn I glimpsed. I know it sounds mad, and it seemed mad at the time, but it was a possibility, as L'Ouverture lived right in town, somewhere in the very direction this bastard was headed. And I wondered if—no, I was sure—my hairstyle and my smooth face informed his choice of insult. I gripped the steering wheel tightly with my newly pampered, manicured hands, dodging in and out of traffic, hoping to catch L'Ouverture's Hummer, if indeed it was L'Ouverture driving the tank. And I hoped it was L'Ouverture, for the sake of that murdered officer, for The Barber, for every person inconvenienced by the cop's death, including those that now walked around with Afros or lopsided haircuts.

Earlier in the day I had purchased L'Ouverture's music, and now that I suspected it was him ahead of me, I slid his disc into the stereo system as chase music of sorts.

I flashed and honked, warning cars to move out of my way, and to my surprise they shifted to the side as if I drove an ambulance. It couldn't be him, I thought. Would a political radical zip through the city in a gas guzzler? Perhaps he kept the car to drive during the revolution he sings about, a time when all the world is destroyed and a new era is set to rise. I felt like the madmen I always admired. The reckless rebels I never had the courage to be.

The tank still headed in the general direction of L'Ouverture's neighborhood, and with each length of pavement that we tore through, I became more and more certain that I was tailing him.

The drums crashed through my speakers and then cymbals and rapid thumping. It sounded urgent. It sounded extreme. Now came a woman's voice, operatic and ethereal. It sounded like an apocalypse.

Just as we crossed over to Hilltop, the tony Northside neighborhood in which L'Ouverture lived, the tank stopped across the street from a deli, a convenience store, a cleaner's, and a seafood spot. I pulled my car up behind his. The door of the Hummer flung open and a man stepped out, slamming it behind him. He had a sturdy build, wore a white tank top, and had neatly trimmed hair. I couldn't see the man's face, as there were bright lights behind him.

I still had no calm, lucid thoughts as he came toward my car cursing and pointing. Emotions and colors whirled through my head. It was only later that they made any sense.

I charged toward the man, barely looking at him, swinging in a fantastic arc, punching him in his thick chest. My blows made a flat slapping noise. He roared and slammed his big fists into my face one by one, bursting my lip. He struck my face again and again, eventually knocking a tooth loose. I became dazed, swinging my hands, not knowing where to strike. My fists hit air, and when I toppled over, they scraped the concrete, tearing skin from my knuckles. The rubber sole of his boot slammed into my face. A mixture of blood and thick snot gushed from my nose. He grasped my dreadlocks and tossed me around. I could feel newly twisted locks unraveling. Pulling hair, I thought, is such a feminine thing to do. I had too much dignity to fight that way. I climbed to my feet, wanting to run, but men don't do that. Do they? No. Again I charged the man, and we clung together in a strange embrace, like weary boxers, though sometimes I wonder if we actually looked like lovers.

Hands pried us apart, and I spit and yelled. My blood stained his tank top. I tried—or pretended to try, I can't be certain which—to charge the man again. What snapped me back into lucidity was a voice from the crowd:

Y'all clowns need to get out of here. I called the police.

The man who spoke was a shop owner, I believe. He came from the deli across the street. I raced to my car, and the man I fought cursed me and called me a coward. People cried out to me, asking if I was all right, but I paid them no mind. I turned my car on and sped off, heading in the direction of my house.

So, was the man I fought really L'Ouverture, the Black Atlas, the Black Nietzsche, the Black Messiah? Of that I can't be certain, and I can't say that I don't care, though I would like to be able to say that I don't care, but the truth is that I still do wonder.

I knew for sure, though, that there was a knurled knot by my right eye and that it would swell. I thought of how angry my wife would be. My lip was torn. There were bruises and cuts along my cheeks and a bleeding space to the right of my front teeth. My hand bled. The skin at my knuckles and my fingers was scraped raw and would later be scarred. The white collared shirt I wore for work was shredded and stained with blood. And I didn't notice it as we fought, didn't at all feel it when it happened, perhaps it was the adrenaline, but I now sported a bald patch at the side of my head. The man had ripped out a handful from its roots. I had lost my soft feminine shine.

Three Insurrections

I went deep into the Wildlands one day, and when they found me, I was near death. My flesh generated enough heat to keep a power plant going for a month, probably. I burned at 107 as if my heart had been replaced by a tiny sun. The doctor tells me brain death begins at 106. He says this ashen-faced, surprised I'm sitting up, conscious, bleary and dazed, but alive.

My parents sit across from my bed in Cross River Hospital Center, the place I was born. Here too I watched my son, Djassi, push himself into the world. I'm hoping the universe is not angling for some sort of sad symmetry, making my place of birth also my place of death.

Monique & Neville Samson, two human beings yet one person. My father reminds me of when I was four and I hit my older brother, Blair. Daddy asked me why I did it and I said, Dad, you know I'm brain damaged.

Now you are, he says, cackling, leaning into my mother as she taps his arm and tells him to hush.

This is serious, Mr. Samson, the doctor says.

He tells me it's probably malaria or Chik-V, or dengue fever or something else you can't get in America. Don't believe any of that, please. I just went into the forest; I didn't leave the country. Though it's true that mosquitos have never been my friend, what's really going on is that Cross River is trying to kill me. The doctor talks and I can feel my heart beating at a rapid speed and the heat from my skin is burning my sheets but not really, that's just the delirium. I think of the times I visited my godmother and cousins with my grandmother—my mother's mother—in Trinidad back when I was young and Granny was still living. The trucks driving by at night spraying white smoke into the air. Smoke seeping through the tightly drawn jalousies. The fleeing mosquitos seeking refuge in the house in East Dry River that my mother grew up in, the same house her mother grew up in. The bugs hide for a while but then all die away. For a week, no mosquitos drink from me, and all my old welts stop itching and fade from my skin. In due time the bugs return, swarming me late into the night. Maybe, I think sitting in that hospital bed, they put something deep inside me that's only coming to life now.

Mr. Samson! the doctor says.

Kin! my father calls.

I look up.

The doctor says: What were you doing so deep in the Wildlands anyway?

I tell the doctor I was looking for myself.

(I don't tell my father when he asks.

Nor my mother.

Nor my wife, Peace.

I whisper it to my son later because he's a baby and thus unable to speak it.

I'm not here to tell you about my time in the Wildlands either, so if you've come for that, then I'm sorry, but you'll be disappointed. Remind me later, though, and I might tell you.)

My father breaks the silence. Only two types of people does go so deep in the Wildlands, you know: fools and madmen.

You forgetting the wolfers, my mother replies.

What you think they are?

What about Blair? I ask. He think he a wolf hunter.

My father schupses.

A set of chupdiness, he mumbles. He a fool too. We only have one sensible child, Monique. Laina would never have go so deep in the Wildlands. Your brother and sister call yet, Kin?

Of course not.

My father sighs.

My father talks, but he never talks, you know. When we get silent and it's just hospital sounds around us, and I ask him to tell me about his father, he

176

pauses and says, What's there to say, boy? Then he becomes quiet and offers to watch Djassi so Peace can visit. Peace is the last person I want to see.

Like, Pop, I say, you tell me the funny stuff, like when that white guy beat up the ref at that soccer game—

Never see a cutass like that.

But what about the other stuff, huh, Dad?

My mother says she'll go to my apartment to watch Djassi. Before either my father or I can object, she's out the door. It's just me and Neville Samson.

What's there to say? he asks again. What you want to know, huh?

Like tell me Dad—(I feel the fever bubbling through me like steam, burning my brain; I imagine it rising from the top of my skull on a bed of hot, white smoke)—tell me how we got to Cross River.

The pipe and the book. Is the book first. And when I forget the book, is the pipe that tell me go Cross River.

Is like history put its hands on my back and shove me from the sidewalk into the street, Kin. I always an athlete, so my mind does go back to that often. Stay on your feet. That's what I keep thinking. Like I'm on the football pitch and some guy's running toward me. I had a coach used to say, *The most persistent rewards go to those who stay on their feet.* But this, this is nothing like I ever seen, you know. These people out there rocking and flipping a car. We like bees, Kin. All of us. Thousands upon thousands of bees waking to find our queen get she head chop off.

You see you, all delirious and half crazy? That's how everybody was on that day. I'll never forget April fifth, 1968. The fourth was like a dream. Fuzzy, confusing. But the fifth was real. Martin Luther King dead.

I couldn't tell you why I was out there, in truth, Kin. Some people want to take a piece of whitey and call that justice. An even trade, you know. Some want the things they can't get on a regular day: television sets, jackets, scarves, food, all that. And then some just out there craving the fire, the burn. I don't know, boy. Maybe I wanted some of all of that. Too much to name, I guess. All I know is that I'm angry like everyone else. Whatever burn in them burn in me. I feel that buzzing like bee wings inside me. Wasn't no, I a Trini and you a Yankee. I a Trini and you a negro. Naw. Before I open my mouth they treat us all like niggers. That's it. Ain't take long to figure that out.

Wait, I go get to the pipe in a minute.

So, Kin, you wouldn't believe the amount of smoke they have rising up above D.C. Smoke for so. People burn cars. They burn stores. They burn apartment buildings. They burn everything. I tell you I ain't never see nothing like it. People running around, in and out the broken windows of stores. Ain't no police nowhere. I stand over there near Florida and Rhode Island, just watching, boy. I live on R Street, so it not too much of a walk. People screaming and waving they arms. I just watch. Taking it all in. Telling myself to stay on my feet.

The fires, though, remind me of the book. The cover self like it on fire. Sure did set fire in my mind when I was in teacher's college back home. *Three Insurrections.* It flit through my head at that moment. I ain't see that cover in about fifty years now, but it like I can see it right there in front me face. I ain't see that book for maybe two, three years when I out there walking in that riot, but it's in my mind's eye clear, clear. I know what I see, Kin; those exact flames from the riot is the same flames on the cover of that book. What they describe on all those pages is what I see in that city. I wish I could go back to that moment in the library at the teacher's college when I holding that book, drinking those pages, yes.

Before I could take in all of the riot, fully appreciate the moment, I feel a bump at my shoulder and is stumble I stumble.

Something in my heart start to flutter as I fall, like I go die right there in that strange city in this strange country. I say to myself, *Neville, boy, what kind of mistake you make coming here?* Like it's a football match and I make the play that lose the game, that's how I feel, but this is serious. I feel a hand grab my arm. Pull me up.

It's Charles. Now, Charles live on my block. He don't say much. Quiet eyes always searching. He sit outside on his stoop most of the time and he sit still, nearly a gargoyle. I bet he out there now. When I see him, we exchange two or three words, but the words got whole worlds inside them. Me and he born oceans apart, but we understand each other, oui.

He hand the only thing stopping me from hitting my head on the concrete.

Neville, what you doing out in all this?

I pull myself to my feet.

The man only talk peace and they shoot him. But what is that?

So you see how they do us? They kill a man of peace. What you think they do to regular negroes, huh? Neville, go home, brother. This all gon' blow over. They'll build the buildings back and then they gon' be stomping us again. Go to class and get your degree and let us handle the shit, man.

Kin, Charles was wrong, you know. They ain't build nothing back. Not for thirty years. Remember when I take you to D.C., begging you like hell to go to Howard. Nearly thirty years to the day, that's when they start taking down some of them buildings and putting something new there. What you think that do to people's minds, huh? How you think they feel living in the capital of the nation and it look like a war just happen?

But I respect the hell out of Charles. That winter before all this, I'm walking home and I see this man's hand. Not Charles, someone else. Something black in it. Black, black, black. Heavy. The thing look impatient. I ain't never see no gun in real life. My father ain't like those things. Never wanted them around.

You got any money on you, sir? he say, polite as ever.

I tremble. I scared. I nod. Reach for my wallet. Slowly. I not trying to anger that gun.

Thank you, he tell me, still with all the politeness his mother teach him. He never meet my eyes. To this day I think his gratitude genuine, oui.

I see Charles the next day and I tell him what happen.

When all this go down? he ask, sitting there cool, cool, cool on his stoop. Yesterday? During the afternoon?

Yes. Bright as day, he jump out on me.

Charles nod. He grunt.

I go to pick up my mail the next day and beside the letters and thing there's my wallet. Everything intact, except the money, of course.

Standing there on that street in D.C. with the riot all around me, I watch Charles disappear into the world. I want to follow. I see the last flicker of him in between the people and I feel swept up. Dust in the gigantic broom of history. This how they want it, huh? They negroes down bottom, frogs running from the river while giant children is chasing to crush them under they foot. Your grandmother used to say all the time—she ever say this to you? *What is joke for schoolboy is death for crapaud.* That was us, frogs scattering from the foot of a great white man.

I walk where I see Charles going; I don't see he, but I walk. Just walk. I don't know where I going. It's just walk, I walking.

This all so different than how yesterday start. Yesterday I walk with purpose, nearly stomping to class. Nothing on my mind but the test I'm 'bout to take. When I get to campus, I see people huddled up. Seem like more people out on the Yard than usual. I don't think nothing of it. No time to think of anything but this chemistry test, anyway. Besides, wasn't nothing unusual about seeing people huddled up in intense conversation on campus. Howard was real. Someone always deep in political discussion. You look out and it's a sea of Afros bobbing up and down furiously. Couple times we take over campus. That's another story though. What I'm getting at is Howard was the center of black life, at least for us, at least in D.C. Wasn't strange to see Stokely Carmichael walking round the Yard. He graduate from there. You know he come from your mother's neighborhood in Port-of-Spain over in East Dry River? You know that, right? She brag they went to kindergarten together. What you laughing at, boy?

But I get by the library and I see Larry, your godfather. He say, Class cancel.

Class cancel? But I stay up all night studying. McGregor playing the ass—

All class cancel. You ain't hear? Someone shoot Martin Luther King.

Shoot? King? Who—

Larry shrug.

That's when the feeling start. That dislocation. It grow out a feeling that I always had with me when I ask myself just what the hell I'm doing here. I still ask myself that when the winter whip in and I think about how your Uncle Alton probably back home on the beach. That day I start wondering seriously why I'm here, though, like why I come to a place where they kill a man of peace just for spite? Not even a year before, the football team at Howard, we play some team down South and afterward we try getting something to eat. Now all of we is Africans or from the West Indies, black, black, black. Wouldn't no one seat us, restaurant after restaurant. The coach, after he come from the last place, he get back on the bus, put he head down, and cry right there.

I ain't want to cry, but I ask myself, why be here? Why I come to some place that hate me? I forget the book. That's the answer to all that.

The book. It flicker in my mind sometimes back then. Little shards of it. When I'm following the crowd in the chaos on that day after they kill King, I think of the book, a little bit. Not much, but I think of it.

When I walk home from campus after hearing King get shot, I start feeling dazed. On fire. You should see all the things passing through my head. I spend the fourth sitting in my room. I do schoolwork. I call your mother. I sleep. Dream. Wake and let myself get tortured by thoughts. Questions. *Why am I here?* Memories.

Right before I step on the plane to come over to America I hear about some negro bodies they find in the South all hung and twist up. Nowhere near D.C., but still. Alton read the article in the newspaper to me in disbelief.

Neville, is sure you sure you want to take this trip?

Naw, Alton, I sure ain't.

But that wasn't the truth, Kin. Your uncle Raoul had long split for Canada. Same with your aunt Janice. And your aunt Maisie was in England. I think Alvin was in Rochester by this time. When I get chance to go Howard, I learn D.C. not too far from Cross River in Maryland. I mean, it's farther than I thought but, uh, I have to see Cross River, the place I read about in the book, the place of the Insurrection.

And since my father pass, I had been going and going and going. I had to slow it down just to get hold of my thoughts.

The fêtes and the girls and the football and the cricket and there was a drama workshop and of course the teaching and teacher's college. I ain't expect to come a teacher growing up, you know. My father was respected in the teaching community. Headmaster of the community school in Tacarigua, and he run the teacher's union for a while. So one of his friends, a fellow teacher, show up after I finish high school and say, Come, Neville, let we take a ride.

Before I know it, I'm at the District Office filling out forms, and that Monday I get a letter assigning me to an elementary school in Tunapuna as an apprentice teacher. Teaching's in our blood, Kin. I was happy when you start teaching at Freedman's University. Your aunt Janice taught and Raoul taught and even Blair for a time. Now he the school resource police at District Central. That's your grandfather speaking through us.

I keep digressing. Where was I? Ah, yes. Out on the street. Me and the crowd. We marching now. Moving like an entity. Every few steps someone join up. Every few steps someone break off. I see people mashing up windows of stores. Some places got *Soul Brother* or *Black Owned* spray paint across the front. The crowd leave those alone. Most people just want to make a little mischief. Then they got some that's taking off with goods. In the truth, I thought about breaking off, running through one of them stores. I just lose my job taking customer calls at the *Washington Post*. It was either play football or take a Sunday shift they ain't schedule me for. Guess which one I pick.

I get help from friends and thing, but it still hard. This before I start driving that illegal taxi for a while back in law school. Why you make your eyes big so for, huh? This after your brother born. You do what you do to survive. If you ain't see that with Djassi yet, you will.

I march steady, steady, though. What go through my head is what my father would say he see me ransacking a store. I imagine Vernon Samson watching me.

My father. Boy, what can I say? I loved him. A lot. We was close. All of us. Everyone have he own relationship with Daddy. He a man without a past. You think I quiet about my old days. I an amateur next to he. After he pass, Maisie tell me a little what she know. His father may have been Indian, half Indian, something, but I never know any of his family. He an outside child and when he come an apprentice teacher, they assign him, coincidentally, out San Fernando near where his father live. Daddy tell his father, I never ask nothing from you and you never give me nothing much, but I getting my career start, I need a place to live out here while I apprentice. His father have a reputation. Lot of people look up to him. The whole world can't know he have an outside child running round, so he tell him, Boy, I can't help you and please don't come back asking for nothing.

So Daddy cut off all ties and ain't speak not once of his father to us. A professor up at the teacher's college one time pull me to the side and he say, You look just like your uncle, boy. I just blink, not sure what he talking about. Later I find out it have a justice in Port-of-Spain, Garvin Samson, but I never knew the man.

Everything about Daddy steady and quiet. He have he own way of teaching you, eh. I tell you, when your father the headmaster, you have to be a little tough. Back in elementary school I supposed to stay in class during the first ten minutes of recess to get some extra help in maths. My friend Kelvin schups and say, Why we have to stay inside while everyone out playing? Well boy, three of us out of seven choose to go to recess when we supposed to be inside. Me, Kelvin, and John. We playing football and laughing it up. We even go by the window and point at the fellas who stay. No one telling us nothing the whole time. Later in the day my father announce that he giving the whole school some free time. An hour to play outside instead of sitting in class. Everyone start clapping and laughing and thing.

We get up and my father say, John, Kelvin, and Neville, please step to the front. Instead of the ten minutes we was supposed to have on lessons we spend the whole hour going over maths, listening to everyone outside, watching people come by the window and point. Daddy, boy.

Now later, when I get older and I'm in line for a scholarship to go London, I make the score, but they give it to some whiteboy in my class. Teacher say, Neville got the brains but he too fast by he mouth. He not England material. Well, Kin, I feel defeated. Deflated. You hear certain things, like one of the Irish priests who teach in my high school always telling us that negroes in America too out of place and thing, but that's the first time I was make to feel . . . look, I wasn't no shrinking violet. I was kinda like Laina, oui. I ain't hold my tongue. Teachers and them don't like that. After that happen, I just stop doing the work. I do it, but I do it in ten minutes before I go play football or cricket, and it show when my marks come.

Daddy call me to his office in the back of our house and say, You comfortable with that?

I say, No. I mean, Kin, what you think I go say?

Then he pause and he look away and he sigh. He say, You shouldn't be comfortable with those marks. But you going to be a big man soon. I can't tell you what you should be comfortable with. You have to decide what sort of man you going to be. Someone who comfortable with these sort of marks or someone who want to show the world what kind of light he got.

He ain't say no more, but I tell you I never brought home marks like that again. He ain't have to rant and yell like . . . well, like I used to when you was being hardheaded. I guess I could take a lesson or two from Daddy, but you was something else, Kin.

It's not long after that—it's not along after that that Daddy—

When he pass, we was all together. Except Raoul. He was off in

Canada already. It was strange for us to all be in the house at the same time. Except Alton, we was all grown or nearly grown. So much running around to do. It was the Christmas holiday or thereabouts, and Daddy come home saying he not feeling too well. I remember he and Mom have a community meeting to attend that night. Mom go without him and let him rest, and it happen just after she get home. I hear she call out, Come, something happening with your father!

We rush in, all of us, and—

Well, boy, that is why you never get a chance to meet your grand-father. I happy as hell I get to wrestle with Djassi and all the rest of the grandchildren. I know your grandfather would have loved y'all like nothing else.

All that going and going and going. Never holding still from after Daddy's funeral to the time I left the island. All that stop me from dealing with how sudden, how unfair it was. Becoming a father ain't even offer me space to deal with it. I ain't even realize that I never reconcile it until you make me talk about Daddy right now. Even after I leave the island, there was school and football and shutting down the campus in protest and getting adjusted to America and then they kill the King.

For that somebody must pay. So the riot happening all around me. It feel like J'ouvert morning. A swarm of us walking down the street and don't no one know where we supposed to end up. I feel protected from the chaos, but a part of it too. Any moment the police go come break us up, I feel. Or someone in the crowd go start something. I don't know these people, but quick, quick, quick, it come like all for one.

Our swarm, it move like a flock of birds. All these beautiful black people in motion. Moving and shifting with a kind of intelligence. When we reach the destination, we just know it. That shining palace on the hill overlooking Rhode Island Avenue. Ha! The Safeway.

We get to the place and all of we stand there watching it. And the manager, a short, little, bald, pink, fat white man in an apron standing out front. I recognize him and his tiny, condescending eyes. A black person ask him questions, and he real curt. That man wouldn't let me return some bad chicken I bought there earlier in the day one time. You think they could act like that out Bethesda? Safeway had a lot to answer for, Kin. I hated going to that place.

Please don't do this, the manager say.

I'm thinking, Why put your life on the line for a bunch of groceries? He must think Mr. Safeway go cry big tears at he funeral. Some guys surround him and they start shoving him back and forth and all around, passing him from man to man like a basketball.

The manager pull away and run into the riot. Bad move. One of the fellas catch he and hit he one—whap!—to the back of he head.

I ain't feel bad about what happen to the Safeway. You go in there, you never see one of us working in front. The meat bad sometimes, and you point that out, you get one cussing from the manager or someone under him. Prices always a dollar, two, three, five higher than some other places like the Giant up Georgia Avenue, but it not easy for me to get to the Giant most times. I never realize it before, but I resent Safeway like hell from the moment I start shopping there until the moment we standing in front of it. No one talking, but as a group we decide the store's fate.

A teenager grab a big rockstone and crash the thing through the store window. I want to say, Hey! We not done deciding, but I guess we finish.

Something in me, maybe is something by my heart, it tell me turn around. Go home. But then I see it clear as clear, the man King standing there on the cover of his book with his arms folded. Title say, *Why We Can't Wait*.

I had it out on my desk in class one day back in teacher's college. I pick it out at the library. You know, you hear bits and pieces about what the negroes in America is doing, striking and sitting down and thing, but I needed to know more.

The teacher come by and she tap my book. This why you didn't do so well on the last test, Neville?

But I get an 80.

Oh, excuse me. I took it from your earlier work that you're not the type of student who is fine with an 80. My mistake. Careful with this stuff you reading, Neville. Careful.

I take it back to the library that day and I ain't read it till I get to America and realize everybody reading these books. Teachers assigning it in class. People talking about *The Communist Manifesto* and thing. Howard was real. That afternoon when I take it back to the library, I supposed to go play cricket, but when I get to the library, I see the book. The Book. The fires burning on the cover. Like an animated thing, you know. Like the whole table on fire, and when I sit down the flames start to speak the pages. *Three Insurrections.* I have a cricket match, you know, but who could remember cricket staring at all that beauty? I miss the damn game to read the book. All the insurrections sewn together like a beautiful garment on each page. The Haitians have a insurrection. The Riverbabies—the Cross Riverians—they have an insurrection. And there is one to come and it's mentioned with the ones that happen like it's a piece of threaded gold passing through the garment. I don't see my name, but I see me. I see you and you don't even exist. You just a vague daydream in the back of the mind of two people who was on the same island, but ain't meet till they travel thousands of miles to go Howard. You was just a sperm that's fifteen-plus years from being manufactured and an egg resting inside your mother.

Something make me left that book in the library, though. Maybe it was too much to take, the way it make my mind spin and spin. I wish to hell I had grab it and run. From then on, Cross River is burn in my brain. I never thought too much about what's to happen with me next. I knew I ain't want to stay teaching forever. Some people expect me to come headmaster like Daddy, take over where he left off, but that's not who I am, I knew that. Whenever I think about the future after that day in the library, I hear Cross River whispering behind my thoughts. Maybe it's always been there. I don't know. I wouldn't doubt it.

But what kind of people is this? I think. These Cross River folks bloody they masters and live free like they not afraid. The book talk about the Haitians too, but I hear about them plenty. The Cross River negroes is new to me. I see my island in a footnote. Some Cross Riverians set off through the Americas, trying to export insurrection. Some even settle in Trinidad, the beauty just hold them, even though they have slaves all over to free. I don't know much about our history before Daddy. Maybe we come from Cross River? How I know our people ain't take part in the Great Insurrection? And that is what draw me and your mother to our homeland, Cross River. Maybe. Who knows, is all I'm saying, Kin.

Something about this book, Kin, you don't read it. You read it, but it make you live it, like a dream. I come a Haitian that day, and then I come a Cross Riverian. And just like a dream I live that third insurrection too, but when I close the book, when I leave the library, I forget what it's like in the third insurrection, and then I must spend the rest of my life chasing it down.

After I read it, I say to Alton, This happen somewhere in America.

I sit there and retell the Cross River part of the book as if I make it up right there. I wasn't sure I didn't.

They burn down the plantation and kill they masters dead, I say. Boy, they ain't teach us none of that up St. Mary's, oui. And I suspect they not going to teach it to you neither.

Alton nod, from politeness more so than interest. When all this happen? he ask me, but I can tell he not that concerned with my answer.

Back in the 1800s, I say. Early part. I go go back to the library tomorrow and get that book for you. They call it the Great Insurrection. Got a town standing to this day in America. They ain't never shut it down. I have to get you that book, boy.

Alton make he lips so and turn from me like he can't be seen with a liar.

The librarian shrug when I go back. It not on the shelf. No record of it ever being in the library, she say.

You sure? I ask.

Perhaps it was a patron's, she tell me. But I don't think it was. I look for it in bookshops off Eastern Main Road. Every time I see a bookshop, I look for it. When I get to Howard, I dig through the library stacks in search of it. I still look for it to this day. Now we got the Internet, and I look for it there too, but no dice, Kin.

The smoke from behind that Safeway, I think it like what I experience when I read the book. You look at me crazy, Kin. When you ever know me to not be rational? I studied chemistry when I was at Howard. I'm a man of science, but you can't tell a feeling nothing about science.

Them people in the crowd start to pelt one set of bricks and rocks and thing at the Safeway, and then when they finish they swarm like a crowd of ants. I ain't hear no sirens in the distance. It occur to me I ain't see not one cop. Later they send the National Guard to lock down the streets, but D.C. belong to us right then.

I think about turning around, leaving the place to the people and they anger. Come back to the Safeway only when I need bread and milk. But the book. The book is the thing.

Someone pull me. A woman. A young woman. Come on, she say. Come on. Don't stand there. Come on.

I don't think of my father. I don't hesitate. I do as she say, as the crowd say. I come right on. You should have seen these people throwing things off the shelves. People with arms full of cheese, socks, heads of lettuce. Anything they can take with two hands.

A man run past me; he bump me with he shoulder. One set of bread go flying all over the place. I apologize and we both on the floor collecting the bread. His ill-gotten bread. He tell me, he say, It's nothing, brother. It's nothing. Don't worry about it. Hurry up and get you something before the pigs come. Don't worry about me. Go on, man. Go on.

So I go on.

I see they got turkeys, but people and them tell me that's what you eat here in November. I ain't know if it's strange to be eating turkey in April. I get to the dairy part. But I don't need no milk, no cheese, no eggs. I turn and see the bread. Got enough bread at home. I just come to this place a few days before white people decide to blow up the world. Not much I need, yes. I had to stop and laugh. I never shop so carefully. Neville, I say, what the devil you doing in here anyhow?

I ain't imagine riots this way. All the upheavals I read about, heard about, and now I was in the middle of one, like the rebellious slaves in the book. Like me when I experience the book. That's what the devil I was up to.

I wander around. Floating. Dislocated. Remembering that I lived through the Haitian Revolution and the Great Insurrection, both. The book make it so. Don't look at me crazy, Kin. I know how it sound.

I stumble to the tobacco aisle. Still empty-handed, but here is the pipe lying on the floor. Finally, the pipe. Someone knock it from the shelf. The wood on the thing look smooth and shiny. Plastic tip on the end. I take it out the bag and rest it at the corner of my mouth.

Lottie, I mumble to myself. Lottie! Lottie! I take on the voice of my blind, senile old grandfather. Living all alone on all that land on Eastern Main Road, and when your grandmother come to visit, me and one or a couple of your uncles or aunts in tow, he always know it she. The old man ain't know much of anything else, not anything about his grandchildren or anything it have going on in the world.

Your grandmother warn over and over before we go inside, Don't get too close. Your grandfather don't have all he wits.

Once on a good day, I could touch my grandfather, but that was early on in my life. By the time I was seven or so, only Mom could touch him or they say he was bound to fly into fits. That was something I ain't want to test. Mom always bring tobacco and dinner mints to calm him, and when she walk in she call, Poopa! Though that magic sense he have already tell him it she. Later when Grandpa get older and more agitated and excitable, he hold a cutlass tight in he hand when we walk through the door and he only relax he grip when he sure it your grandmother and not bandits come to raid the house.

This day I watch the madman and his smoky black eyes. This man who know nothing but his daughter and his short corncob pipe. That pipe. That pipe. It look nothing like the one I hold in my hand in Safeway, but it everything like it if you ask me in that moment I'm standing in the aisle pretending. Granddad's house burn of urine and hot air hanging heavy. He call her name and his voice take on an edge until she respond or sometimes she just put a hand on he back.

Then he sit in his creaky chair and settle himself before reaching into the coal pot at his side to flip a piece of coal into his pipe. A couple puffs at that thing and he'd be content, peaceful. Granddaddy was always so precise, not just for a blind man but for any man, that burning ember flipping through the dark. It never burn him. Never spark on the ground. Always flip into the mouth of that pipe.

This time it's me and Raoul and Mom. She wander about straightening up, and then she go off to the kitchen to cook Granddaddy's food. I think is whisper I whisper when I turn to Raoul and say, Granddaddy's gonna burn this place one day.

Neville, you hush your mouth, your granny call from the next room.

Neville, you better hush your mouth, I mumble to myself in that Safeway tobacco aisle, and I'm back there smelling the smoke coming from the street. Raoul disappear and then my mother disappear and then my grandfather once again he dead and gone, always like a spirit in a cloud of smoke. Sirens start screaming in the distance. There's a riot. A dead king somewhere shaking he head at all that burn in he name. There's the book and another insurrection somewhere, sometime. Police out there, maybe coming to save the Safeway, and they don't mean no good for no one.

I stuff the pipe in my pocket and run from the store back into the smoky streets and I ain't stop running till I at my door. All the while, my heart is beating fast, fast, fast in my ears like history shouting loud enough to deafen me.

Not a day that go by after that I don't think about Cross River. That pipe, every time I look at it, it remind me that the book exist somewhere and another insurrection go be happening sometime. Thinking about Cross River make me late to my wedding. Laugh, Kin, but you almost wasn't made because of Cross River. We flirt with moving back to Trinidad, moving to upstate New York, but the only thing we take serious is moving to this town. I go to law school at Howard again and get a job and thing, but then when your sister is three or four and your brother is five or six, we pack up all our things, no job, no nothing. People tell me it have a big Caribbean community in Cross River, and is true and that nice and thing, but that not why we move here. People ask me why I go Cross River, I say, We come to see the Insurrection.

I don't know what we think we go find; I don't know what we did find, but we find it.

I want you to remember this, Kin: You are the only member of this family that is born into Cross River. The rest of we adopt it. Cross River is you. That moment in the aisle is you. Tell you the truth, when your brother, Blair, come a cop, I get disappointed. The son of Neville Samson a police? Naw. I feel like I ain't give him enough of what was in me in that moment during the riot. And your sister too damn reasonable for her own good. Sometimes, Kin, I think I give you too much of what was in me in that Safeway. You too damn miserable, but you, Akinsanya Abel Samson, you are the Cross Riverian Dream. I know you say that sound corny and thing, but when them people wrench themselves free, is you they think about.

We sit in silence listening to the hospital machines beeping and sighing. I wonder if the thoughts spinning wildly and crazily around my head are from the delirium or from my father's crazy tale.

He breaks the silence first by drifting off into a snore that startles and wakes him. I think of how much all this recollecting must have cost him.

Now you, he says.

Huh?

Tell me a story.

I don't have no stories like that.

Don't play the fool, Kin. You know what I mean. Tell me why you go quite out in the Wildlands.

Is nothing, boy, I say, mimicking my father's accent, his voice, the shrug of his shoulder and the wave of his hand, the same way my face has always mimicked his own. Playing dead to catch corbeaux alive.

Acknowledgments

First, I'd like to thank all the readers who opened their minds and their hearts to these words. I wrote them especially for you.

Thank you to the people of Cross River, Maryland, for letting me into your world.

I would like to thank my wonderful editor, Lisa Williams, for choosing my book and then approaching each story with enthusiasm, care, and a sharply critical eye. Whenever I figured I'd done enough, she showed me ways in which the words could do more. Thank you to everyone at the University Press of Kentucky.

Thank you to all the editors who gave these stories a home in their literary magazines, and even to many who declined to publish early versions but provided a kind word or a helpful suggestion.

Support provided by Kimbilio, the Pan-African Literary Forum, and Bowie State University kept me going.

Many of these stories were written while I attended George Mason University's MFA in Creative Writing program and quite literally wouldn't exist without the spark and encouragement of my brilliant professors Susan Shreve, Alan Cheuse (RIP), Courtney Brkic, Mary Kay Zuravleff, and Steve Goodwin. Thank you also to my classmates, fellow writers and friends Ryan Call, Alyson Foster, Eugenia Tsutsumi, David Conner, David Heath, David Rider, Becky Bikowski, Mike Scalise, and Sara Hov. Thank you to everyone who's ever been in a workshop with me.

Bro Yao, your heartfelt words of encouragement have been just golden and so necessary, especially when I can't see around the dark corners.

Acknowledgments

Thanks to Mensah Demary for the laughs and the literary camaraderie.

Thank you to Kyle Minor for the encouraging messages, which were just minutes of his time but always seemed to come right at the moment I needed them most.

If I extended ten thousand thank-yous to the incomparable human being known as Kima Jones, I would still come up short.

Thank you to all the good people on Twitter who allow me to waste time with them.

Thank you, Rickita Perry, for being such a good reader, but most importantly such a good friend.

Thank you to my parents, Nigel and Monica Scott, for their ongoing unconditional love and support. None of this is possible without their emotional, material, and spiritual backing. My big brothers, Duane and Omar, were my original readership, and to this day they are my most loyal readers. I'll never stop wanting to be like my big brothers. Thanks too to my sisters-in-law, Tracy and Tara, my nephew and nieces, Zavier, Sasha, Nia, and Maya, and my cousin Brian.

Thanks to my Abdur-Rahman family in New York. It's incredible how much richer my life is with you all there.

Special thanks to my father for letting me interview him about his journey. I got a couple of stories out of our talks, but I also got so much more.

My grandmother used to sit with me and tell me all about her childhood, her travels, the pains still fresh after decades and decades, how she grew to be a master seamstress, and how much she loved my mother. All of this is in here somewhere and for that I am grateful. I miss her dearly.

My son, Samaadi Cabral Scott, the funniest little comedian on the planet, Daddy loves you.

Eternal thanks to my wife, Sufiya Abdur-Rahman, for reading every word, critiquing every syllable, and most of all for loving me.

194

THE UNIVERSITY PRESS OF KENTUCKY
NEW POETRY AND PROSE SERIES

This series features books of contemporary poetry and fiction that exhibit a profound attention to language, strong imagination, formal inventiveness, and awareness of one's literary roots.

SERIES EDITOR: Lisa Williams

ADVISORY BOARD: Camille Dungy, Rebecca Morgan Frank, Silas House, Davis McCombs, and Roger Reeves

Sponsored by Centre College

CENTRE
COLLEGE

CPSIA information can be obtained
at www.ICGtesting.com
Printed in the USA
BVOW08s0510050717
488510BV00002B/5/P

9 780813 174402